WARRIOR

WARRIOR

Book Two of the Legacy Fleet Trilogy

Nick Webb

www.nickwebbwrites.com

Summary: We repelled the Swarm, for now. But they won't stop:
they're inhuman. They have no inhibitions. No conscience. And no
mercy. But from the crucible of battle has risen an unlikely hero.
Captain Timothy Granger, at the helm of another time-tested battleship, will take the fight to the enemy. He'll discover their secrets.
Find their homeworld. Destroy it before they destroy ours. He will
save us all. He must. Or we'll die. WARRIOR

Text set in Garamond
Designed by Jenny Webb
http://jennywebbedits.com

Cover art by Tom Edwards
http://tomedwardsdmuga.blogspot.co.uk

ISBN-10: 1519465912
ISBN-13: 978-1519465917

Printed in the United Sates of America

For J., L., and C.

CHAPTER ONE

New Dublin, Eyre Sector
Planetary Command Center

GOVERNOR WOLFRAM WRUNG his hands nervously. Sweat beaded on his shiny forehead but he didn't even bother wiping it. Power was being diverted away from luxuries like air conditioning to more useful things like planetary shielding and orbital plasma-particle beams.

They were coming.

And fast, he noticed, watching the flurry of large dots on the tactical readout, each indicating a massive Swarm carrier, all likely full of thousands of fighters, rapidly approaching the inner system defenses.

"Any response yet from CENTCOM?" he barked at the admiral huddled with his commanders near the tactical station.

From his tight smile and furrowed brow, Governor Wolfram could tell the admiral was annoyed. "No, sir. We only just sent out the meta-space distress call an hour ago. We're expecting a response any moment now." Admiral Azbill resumed the coordination of the New Dublin planetary fleet defenses.

Wolfram nodded, and turned back to the tactical readout nearby. Ten ships. *Ten.* The fleet that had attacked Earth just over two months ago had numbered ten, too. A first wave of six, followed closely by four more. In all the Swarm incursions since that battle, they'd only sent in smaller strike forces now that they knew Earth knew how to fight back. Two ships here, three there, always striking at smaller settlements on fringe worlds where they were assured a quick victory and a sharp, devastating raid before they melted away, disappearing to whatever star systems they were originating from.

But New Dublin was not on the periphery, and ten ships meant they were coming for blood. This was the real deal.

He wrung his hands again, and watched as the last defense outpost about halfway out to the nearest planet—a handful of automated laser turrets mounted to a smattering of small asteroids orbiting their sun—disappeared from the tactical readout, and the flurry of large dots resumed their course to New Dublin.

Less than an hour away.

There was no hope. If CENTCOM was only now receiving and responding to the meta-space distress call there would never be enough time to dispatch a rescue force.

They were doomed. In one hour. With ten Swarm ships incoming, there was no way any city or town on New Dublin would survive. Their planetary defense fleet was simply no match for that much firepower.

He'd often wondered why the Swarm came at a planet with conventional inertial thrusters, rather than q-jump all the way into a system. Q-jumping would give their targets far less time to assemble and organize any sort of defense. But Admiral Azbill, the IDF commander in charge of the New Dublin force, assured him it was not because of any sort of technical shortcomings on the Swarm's part.

No, he believed they did it to sow fear and terror in their victims. Let them see you coming for hours. Let them stew in their own juices, painfully aware that their end was coming very, very soon. Let them run around in a frenzy, inciting confusion and distress in the population, allowing for maximum disorder and mayhem and destruction when the Swarm finally arrived.

Why would the Swarm do this? Why would they care? Nobody knew. Nobody seemed to know *anything* about them, as far as he could tell.

How could you fight an enemy you knew nothing about?

The blood drained from his face as a new dot suddenly appeared on the tactical screen, just a hundred thousand kilometers from New Dublin. Damn. Maybe they'd changed their tactics. Were they sending in an advance warship to soften them up before the main body of their fleet arrived?

The new dot swooped in, terribly fast, toward a low orbit.

It was massive. The energy readings coming off the ship indicated it was charging weapons and preparing for a fight. Wolfram's stomach tensed. The end would come sooner, rather than later, it seemed.

He heard a whoop off to the side, and snapped his head toward the officer who'd made the sound, bouncing excitedly at his station. The comm station.

"Admiral! It's the *Warrior!* It's Granger himself!"

Admiral Azbill's face immediately transformed from that of a grim, harried commander to an expression of something Governor Wolfram had not seen in quite some time.

3

Hope.

"Amazing," Wolfram muttered. "He's managed to assemble his strike force and get here already? But where are his other ships?"

Admiral Azbill shrugged. "Patch him through."

A few moments later, the officer at comm nodded. "You're on, Admiral. We've got visual, too."

"This is Admiral Azbill of New Dublin Planetary Command. That you, Granger?" They all turned to the viewscreen covering half of one of the walls.

An image of an older man, his faced lined and dark bags sagging under his eyes, snapped onto the screen. And in spite of the lines and scars and obvious signs of months of battle, he was smiling.

"Good to see you, Azbill. I understand you're in need of some assistance?"

Admiral Azbill gave a hollow laugh. "Yeah, you could say that."

Granger's smile widened. "Well then, let's get this party started. I'd like to send one of my people down to you to help coordinate and integrate with operations on the *Warrior*. You've got your planetary defense fleet assembled, I presume? We're going to need them."

Azbill hesitated. "Captain, where's your strike force? They coming in right behind you?"

Granger shook his head. Oddly enough though, his smile deepened. Governor Wolfram felt his stomach tighten. *No fleet?*

"The Swarm is putting us through the wringer today. Three separate incursions. I've sent my fleet on to the Johannesburg Sector to deal with the four Swarm ships there, and Admiral Zingano from CENTCOM is personally dealing with a Swarm raid in the Centauri System with the strike force based at Sol."

Azbill's back stiffened. "Am I to understand, sir, that you're it? No one else is coming?" Governor Wolfram thought it odd that an admiral was addressing a captain as *sir*. Was the man's reputation and mythos that powerful? Granger had become something of a legend in the past two months, as he was able to repel invasion after deadly invasion. The man seemed to have a knack for dealing with the Swarm.

Not to mention his inexplicable return from the dead. The *Constitution* had disappeared—the satellite cameras had broadcast the event to the entire Earth. One moment she crashed and disappeared into a singularity, taking out three Swarm carriers with it, and the next moment she'd reappeared, careening through the atmosphere.

"That's right, Admiral. The *Warrior*'s it."

Silence fell on the previously busy command center. He heard an officer cough nervously behind him. *One ship?* Wolfram thought. *One ship against ten swarm carriers! The man is mad.*

Admiral Azbill was becoming agitated. "Granger, is this a joke? Your fleet is right behind you, I hope, for all our sakes. In case CENTCOM didn't update you, we've got *ten* Swarm carriers incoming. *Ten.*"

Granger leaned in slightly to the viewscreen. "No joke, Azbill. They've got ten carriers. But we've got your entire planetary defense fleet, one *ISS Warrior* ... and one *me*." Governor Wolfram almost missed it, but Granger actually winked at them. The man had style. And balls. "I'd say the odds are about even."

CHAPTER TWO

New Dublin, Eyre Sector
Bridge, ISS Warrior

CAPTAIN GRANGER NODDED toward the comm officer on duty to cut the transmission, and swiveled his chair to face Proctor.

"You ready, Commander?"

She nodded, and stood up to leave. "I'll get down there right away."

It was always painful to have her leave—fighting without Proctor was like tying your good arm behind your back during a fist fight—but he needed the coordination with the surface forces only she could provide. The woman had a knack for getting things done—quickly and efficiently. And besides, excluding himself, she had the most experience fighting the Swarm. Her capabilities would be the most valuable directing the response of the rest of the defense forces planet-side.

He swiveled back to his station. "Should be just like Tau Ceti," he said. "Swarm'll never know what hit them."

She paused at the door. "Tim, this is hardly like Tau Ceti. We fought four ships there. We've got *ten* incoming."

"But New Dublin's defense force is far more capable than Tau Ceti's."

"True," she conceded.

He glanced over at the tactical station, motioning to Lieutenant Diaz, the tactical officer, to join him. "Don't worry, Commander. The bastards will never know what hit them. This time tomorrow we'll be back to planning Operation Battle-ax."

Proctor stayed at the door a moment longer, then left. He knew what she wanted to say: *You're being too cocky, Tim.* She'd warned him several times over the last few weeks. She thought he was being too overconfident. Too brash.

And the truth was, he felt it. His confidence brimmed over, and he knew, *he just knew* he was going to crush those bastards. Ever since he'd woken up on Proctor's shoulder as she carried him down to engineering in a flaming *Constitution* careening through the atmosphere. Ever since the cancer had left.

Ever since those missing three days. Or fifteen seconds, depending on how one looked at it.

Somehow, the miraculous nature of the circumstances, and the fact that he and Proctor had almost single-handedly saved Earth, granted him the knowledge that they'd be ok. They would survive. More than survive: they'd win so convincingly that the Swarm would either never attack them again, or be wiped out so utterly that the win would amount to a genocide. And Granger was ok with that. That vague feeling, that voice in the back of his head, it gave him confidence. Swagger.

He didn't stifle the swagger. On the contrary, he flaunted it. His people ate it up. They needed it. Craved it. And in the aftermath of the invasion of Earth, he'd gained—and cultivated—an almost legendary status.

The Hero of Earth. He found that by acting the part of the legend, his people responded in kind with legendary performance. He acted the part for *them.* They wanted a hero? Then, by god, he'd give them one, if it meant the Swarm would be destroyed and humanity saved.

"Helm, report."

Ensign Prince, whose red, raw face just recently emerged from the bandages that had covered the severe burns he suffered during the previous week's engagement with the Swarm, cocked his head to the side in answer. "Assuming a low orbit. We'll be swinging around the limb of the horizon just as the Swarm arrives, sir."

"Perfect." He glanced to the side. "Tactical?"

"All mag rails primed and ready."

"Any more trouble with the new ones they installed last maintenance?"

IDF had upgraded the *Warrior* with over one hundred new mag rail guns, more than doubling her complement. That meant over five hundred new crew members to manage and worry about, but it was well worth the extra firepower.

"All power conduits are reading normal. Looks like Rayna's got them all under control."

A voice chimed over the comm system. "Cap'n, my baby's ready for you. Treat her nice or I'll be grumpy tomorrow."

Speak of the devil. He cleared his throat and raised his head. "Thank you, Commander Scott. Your baby's my baby."

"Uh, sir?" He could hear the smirk in her voice. "I'm a married woman."

"You can't marry a ship, Rayna. Granger out." He smiled and swatted at the comm button. He glanced at the new communications officer, a young man straight out of the Academy. Top of the class. Ensign Prucha. "Is Proctor down there yet?"

Prucha checked his console, and nodded. "Just arrived a moment ago."

"Good. Once you two have a system link set up, we can get this show on the road."

He checked the status board, confirming that all crews were ready for combat. One more senior officer to report in....

As if on cue, a patrician British voice chimed over the comm: "Captain Granger, all fighter crews ready."

"All four hundred? I'm still amazed you found a way to pack that many in there, Commander Pierce."

The CAG's calming accent contained the smallest quiver. "Desperation is the father of genius, sir." He hesitated. "Will we be deploying *all* fighters this time around?"

Pierce, while being the best CAG Granger had ever served with, still hadn't recovered from the loss of his father, who'd commanded a British warship before encountering the initial Swarm invasion force. Or was it deeper than that? Could it be that the other man just couldn't live with losing his pilots? As Captain, Granger knew it was never easy: they lost a handful of people in every engagement. The Flight Academy could hardly keep up with the attrition rate. Granger could understand the man's concern.

But this was not a time for hesitation. "All fighters, Commander. Will that be a problem?"

A brief silence on the other end. "No problem, sir. All fighter squadrons reporting ready."

"Good. Granger out." He thumbed the comm off.

He gripped his armrests, suppressing the rising tension. Playing the part of swaggering hero for his people was one thing. Fooling himself that the upcoming battle would be a cakewalk was another entirely. This would be the battle of his life, and while he was confident they would prevail, he knew he'd lose people. A lot of people. And New Dublin would face heavy casualties, too. It was unavoidable. War was hell, and modern space warfare was fiery, brutal hell on an epic scale.

The time ticked by. Granger busied himself with the last minute details of battle preparation, but it was all window-dressing. They were ready. The guns were primed. The missiles loaded. The lasers powered. All they needed was a target.

"Sir! Coming up over the limb of the planet now. Visual contact with the Swarm fleet."

"Shelby, I hope that was enough time for you," he said under his breath.

Diaz gawked at his screen, waving emphatically at Granger. "Sir! Detecting *thirteen* Swarm capital vessels."

Thirteen?! Damn.

CHAPTER THREE

New Dublin, Eyre Sector
Planetary Command Center

PROCTOR DASHED DOWN the lowering ramp of the shuttle as soon as it was safe, rushing abruptly past the Commander who'd been sent to receive her and making her way briskly toward the command center. Granger's idea. Show them, with urgency, who was in charge and who'd be calling the shots. Even though she didn't know where the command center was.

"Commander Proctor!" said the short man, running after her. His uniform was too tight, as if he were someone who vainly and stubbornly clung to his older, smaller clothing despite gaining fifty pounds.

"Please keep up, Commander," she replied, without slowing or turning around. With no idea of how to get to the command center, she needed him to catch up faster, but she wasn't about to slow down to wait.

He huffed, breaking out into a jog, falling into step alongside her. "Commander Proctor, why did CENT-COM only send the *Warrior?*"

She looked askance at him, raising a single eyebrow. "Actually, Commander, CENTCOM wanted to send in the *Warrior*'s whole strike force. Captain Granger convinced them not to."

Proctor almost laughed as she saw the man's jaw drop a full inch. But she kept moving ahead until she reached a T in the hallway that forced her to slow down momentarily to await his direction.

"But ... why?"

She saw a sign pointing to the command center and quickened her pace now that she no longer needed his assistance. "Two reasons. Both of which the captain already told Admiral Azbill. He felt the strike force was needed in the Johannesburg Sector, and he's confident that the combined strength of the *Warrior* and the New Dublin fleet will be more than sufficient to meet the threat."

"But ... but that's ... that's just mad!" The man looked flustered, his thick face turning red either from the jogging or disbelief at what she was saying.

"Mad? Probably. You'll find that Granger's tactics have become a bit ... unconventional as of late. But he's also effective. We've actually got great odds."

"And just what do you place the odds at?" They passed the doors to the command center, which opened right in time to receive them.

"Oh, twenty-five percent? Thirty? Hard to tell."

She was kidding, of course, but the expression of dread spreading over the commander's red face was priceless. The real odds were far higher. Fifty fifty, just like Granger had said. But he'd had an incredible streak of luck the past few months. Maybe this was the battle that would restore some balance to their track record.

Admiral Azbill greeted her with a curt nod. "Commander Proctor." Although he projected the confidence befitting a senior commander, she could discern several subtle signs of stress. He squinted. His eyes flickered between her and the status screens on the wall behind her. He was in over his head, and he knew it, but he was not about to let anyone else know it. This could be tricky—she needed operational authority if they were going to pull this off, but he might just be the type to stubbornly refuse.

"Admiral Azbill, I'm honored to be here—Captain Granger has spoken very highly of you. He asked that I coordinate the *Warrior*'s efforts with your forces. The experience we've gained engaging the Swarm will be best implemented if I assist you directly down here." She translated in her head: *Granger asked that I come and take over your fleet so you don't, in his words, piss away our victory and kill us all.* She looked him up and down. A career IDF man. Probably served at a desk job for ten years in the old Miami HQ, deep in the bowels of the bureaucracy. Most definitely not one tactically-adept bone in his body.

"Commander, what in blazes is Granger playing at? We don't stand a chance against that fleet and he knows it. We just detected an extra three ships q-jumping in to join the other ten, and all CENTCOM sends is *one* ship as backup?" He waved his arms, clearly agitated.

He was absolutely right, of course. It was insane. By all rights they should have arrived with an armada of ships to repel a Swarm incursion of this size. But they couldn't spare them. Operation Battle-ax depended on it. If Granger was right, that plan would put an end to the Swarm threat forever. They just had to survive the next few months before they could implement it.

"Admiral Azbill, I understand your concern, and I share it. But believe me, we can do this. Just give me operational authority down here and by the end of the day we'll be clinking glasses down at the local pub."

His eyes narrowed and she could feel him fume. "*Commander Proctor—*"

She held up a hand. "Fine. Keep operational authority. But please, allow me to coordinate your forces with the *Warrior*, and I promise we'll pull through." She paused, watching the officers all around her. They were desperate. Death was visible on their viewscreens: thirteen dots converging on their position so rapidly that they'd barely have enough time to mount any kind of effective response. They needed hope. They needed a legend on their side. They needed *The Hero of Earth*. She continued, "Captain *Granger* promises we'll pull through. Believe me, if it were anyone else, I'd say retreat as fast as possible. But that man is more than just some washed-up fleet captain. He's a genius. Pure grit and genius. If anyone can save us, it's him."

The words felt hollow and stale in her mouth. He was, after all, just a man. A man who made mistakes and bad calls just like every other officer in the room.

But that's not what these people needed to hear. It's not what they wanted to hear.

And besides, he really did have grit. Grittiest old bastard she'd ever met.

Admiral Azbill nodded. "Fine. I'll keep operational authority," he nodded to all the officers scattered amongst the stations in the command center, "but you are all to do as she says." He turned back to her and waved an arm to the command station. "Commander, after you."

She didn't skip a beat. "Direct three of your frontline ships to make a point blank full-throttle charge against the incoming fleet. All weapons firing at full spread, targeting their lead ship. Mag rails to puncture, lasers to rip into the wounds."

The ensigns at the comm immediately began chattering into their headsets, relaying instructions to the planetary defense fleet, while Admiral Azbill sidled up to her, still nodding at the comm station as if to confirm her orders. "Commander ... *three* ships? They'll be slaughtered."

Proctor pressed her lips together, and nodded once in answer. "Maybe not. But it's part of the strategy. Not only will it soften up their lead ship for the *Warrior*, but it acts as a feint. We've been conditioning the Swarm for two months to expect certain strategies, giving them patterns to look for and adapt to."

Admiral Azbill lowered his voice. "You're engaging in psychological warfare with a species that we know nothing about?"

"On the contrary. We know something very important about them."

"And what is that?"

She glanced at him with a gallows humor wink. "That they want us dead. At all costs."

CHAPTER FOUR

New Dublin, Eyre Sector
Bridge, ISS Warrior

THIRTEEN SHIPS.

Aware that every head was turned toward him, watching and scrutinizing his reaction, Granger shoved his fear deep into a corner and forced a smile, standing up slowly and clasping his hands behind his back. Calmly. Deliberately. *Give them a good show, Granger.*

"Good. An extra three ships to beat the shit out of. Full thrust, Ensign. Bring us in hot. Be ready to execute maneuver Granger One."

Every head turned back to their station, brimming with confidence. He could feel the energy in the room. The bridge crew worked with a seamless discipline and coordination. It was show time.

"Any word from Proctor?" Granger glanced at his command console, scanning for signs the New Dublin defense fleet was taking orders from his first officer.

"Aye, sir. Three New Dublin ships are converging on the Swarm fleet. One minute until direct engagement."

Granger nodded. Good. Proctor had things under control on the surface. Now it was time to make sure the impending sacrifices of the day would not be in vain. "Time until maximum weapons range?"

"Weapons range in seventy seconds," said Diaz.

"Commence fire when ready," replied Granger, sitting back down.

"Aye aye, sir."

He glanced at the clock. Sixty seconds.

Fifty.

Forty.

Another stirring speech? There was still time, given his tendency toward brevity. No, they were ready. Another quick readiness review of the weapons crews? No, only thirty seconds left. That would take at least another five minutes.

Twenty seconds. The Swarm fleet began to resolve on the screen, shifting from pixellated blobs to menacing, multi-nacelled behemoths that were already disgorging thousands of fighters.

"The three New Dublin ships have engaged the Swarm, sir."

He watched the screen as the three sacrificial lambs plunged swiftly into the fray, forcing the Swarm fleet to suspend its approach to New Dublin and deal with the defenders.

But despite the new iridium armor plating and the upgraded smart steel defenses—which now worked much better thanks to a reset of the modulation frequencies that the Swarm had somehow decoded for their first run at Earth two months ago—the defenders sustained punishing fire, and the lead cruiser burst apart in a dazzling, sickening bright blast.

"In weapons range, sir."

"Fire."

Every mag rail gun aboard the *Warrior* blazed as hundreds of high-velocity projectiles leapt out from the hull and slammed into the nearest Swarm vessel. The view on screen pulsed with brilliant explosions as the slugs rammed into the other ship, which began disgorging fire and debris as the mag rail projectiles ripped through its hull.

"Retarget. Hit the next ship with the mag rails. Laser crews target the holes in the first."

"Aye, sir," came the reply from the tactical station, and Lieutenant Diaz coordinated the new orders.

Granger glanced at the clock, cringing as he realized the time was nearly up for their first pass. The ship rumbled and jolted as the Swarm fleet understood it was being attacked from a new vector. Granger watched on the viewscreen as the enemy vessels grew large, then began to shrink as the camera switched views, indicating that the *Warrior* had sailed right on by the pitched battle.

The ship rumbled a few more times as the Swarm ships managed to fire off a few more shots—the viewscreen flared up with an intense green glow every time the deadly pulses made contact with the hull—but soon the other ships receded completely from view, falling behind the limb of the planet as the *Warrior* continued its blazingly-fast orbit around New Dublin.

"Right. First pass complete. Time to second?" he said, turning to navigation.

"At this speed, six minutes."

It wasn't fast enough. They'd planned on ten ships. Not thirteen. "Increase thrust to one g, aft."

Ensign Prince swiveled in his chair to look at Granger with a raised eyebrow. "But sir, that will require a steady increase in thrust radially inward toward the planet. That'll take us over the safety threshold within three minutes."

"You heard me, Ensign."

From deep within the deck plates, the ship groaned as it tried to keep up with the increased gravitational stresses. Granger placed his hand on the console. She was no *Constitution*, but she was just as good. He didn't want to openly admit it to himself, but she was actually a whole lot better, given her extensive refit after the battle over Earth two months ago.

"ETA now three minutes, sir."

"And the Swarm? Have they resumed their course?"

Ensign Diamond at sensors studied his readings. "Yes, sir. The three ships in the first wave are destroyed. But the second wave is intercepting now."

He suppressed the pit in his stomach. No time to feel guilt. No time for remorse. There was only time to survive. After survival, there would be time for luxuries. Luxuries like feeling.

"Adjust heading to meet them."

His fingers drummed the seconds away. On the screen, the planet rotated serenely, almost blissful in its apparent ignorance of the destruction and carnage occurring far above its peaceful atmosphere. New Dublin was a beauty, for sure. Green and blue and cloudy. Why in the world the Swarm wanted this planet so badly—enough to send *thirteen* ships against it—made him wonder. The planet, and the sector, held modest strategic importance. It was relatively centrally located. It had some resources, but no more than any other average world. It was almost identical to the other three planets being assaulted today in the Swarm's four-pronged attack, but the fleet attacking it was the largest by far. What was he missing?

"Ten seconds," said Prince.

Granger shook his head. There would be time for solving mysteries later. He would make sure of it.

"Fire."

CHAPTER FIVE

New Dublin, Eyre Sector
Planetary Command Center

"ADMIRAL AZBILL, THE *Praxis*, the *Harrier*, and the *Crenshaw* report engagement with the Swarm!" reported an officer at the tactical station.

Azbill furrowed his brow. "Where's the *Warrior*?"

Proctor motioned him over to one of the command stations she'd commandeered. "Take a look, Admiral." She pointed to the tactical schematic. The *Warrior*, still advancing under the cover of New Dublin's horizon, was bearing down on the pitched battle with blazing speed. Far faster than a regular orbit at that altitude. "She's orbiting at a two-x low-orbital speed. In a few seconds, the Swarm'll never know what hit them."

He frowned, pointing to the area on the screen where the invading fleet had momentarily stopped to deal with the three New Dublin ships. "But what about the—"

One of the dots disappeared, and Azbill's hand jerked away.

"Sir! We've just lost the *Praxis*!"

Azbill pounded Proctor's command console. "Dammit, Commander, there were five hundred people on that ship!"

The tactical officer called out again. "The *Harrier* is reporting hull decompression. They're not going to make it much longer. The thirteen Swarm vessels have them completely surrounded." He typed in a few commands, and the view on the screen that comprised one of the walls of the command center was replaced by the camera feed from a satellite passing the field of battle.

The *Harrier* and the *Crenshaw* flitted in and out of the enemy ships, targeting all their mag rails and lasers on the cloud of fighters belching out of the Swarm carriers, moving between the massive vessels as quickly as possible—just as Proctor had instructed them. Their job was to interdict and impede, at the expense of their lives.

And they were doing a hell of a job. The fleet of Swarm ships buzzed like an angry bee's nest.

"Here she comes," murmured Proctor.

The satellite's camera angle widened, and from the right side of the screen the *Warrior* blazed in, all guns firing, making a ferocious dive for the Swarm ship in its sights.

And Proctor grinned—the Swarm ship was getting the snot beat out of it. Multiple deep gouges sprouted in its starboard hull, which exploded as the *Warrior*'s laser crews trained their guns on the erupting wounds.

A second Swarm ship soon found itself on the receiving end of the *Warrior*'s guns. And the next moment, she was gone as she disappeared behind the limb of the atmosphere, leaving destruction in her wake.

Admiral Azbill paused, his mouth temporarily gaping open. "Lieutenant, status of those two Swarm ships?"

Some fumbling with the controls, and a moment later the woman replied, "No active energy readings from that first ship, sir, and reading massive power failures and structural integrity fluctuations in the second. Though it is still firing at the *Harrier.*"

A moment later the satellite's camera, just before it passed out of view, revealed the remaining Swarm ships descending on the *Harrier* and the *Crenshaw* in a tide of green anti-matter pulse beams. The *Harrier* exploded, and the camera cut out.

"Fine. That's one and a half enemy birds out of commission." He turned to glare at Proctor. "But at the cost of *three* of our best ships? Three ships that we just tossed out there as cannon fodder? Over fifteen hundred officers and crewmen?"

She met his gaze, and held it. "Yes. Three ships. We've tried one, but they don't stop for one. They don't stop for two. They stop for three, and so three is the number we sacrifice so that the rest of us have time to fight."

The room fell to a quiet murmur as she spoke. The statistics were grim. Sobering. Ghoulish. But they all knew she was right. The unspoken historical statistics were far more grisly. At Earth, two months ago, over thirty of IDF's best ships fell before they'd even made a dent in one Swarm vessel.

She swiveled toward the tactical station. "Send the next three from their holding pattern in low orbit. Direct intercept course. Same as before."

The officers at the tactical station paused, and looked to Admiral Azbill, who, frowning, finally nodded.

"This had better be worth it, Proctor, or—"

An alarm started blaring, and Proctor didn't have to ask what it meant. On the wall's viewscreen, from the camera of one of the ships approaching the Swarm invasion fleet, she saw the tell-tale bright shimmer.

They'd initiated a forced quantum singularity.

CHAPTER SIX

New Dublin, Eyre Sector
Bridge, ISS Warrior

THE SHIMMERING SPHERES hovering amidst the invading fleet could only mean one thing. Fortunately, it was the last thing Granger worried about at that point of the battle. "Commander Pierce, deploy all wings."

"Aye, sir."

He turned to navigation. "Ensign Prince, full reverse. Slow us down for direct engagement."

The ensign keyed the commands in, and Granger could feel the scarcely perceptible sway of the internal gravity field as it adjusted to keep up with the changing inertia. It was strange—during his brief battle with cancer, one that he should have lost, he could feel every turn, every imperceptible shift. Even the slightest change in acceleration had registered with him on a visceral level. Something about the tumor in his brain had affected his balance, but in turn had let him detect even the slightest change in momentum.

Now, that was all gone. He was healed. Whole.

But how? The mystery had remained unsolved, and, frankly, he didn't have time to sit around philosophizing about it. Especially right now.

An alarm blared, and he chided himself for his momentary lapse into thought. The flashing indicator on his board told him they were nearly there. "All gun crews, prepare for operation Granger Two."

He glanced at the tactical stream relayed from the planet by Proctor. Mentally crossing his fingers that she'd managed to set up her end of operation Granger Two, he did a last minute check of their capacitor banks. Eighty-five percent.

Good enough.

"Sir, contact with thirteen New Dublin ships. They're rising up through the atmosphere below and behind us."

Granger smiled. *Good work, Proctor.*

"Continue braking maneuver, and open fire on my mark."

He watched as the blips on their sensors grew larger, and then the viewscreen on the wall split to reveal the thirteen New Dublin planetary force cruisers soaring up through the atmosphere like comets. Ultra-compressed gas streamed out behind them as they accelerated to speeds far greater than what was considered safe and prudent for an atmospheric ascent. Within another ten seconds, he supposed all of their exterior guns would be useless, just as their sensors, cameras, and anything else attached to the exterior hull were all long burned away by now.

But it wouldn't matter. All that mattered was the sacrifice of those skeleton crews. And what that sacrifice would accomplish.

"Adjust speed, Ensign. Keep us right between our boys down there and the Swarm."

"Aye, sir."

He raised a hand, finger pointing toward the screen, poised to give the fire order. He glanced at the tactical readout. Five more seconds.

Three.

One.

"Fire."

All the mag rails opened up, unleashing a storm of high-velocity slugs on the still-advancing fleet. In response, half the Swarm vessels returned fire. Over a dozen green beams lanced out, slamming into the *Warrior* head on. The ship rocked, and the deck plates bucked.

"Brake. *Hard*, Ensign!" He sat down and grabbed his armrests, but didn't buckle his restraints. He'd ride this out like a captain on an old sailing ship buffeted by hurricane force winds.

The *Warrior* slowed dramatically and everyone aboard the bridge lurched forward as their momentum caught up with the ship's.

And from behind the *Warrior* came the New Dublin fleet, hulls still glowing faintly red from their destructively fast ascent through the atmosphere, accelerating like bullets toward the Swarm ships.

All the green anti-matter beams ceased, and for a moment Granger could almost imagine the confusion on the faces of the Swarm upon seeing the thirteen ships blaze out of nowhere. Until he remembered that they didn't have faces.

What the hell did they have? It was a mystery he knew they'd have to figure out before they would have any chance of permanently defeating their enemy. They had to be more than blobs of green slime.

"All enemy fire now directed at the New Dublin Planetary fleet task force," said Lieutenant Diaz.

For all the good it'll do them. He watched as the thirteen ships approached their targets. No more than seven seconds away. They continued to accelerate. One exploded under the intense onslaught of the anti-matter beams. Then another.

Each ship—or fragments of a ship—careened closer to its target, each one dwarfed by the massive Swarm carriers looming ahead.

A voice scratched over the comm. Admiral Azbill's. "This had better work, Granger. Even a high-velocity suicide run by one of our heavy cruisers won't be enough to destroy a Swarm ship."

"We don't have to destroy them. Just watch, Admiral."

And it was time. Two more heavy cruisers had exploded into fiery pieces, but it was too late—each one found its target. Each plowed into a Swarm vessel, initiating massive explosions that made the enemy ships shudder and convulse. The explosions were insignificant compared to the sheer size of the Swarm carriers, but it wasn't the size of the explosion that mattered.

It was the location of the explosions.

"Lieutenant?" He turned to the tactical station, eyeing the man at sensors.

Diaz's eyes darted over his readouts, and he nodded. "Confirmed. All main fighter bays destroyed."

Granger leaned back and smiled. "Commander Pierce, scramble fighters. Get rid of those singularities, then beat the shit out of the capital ships." He raised his head. "Admiral? Feel free to deploy the rest of your fleet. Target at will."

A silence. Granger supposed the man was deciding whether to cuss him out for losing sixteen of his largest ships or acknowledge that the odds were suddenly far more even. "There are still fighters coming out of those things, Granger, I fail to see—"

Granger broke protocol and interrupted. "Each carrier has several fighter bays, yes, but the main one holds over seventy-five percent of their craft. Moreover, compromising their hulls in this fashion disrupts whatever they're using to block our lasers—their ships are now vulnerable to our full suite of weaponry. What was before an unwinnable battle is now tipped slightly in our favor, but by no means won. We need the rest of your fleet out here now, Admiral. Target their weapons batteries first, then move onto the next. Rinse and repeat."

Another brief silence. "Very well, Granger. Azbill out."

Granger raised an eyebrow, then turned back to tactical. "Target every single gaping hole with lasers and open fire. Boil the bastards from the inside out. Send out some nukes for good measure."

"With pleasure, sir."

He glanced back at his command console, looking for the timer that would indicate when the first singularity weapon would most likely launch. Damn. Less than a minute. And there were six of them—each one capable of completely annihilating the largest city on New Dublin and the towns surrounding it for hundreds of miles around.

The fighter pilots would have their work cut out for them.

CHAPTER SEVEN

New Dublin, Eyre Sector
Low Orbit

LIEUTENANT TYLER "BALLSY" Volz pushed his fighter's throttle to the limit. Thankfully, the morning's hangover was a distant memory, and he was ready to kill stuff. The more stuff, the better.

The Swarm carriers loomed ahead, forbidding and threatening, in spite of the fire and debris gushing out from their midsections where the main fighter bays should have been. Enemy fighters buzzed around them like bloodthirsty insects, but not nearly as many as there would have been without the sacrifice of those thirteen cruisers.

"Spacechamp, on me. Pew Pew and Fodder, take the wings and prepare to deliver your cargo." He glanced at his sensor map. "Bogey engagement in five. Look sharp."

Before he focused on the enemy fighters bearing down on them, he risked a glance to his side, toward one of his wingmen. Pew Pew, who'd replaced another nameless pilot Volz had lost the week before, held a tight formation despite the bulky cargo strapped to the under-carriage of the craft.

The cargo: a brick. A brick of solid osmium. Only about two meters long and one wide, it was easily twice the mass of the rest of the fighter. And therein lay the key to their best defense against the unthinkably destructive Swarm singularities.

Mass. Enough to close one of the miniature black holes before it launched toward the surface or the *Warrior* or whatever else the Swarm targeted.

From within the cockpit, Pew Pew turned his head briefly and gave Ballsy a thumbs up. And with that, the alarm rang out, indicating enemy weapons fire in close proximity.

It was time.

In a tightly-coordinated and thoroughly-practiced maneuver, all four of them dove down, split off from their vector, curved out in a tight loop, and converged on a new vector: the nearest singularity. They ignored all the fire strafing across their path.

"Watch your three o'clock, Fodder," Ballsy said. He pushed his fighter into another tight loop, trying to shake off a bogey who'd latched onto his vector. "Pew Pew, I need help here—" he started to say, but a muted explosion out of the corner of his eye cut him off.

"Already taken care of, Ballsy. Pew pew!" said the other pilot, adding his customary sound effect. If there was anyone that liked to shoot stuff more than Ballsy, it was Pew Pew.

He grunted an acknowledgement, then redirected his sights back on the glimmering singularity. They were remarkable things, really, no bigger than a smaller-than-average grain of sand. But the swirling glow of in-falling material extended out several centimeters and was so bright that it could be seen for dozens of kilometers around. While not massive, it nevertheless would rip apart anything that got within a meter, absorbing its mass and growing even larger.

And it was toward one of these monsters that Ballsy now accelerated. One of the shimmering beasts that had swallowed Fishtail whole. Jessica Miller. He knew her name. All of it. He still had nightmares where she fell into a fathomless black pit and the only thing he could see was her contorted face screaming out for him.

He was half tempted to accelerate further and plunge straight in. Fishtail had done it, on Commander Pierce's orders. And Granger had done it himself and returned just fine. If the old man could do it, why couldn't Fishtail? He wanted desperately to believe she was just on the other side, her fighter hobbled and broken down, waiting for someone to come retrieve her.

"Ballsy, what are you doing?" The voice was a woman's. *Fishtail?*

No. She was dead, of course. It was Spacechamp, who was tailing him, escorting him and his cargo to the monster.

"Ballsy, pull up!"

He stared at the pulsing light directly ahead. He could almost feel its gravitational pull increase—though the rational part of his mind knew that was impossible this far out. But he was plunging in toward it with alarming speed.

Why shouldn't he go in? Why shouldn't he go save her? He glanced at the picture sticking up out of a seam in the dashboard. A small boy. *Her* boy. Holding a miniature toy model of a space fighter—the same fighter that Fishtail had piloted to her death.

"Ballsy!"

He closed his eyes and pressed the release trigger, and immediately he felt the mass of his fighter decrease by two-thirds as the osmium brick flew toward the singularity. With a jolt he pulled the flight controls up, veering away from the beast at the last moment.

With his maneuverability suddenly restored, he pushed hard on the accelerator, darting his small craft away from the singularity like lightning, and moments later it exploded in a piercing white blast. Glancing behind, he confirmed it was gone.

"What the hell was that, Ballsy? That was way too close!" Spacechamp said, clearly irritated.

"Last time I launched too early the cumrats blasted the brick before it hit. Just wanted to make sure it went in this time."

Spacechamp snorted. "By sticking your bloomin' nose into it? Seriously, Ballsy, it's like you've got a death wish or something."

He shrugged. Death would be a relief, these days. Nonstop engagements. Near daily skirmishes with the Swarm. More flight missions than he could count. Little sleep. Severely rationed food.

And the friends. All the dead friends. Pilots he'd get to know for a few days before they were snuffed out by relentless Swarm fire.

"Death? Not today, Spacechamp." He glanced at his sensors. Of the six original singularities, four had been dissipated. The other squads, however, were being harassed by enemy fighters. "We've still got two more of these bungholes. Looks like squads Delta and Wolf need help with theirs. Fodder, Pew Pew, Spacechamp, on me. Let's go blow shit up."

CHAPTER EIGHT

New Dublin, Eyre Sector
Bridge, ISS Warrior

THE REST OF THE New Dublin Planetary Defense Force descended from their higher orbit and joined in the fight. Granger nodded in approval as he watched them engage the Swarm, taking heavy damage but dealing out their share too, wantonly blasting at the anti-matter cannons dotting the surfaces of the Swarm carriers with mag rail and laser fire. The debris field was so dense that the paths of the normally invisible laser beams glittered with intense blue light.

"Tactical, focus on those three ships at twenty-eight mark four. They're still capable of singularity generation."

The *Warrior*'s mag rails showered the three Swarm carriers with thousands of slugs while dozens of IDF fighters engulfed them in small weapon's fire, and soon the three hulls were ablaze with fire and debris spinning off into the deadness of space.

It was going well. Very well. Far better than he'd hoped, especially given that there were thirteen Swarm ships instead of the expected ten. The *Warrior*, her fighters, plus a few dozen heavy and light cruisers from New Dublin and their fighter wings were pulling off what would have been thought impossible a few months ago.

A victory. An almost easy victory.

But with the smart-steel armor now capable of enduring more than two blasts of the Swarm's anti-matter weapon, the odds for each battle were now far greater than they'd been over Earth two months prior.

Victory, yes. But it reminded him of the cost. The sacrifice. He'd written off the lives of the crews of sixteen entire ships. Used them as bricks. The brick-layer—that's what scuttlebutt said his new nickname was these days. Hero, yes. Legend, sure. But a butcher who wantonly threw his people's lives away so that he could keep fighting? Dammit—no, he couldn't think about that. No hesitation. No worry. Only focus. Thinking otherwise would make the sacrifices all vain.

And the treachery—they had a traitor in their midst. No other explanation could satisfy why updating the smart-steel algorithms two months ago was enough to make it suddenly effective against the Swarm's fire. Someone was collaborating with the enemy. Someone up top.

"They're on the run, sir," Lieutenant Diaz said with a wide smile. "The remaining five ships are pulling away. Slowly—their drives seem to be damaged."

Granger nodded. "Good. Order pursuit. None of those five get out alive." He scanned his sensor readout. "And the first ship? The one we disabled on our first pass?"

"Still in high orbit, sir. But it looks like they've fixed their drive and they've set a course out of the system."

He nodded again. "Just as they should. Relay orders to the New Dublin fleet to ignore that one. Proctor should have taken care of it, but we need to be sure Admiral Azbill understands that—"

"Sir!" Ensign Prucha waved a hand. "Admiral Azbill is on the comm. He doesn't sound happy."

"Speak of the devil." Granger sighed. "Patch him through."

The angry voice boomed over the speakers. "Granger, what in the *hell* are you playing at?"

Granger kept his voice neutral, in spite of his desire to blast the comm speaker with his sidearm. "Admiral?"

"Why are you letting that carrier escape? Are you batshit crazy?"

"Batshit crazy?" Granger grinned. "Sounds about right. I had a plush retirement planned down on a Florida beach, and somehow I let Zingano convince me to stay on for another tour."

Azbill huffed. "A Florida beach that no longer exists, Tim. The lower peninsula is gone. The panhandle's a wreck—almost uninhabitable. Tens of millions dead, and our asses out here are on the line because of these Swarm bastards, and you're *letting* it get away?"

"I am. And you should too," Granger replied, struggling to keep a dangerous note out of his voice.

"Excuse me, *Captain?*"

Granger stood up. "I have direct orders from Fleet Admiral Zingano. We are to ignore that carrier. It poses no threat to us, and will be allowed to escape."

A long pause.

"I don't believe you. Azbill out."

Granger's eyes widened, and he swore.

"Sir, the flagship and several more New Dublin cruisers are pulling off and laying in a pursuit course for that first carrier."

Granger spun toward navigation. "Ensign, intercept course. Full speed. Head them off."

It was the key to the whole operation. Save New Dublin? Fine. More than fine—millions of people lived down there. But save humanity? Even more important. But until they knew where the Swarm homeworld was, or for that matter, *any* Swarm planet, all they could ever do was defend. Defend, and lose. Strong defense never won a war by itself. Without an actual offense, the war was as good as over.

That carrier *had* to get away. Granger glanced down at his command console and confirmed: the *Warrior* had launched a small tracking device on its first pass and it had attached itself to the Swarm carrier's hull. It now streamed a constant, low power telemetry signal.

And when the carrier q-jumped away, Granger would know exactly in which direction it had jumped, and how far.

But he couldn't tell Azbill that. The plan was highly classified. Only a handful of his bridge crew even knew about the tracking device, and of his senior staff only Proctor knew the full plan. Hell, even *he* didn't know the entire plan. Zingano and President Avery were holding that pretty close to their chests.

But he knew it involved him, finally, going on the offensive. And he'd be damned if he'd let some stuffy ego-inflated admiral deprive him of the joy of going on the offensive against the Swarm.

"Time?"

Ensign Prince glanced at his navigational board. "Two minutes."

They wouldn't get there in time. On his own sensor readout he saw that the New Dublin ships were nearly there, less than thirty seconds away. The Swarm carrier wouldn't survive more than a few dozen peta-watt laser blasts.

He turned to the comm. "Patch me through to the flagship."

After a moment, Ensign Prucha nodded. "You're on, sir."

"*ISS Galway*, stand down. I repeat, *stand down*. On Fleet Admiral Zingano's authority himself. There's still five ships to take care of down in lower orbit—plenty of ass-kicking to go around. I repeat, stand down."

Granger drummed his fingers on his armrest. No response. The first mag rail slugs shot out from the bow of the New Dublin flagship.

Dammit! He watched as his hopes melted away with every slug that collided with the hull of the Swarm carrier. All the sacrifice and loss that day, wasted. If that enemy bird didn't get away, if *Warrior* couldn't track it, they'd be back at square one.

They'd allowed half a dozen Swarm ships get away over the past month, and they'd managed to zero in on a few quadrants of space out toward Ursa Major. But it was still far too much space to search through planet by planet. They needed to triangulate better, and for that they needed at least a few more Swarm ships to escape.

"Reading massive internal explosions in the Swarm carrier, sir."

Granger debated telling Azbill over the comm why they were letting the carrier escape. But no. Far too risky. If the Swarm overheard that conversation, and transmitted it back to their homeworld through a meta-space signal, then it was all over. IDF would never learn where the Swarm was coming from, and humanity would be pounded relentlessly into submission, then oblivion.

He had to block that mag rail fire.

"Ensign, move the *Warrior* in between the cruisers and the—"

"Captain!"

Granger spun around to the sensor station at the officer who'd just yelled. The man's face was flustered. Bewildered.

"What?" said Granger.

"More ships, sir. Reading ten—no—fifteen new signals."

Dammit.

"Swarm?"

The officer screwed up his brow. "I—I'm not sure."

"Visual?"

The officer nodded, and punched in a command.

Granger turned toward the viewscreen at the front of the bridge. It flickered, changing views from the bombardment of the hobbling Swarm carrier to the newcomers.

Not Swarm.

Not IDF either.

Russian? Chinese Communion?

Ensign Prucha called out from the comm. "We're being hailed, sir. Video feed."

Granger nodded for the man to put it up on the viewscreen, and within a moment he found himself staring at something he'd thought he'd never see in his life.

Aliens.

A man, or at least, a head attached to a vaguely reptilian torso, looked Granger up and down before opening its mouth. It spoke only one word, and Granger didn't even think to wonder at the fact that it spoke English.

"Leave."

Granger paused as he tried to process what he was seeing and hearing.

The alien spoke again, this time leaning in threateningly toward the screen, its voice twisted in an accent that spoke both of its difficulty with English and its utter foreignness. It was definitely *other*.

"Leave. Or die."

CHAPTER NINE

New Dublin, Eyre Sector
Low Orbit

EVEN THOUGH THE MAIN fighter bays of the Swarm carriers had been destroyed, it seemed that several hundred craft had surrounded the remaining two singularities in an attempt to blockade the sabotage runs. A storm of weapons fire flared all around Ballsy and his crew as they angled through the melee.

"Delta squad is gone. Beta squad is on its way. Our orders are to run interference for them until the package is delivered." Ballsy cranked hard on his control stick and dove down through a formation of enemy bogeys, letting Pew Pew and Fodder savage them with two streams of rapid-fire ordnance. Spacechamp picked off the stragglers. Spatters of rapidly freezing Swarm goo streaked across Ballsy's viewport.

A few moments later Beta squad arrived, and Ballsy and his crew careened toward a dozen bogeys converging on the new-comers. It seemed the Swarm knew exactly which fighters posed their super-weapon the greatest threat as they targeted the fighter with the osmium brick attached to its undercarriage.

"Pew Pew and Fodder, peel off and take out the wings. Spacechamp, cover me."

"No problem, boss. And Ballsy, remember, don't fly like my brother," said Pew Pew.

"Yeah, well don't fly like *my* brother," replied Fodder.

The two fighters sped away in opposite directions. Two brothers. Each headed toward half a dozen enemy fighters. *Don't fly like my brother.* They actually were brothers, something Ballsy had figured out only recently. They always said that when they were in a morbidly cavalier mood—something that came when they faced down hopelessly dangerous situations. Ballsy scanned the wings. There were more bogeys than Ballsy had initially realized, and he suddenly worried that he'd sent them to their deaths. Fodder was always complaining about that—hence his callsign—but a sick certainty hit Ballsy as he became sure he'd finally sent his fellow pilot to his death.

Yet there was no time to worry. He was in the midst of them now, and a sudden jerk told him he'd been hit. But the damage was light, and before another slug could connect he looped around in a tight curve, allowing Spacechamp to blast a few bogeys that had started to tail him. He finished the loop and ended up on her tail, returning the favor as she'd taken on two shadows herself.

"Ballsy, you're hit," said Spacechamp.

He craned his neck around and saw the smoke billowing from his right wing. Technically, he didn't need the wing, so long as he didn't have to re-enter the atmosphere, but if the internal pressure was compromised, or if the starboard stabilizers were damaged, he'd have a hell of a time in the coming minutes.

41

Testing his maneuvering thrusters, he satisfied himself that he was good to go, when suddenly the world seemed to explode. *Am I hit? Damn.* He couldn't even see.

A whooping cheer made him realize that it wasn't him that had been hit. It was the singularity. Beta squad had delivered its package. He breathed a cautious sigh of relief.

"Why are those bricks made out of osmium, anyway?" said Spacechamp as the light from the explosion died down. She was often distracted by details like that, and Ballsy hated it when she wondered things out loud in the heat of battle. How anyone could be distracted during such an intense situation was beyond him. He shrugged the question off, but Fodder answered for him.

"Comes from the asteroid mining ops. They use all the other heavy metals in ship hulls, but the osmium is useless. They just dump it all out in the asteroid belt. But now they finally got a use for that crap."

Ballsy sighed again in relief. Hearing his voice meant that Fodder was alive. He scanned his readout looking for Pew Pew, but didn't see him. He squeezed off a few rounds at a stray bogey as it passed, and searched the field of battle for their next target.

"But isn't that shit poisonous? Osmium?" Spacechamp continued. Ballsy was half tempted to reprimand her for distracting them, but before he could say anything a fireball exploded right behind him.

A bogey, caught in Spacechamp's deadly sights. Damn. The girl was good. Guess she could wonder about trivia and blast cumrats out of the sky at the same time.

"You seen Pew Pew, Spacechamp?" He pulled hard left to avoid running into the smoking skeleton of an IDF light cruiser, then wrapped around hard and blasted two bogeys trailing Fodder to oblivion.

"Nope."

He craned his neck around again, searching for Pew Pew. "Fodder, where's your bro?"

"Don't know, man."

Fodder's voice sounded nonchalant, at ease, as if his brother had just gone outside for an evening smoke. Those two had far more confidence than Ballsy. Hell, what had happened to him the last two months? He was distracted, his confidence wavered—he was nothing like the balls-to-the-wall young space jock he remembered being after graduating from IDF Flight Academy.

He glanced back at the picture of Fishtail's boy holding the toy fighter propped up on his dashboard. *She* had happened to him. He couldn't stop thinking about her, about her son, about that day he'd told the kid her mom wasn't coming home. The whole experience had knocked him on his ass. It surprised him—he was the battle-hardened space jock. He lived for the thrill. He didn't get hung up about women, and he didn't get hung up about lost friends.

But he was hung up.

The new orders flashed up on his console. *Engage the carriers.*

Commander Pierce's voice blared over his comm set in confirmation. "All birds engage the remaining carriers. Fly interference for the New Dublin cruisers. Ignore the fighters as much as possible. Focus all firepower on the carriers. CAG out."

Damn. They'd have to track down Pew Pew later. "You heard him, boys and girls," he said, peeling hard to the right and setting his attack vector on the nearest Swarm carrier. It was just a kilometer away, billowing smoke and debris as the *Warrior* pounded a gaping hole in its side with nearly invisible laser beams. They may have been invisible, but they would incinerate his fighter within a second if he strayed too close.

An anti-matter beam lanced out from the carrier and slammed into the *Warrior*, followed by half a dozen more beams. One of them shot out and caught a New Dublin cruiser right in the bow, initiating a massive explosion that rocked the ship as it passed.

Fodder's voice came over the comm. "Let's go pick off those turrets."

"Agreed," replied Ballsy. "Spacechamp, back us up."

"Aye aye, Ballsy, sir, cap'n lord commander!" Her voice was playfully ironic. For a moment it reminded him of Fishtail. Hell, it seemed everything was reminding him of Fishtail these days. Fighters reminded him of Fishtail. Sleeping and breathing reminded him of Fishtail.

They dove in, streaking and zooming back and forth to avoid the incoming fire from the enemy bogeys swarming them. He tried to remember Commander Pierce's lessons. The CAG held a weekly training session for the seasoned pilots, and they'd just had one that morning. *Keep it random*, he'd said. *If you're predictable, you're dead.*

He bounced back and forth, up and down, as randomly as he could, bobbing and weaving through a cloud of fighters, picking off the occasional target as he often as he could, but keeping his heading toward the carrier. At last, they were there.

"Send a torpedo at that tower, Fodder. Spacechamp and I will cover."

Fodder's fighter leapt forward. A dozen or more enemy fighters careened toward him, and Ballsy shot around them in a gut-churning high-g loop, picking them off one by one with Spacechamp, who matched his moves.

Fodder managed to thread his way through the melee, though Ballsy didn't see how—the cloud of bogeys was thick. This was possibly their most hopeless and deadly skirmish yet, even though the sacrificial cruisers took out over three quarters of the enemy birds in their own fighter bays. A lone torpedo blasted off from Fodder's left wing and slammed into the anti-matter beam tower, even as a green beam lanced out from the turret and slammed into a passing IDF cruiser.

The cruiser and the beam turret simultaneously exploded, and Ballsy flinched as he soared through the expanding cloud of dissipating debris.

"Aw yeah. On to the next, pardner," said Fodder.

They blasted away toward the next tower, halfway down the length of the carrier, and cringed as they saw the dozens of bogeys swarming around it—apparently they were expected.

"Right," Ballsy began. "Nothing for it but to—"

Fodder didn't wait for Ballsy to finish. He accelerated toward the swarm of fighters, guns blazing. "Yeehaw!"

"Careful there, Fodder, don't take your callsign literally," said Spacechamp.

"Babe, this is how I *got* my callsign. Full speed ahead, bitches!"

He plunged right into the thick of the horde, swerving and blasting them to pieces. A handful of slugs caught his tail and wings, but he kept on looping and firing. Ballsy swore and plunged in after him, Spacechamp close behind.

He took a hit. And another. Damn. This was going to be his last flight, he knew.

"I'm hit!" Spacechamp screamed into her headset. "Losing control—" Ballsy watched as a pair of fighters bore down on her, pelting her with several more slugs. But he had his own bogeys to deal with.

They were going to die.

Out of the corner of his eye flashed a bolt of shining metal, weapons fire screaming off its turrets. It was missing its right wing, and Ballsy wasn't sure how it was still navigating, but sure enough it looped around and picked off Spacechamp's tails before shooting straight at Ballsy, who dropped low for it to pass, and as it streaked by it nailed two of his own tailing bogeys.

"Hot enough for ya'?" came Pew Pew's voice. Ballsy sighed in relief: he was still alive, and so was Fodder's brother. Unlikely as both events seemed.

"I told you, don't fly like my brother," said Fodder, who had punched his way through the melee and now launched another torpedo at the second turret. It exploded in a convulsive blast.

The four of them peeled away toward their next target.

"Where the hell is the *Warrior*?" asked Spacechamp.

Ballsy glanced at his scopes, and sure enough, it was gone. Only a few dozen New Dublin cruisers, and all of *Warrior*'s fighters could be seen, pounding away at the five remaining Swarm carriers.

CHAPTER TEN

New Dublin, Eyre Sector
Bridge, ISS Warrior

CAPTAIN GRANGER BOLTED out of his seat. The sight of the individual on the screen—obviously not human, yet speaking Granger's own language—spurred him to action. Or at least to tactically stall until he could find out who, or what, they were dealing with.

"Who am I speaking to?"

No answer. The person on the screen stared at Granger. The eyes reminded Granger of a cat—slitted, dilating, and then shrinking in response to some stimulus Granger wasn't aware of. Slowly, dangerously, it bared its teeth—yellow, spiked teeth that looked like they could cut a man's neck clean off.

"Who are you? This is Earth territory, and this planet is under our protection. I advise you to—"

The alien interrupted. "Stop your attack on our ally. Then leave. You have—" It paused, as if thinking, or considering its words. "—Sixty seconds."

Granger stared at his opponent, then motioned to the comm. "Admiral Azbill. Now."

Ensign Prucha nodded, and frantically called into his receiver. Moments later, Admiral Azbill's voice once again came through the speakers on Granger's station. He motioned to the ensign to mute the audio on the alien's video feed.

"Admiral, are you seeing this?"

"Yeah, Tim," Azbill replied. "Those Russians with masks on?"

"No. This looks like the real deal. Ship design is completely foreign." He glanced at the intel station to be sure, and the officers there all shrugged. "We've got nothing on these guys. You?"

Azbill cleared his throat. "Negative."

Granger looked at the countdown timer one of the tactical crew had enabled on the front viewscreen. They had less than twenty seconds to comply. Twenty seconds to see if those fifteen new warships were as dangerous as they looked. Allies with the Swarm? The idea boggled his mind. If it was true, it could derail their entire war strategy.

"Admiral, we've got to hold fire on that fleeing carrier. Let's see what these people want. Who they are. What they're doing here."

After a short pause, Azbill swore. "Fine. I'll send word to the *Galway*. You're close to them—get a full sensor work up. Full sweep, all frequencies. Neutron scan. Meta-space monitoring. Everything. We need to know what we're dealing with."

Granger nodded, and after a quick glance to Lieutenant Diaz, to make sure the tactical crew was on top of the scans Admiral Azbill had ordered, he motioned back to the comm to un-mute the alien's audio.

He looked back up at the vaguely reptilian man—at least, he assumed it was a male—on his screen. "We have complied. We no longer attack the Swarm vessel."

The alien looked to the side, probably to someone off-camera, for confirmation. Then, turning back, he rested his hands on the table in front of him. "Now leave."

"First, I want to know who you are, and why you've come." Granger knew it would take at least a few minutes for the scanning crews to get anything approaching a useful data set, so he'd have to stall to give them enough time.

"We have come to our ally's aid. Who we are is not relevant."

"It is relevant, sir, as this is our space, and you are the guests. It is not polite to withhold your identity from your host."

It was difficult to read the alien's facial expressions, but to Granger it looked as if the other man scowled. "Guests. We are not your *guests*. We are your adversaries. You are enemies of our ally. The Valarisi have been our friends for ... time. For all time. You will submit to them if you are wise. Continue to resist them at your peril."

Valarisi? Was that what the Swarm called themselves? Odd that after seventy-five years and two devastating invasions, they hadn't even learned the name of their foe.

"And you? What do you call yourselves?"

"We are Dolmasi. Of the Concordat of Seven. The first allies and friends of the Valarisi."

Granger stroked his stubble. "Concordat of Seven? What is that? Are there more civilizations than the Dolmasi who are friends with the Swarm? What are your intentions toward us?"

The alien smiled—at least, as good a approximation of a smile as the face could manage. Granger couldn't tell if it was a natural expression, or if, like the alien's ability to use English, the rudimentary facial expressions were a learned skill.

"Our intentions are to stand by our allies. Our allies wish to bring you into submission, so that is what we will do. We are the second house of the Concordat of Seven. We and our brothers will bury you, unless you lay down your arms, abandon your ships, and welcome the most high Valarisi—the first house of the Concordat of Seven—onto your worlds with open arms."

Granger's fist clenched behind his back. He had half a mind to order a mag rail bombardment right then and there on the lead vessel and teach these people a lesson: you did not come barging in to Earth's territory on the Swarm's behest and expect a warm welcome.

But the exchange bought them some valuable information. Crucial information.

The Swarm could be negotiated with. Communication was possible.

He tossed a questioning glance toward the sensor station at tactical, and the ensign in charge there, Ensign Diamond, shook his head. Damn—they still needed time for their scans. They needed to know everything possible about this new enemy. In case they had to fight them.

"And might I ask your name, sir?"

The alien inclined his head. "Vishgane Kharsa. I am Vishgane of this vessel and all the vessels you see here, and fifty others."

"Vishgane." Granger repeated the word. It must have meant Admiral in whatever language the Dolmasi spoke. "I am Captain Timothy Granger of the *ISS Warrior*. The Swarm—the Valarisi, as you call them—have invaded our space and killed our people. We will expel them. Do not make me expel you as well."

The alien made an odd noise, almost like a grumble or a cough, and it took a moment before Granger realized he was laughing. Interesting—he'd taken the requisite course at IDF Academy for first contact which included topics like xenobiology and xenosociology, and it never occurred to him that an alien would ever develop the social custom of laughing like humanity had. Or was this another learned skill again, and if so, how much had they learned?

"You are in no position to expel us. You command one ship that has the potential to harm us and another twenty that don't."

He shot a quick glance at the sensor station, and made a questioning face to the crew there. With a grimace, the ensign nodded. Apparently they'd had time to parse some of the sensor data and confirmed that the new enemy vessels did indeed pose a threat. A significant one, by the look on Ensign Diamond's face.

Granger glanced at his tactical screen, at the fifteen ships that floated ominously just kilometers away, between them and the lone Swarm carrier which hobbled away at a fraction of its optimal acceleration. He wondered whether the tracking beacon had been damaged in the assault, and if the vessel would be able to q-jump away.

"Perhaps not, Vishgane Kharsa. But would you like to test that theory? I daresay many of you will not survive your encounter with the *ISS Warrior*." He cocked his head toward tactical and murmured, "*Ready anti-matter torpedo.*" They'd never been fielded before—IDF weapons research division had only given them a handful to test—

but he suspected a regular nuke wouldn't be enough to scare them off.

Another coughing grumble, and Vishgane Kharsa spread his arms wide in what Granger guessed was a sign of confrontation. "We care not for survival with the Valarisi as our ally. We sacrifice and die at their command, as is our glorious right."

"So you are slaves then?"

A hiss. That sound and its meaning were obvious. "Slaves? We are no slaves. It is a prestige and an honor to serve the Valarisi. We are the most honored and loyal of their allies."

"Interesting. Your allies seem to have about as much sway over you as a master to his slave." He nodded toward tactical. "Give them a demonstration, Lieutenant. Zee minus ten kilometers. Right under their ass."

"Firing, sir."

On the viewscreen Granger watched as a small projectile shot away from the *Warrior*, and it angled down from the bow until it raced away from them and approached a point several kilometers below the Dolmasi fleet.

A shimmering green beam lanced out from the lead ship and vaporized the torpedo, and it erupted in a muted explosion, its antimatter pod apparently untouched by the detonation.

"Very impressive, Captain Granger."

Granger cringed on the inside—apparently his opponent had not only mastered English, but sarcasm as well.

"We've got thousands more," he bluffed. "Are you willing to take your chances? Leave now, and I promise we will allow you to escape without further violence. But if you stay, be prepared to—"

More coughing laughter, and the Dolmasi Vishgane threw his arms wide again, this time even more aggressively.

"Now it is our turn for a demonstration, Captain. Prepare yourself, if you can."

Granger stepped forward and touched Ensign Prince's shoulder. "Evasive maneuvers, Ensign. Tactical," he motioned toward the station, "full spread of RPO fire. Intercept whatever they're sending at us."

"Aye, sir."

The tactical crew was abuzz with activity as the dozen or so officers coordinated the efforts of the rapid-pulse-ordnance crews down below. Granger turned back to his console to scan for whatever the Dolmasi were sending at them.

He saw it just as the sensor officer called it out.

"Sir! Forty more ships just q-jumped in. They're right on top of us!"

CHAPTER ELEVEN

New Dublin, Eyre Sector
Bridge, ISS Warrior

"MORE DOLMASI? SWARM?" Granger asked.

Ensign Diamond at sensors shook his head, examining his board, and then smiled. But Ensign Prucha beat him to it. "Sir, Fleet Admiral Zingano aboard the *ISS Victory* is hailing us."

Granger relaxed. Finally. He watched the other vessel—almost a carbon copy of both the *Constitution* and the *Warrior*—sail into the midst of the confrontation. IDF's shipbuilding program had not only swung into high gear the past two months, it was several orders of magnitude past overdrive as Earth's entire population—and that of dozens of other worlds—swung into a total-war footing. *Victory* had only been space-worthy for a week, but had already notched two wins. Three, if Zingano had been successful at Centauri earlier in the day.

"Patch him through."

A moment later Zingano's voice boomed over the speakers. "Looks like you could use a hand, Tim."

"Looks that way, Bill. Your arrival is ... timely."

Admiral Zingano grumbled. "The assault at Centauri was a feint. They immediately pulled those ships back and from their q-jump vectors it looked like they were coming in your direction."

Granger nodded. "Thirteen showed up instead of ten."

"And it appears they brought some company. But our new friends seem to be making themselves scarce."

Granger glanced at his tactical readout, and sure enough, the fifteen Dolmasi vessels were pulling back, falling into formation with the lone Swarm carrier as if to escort it out of the system.

Admiral Azbill's voice came over the speakers. "Bill, they're getting away. They could q-jump out of the system at any moment. We need to strike now while their backs are turned."

"No, Admiral," Zingano's voice replied. "We have no idea what the capabilities of those other ships are. If they're leaving without a fight, then we're not going to give them one. Not without more tactical knowledge."

"But, sir! They've destroyed over two dozen of my best ships! Our safety depends on us taking out as many of them as—"

"No, Russell, your safety depends on following my orders to the letter. Or was that not clear when you accepted your admiral's bars? End of discussion."

Ensign Diamond caught Granger's attention. "Sir, they've made their q-jump. All the Dolmasi ships are gone."

He waited expectantly for the key piece of information. "And? The Swarm carrier?"

"Gone as well."

"Please tell me the tracking beacon was still functional."

Diamond tapped a few more controls on his console, furrowing his brow.

He smiled, and looked up.

"Toward Polaris, in the Jorgun Sector."

Granger turned back to the comm. "You hear that, Bill?"

He could almost hear the other man smile on the other end. "I did. I think that's enough for us to enter phase two of Operation Battle-ax."

Admiral Azbill's voice blurted out onto the channel. He was starting to really annoy Granger. "Operation Battle-ax? Why wasn't I told about this?"

"Need to know, Russell. That shouldn't surprise you."

"But this is *my* world they've been attacking today. Governor Wolfram will want to know about your plans to maintain New Dublin's security and—"

Zingano interrupted, his voice approaching impatience. "Russell, we're here to protect humanity. Inasmuch as that means protecting New Dublin, then that's what we do. But I do *not* share operational details of strategic plans with officers that don't have a need to know. Never have, never will. Is that clear? Now get your ass back to New Dublin—"

"I am on New Dublin—"

"—and organize your defenses—the Swarm don't like losing battles like these—you can bet your asses they'll be back within the week. It's their way." Zingano talked right over him until the other man fell silent. The war was clearly getting on everyone's nerves.

"But you include *him* in your plans. The man that came back. The friggin' brick-layer. The one who's probably a Russian agent. Don't deny it, Bill. Even the president has her doubts."

A long pause. Granger smirked at his bridge crew, and a few of them smiled back.

Zingano sighed. "Admiral Azbill, you're relieved. Report to IDF CENTCOM on Earth in two days. Your replacement will arrive then. Zingano out."

The comm crackled, indicating at least one of the lines had terminated.

"Tim, you still there?" came Zingano's voice.

"Yeah, Bill."

"We need to talk. You, me, Proctor, everyone on the war council that I trust."

Interesting. Interesting that he included Proctor in there, and interesting that he distinguished Granger and Proctor from the others with the word *trust*. Trust was a rare commodity at CENTCOM these days, in spite of the total war footing and President Avery running the country and its associate planets like one giant wartime industrial engine.

"At the waypoint?"

"Yes. See you there in one day. Zingano out."

The waypoint. The secret coordinates that only a handful of people knew about. Granger, Proctor, Zingano, and only two or three other admirals. President Avery as well.

He addressed Ensign Prince but remained standing, facing the empty XO's chair. "Get back to New Dublin. We need our fighters and our XO. All hands, stand down from battle stations. Commence repair and recovery operations."

CHAPTER TWELVE

New Dublin, Eyre Sector
Low Orbit

TWO CARRIERS LEFT. They had this in one the bag—against all odds. Volz's face was sweaty and dripping—one of the hits his fighter had taken had knocked out the environmental controls so the cockpit was overheating. Thankfully, his flight suit was fully contained and had enough oxygen to last at least a day, but damn it was hot.

His squad finished off the last anti-matter turret on the closest carrier, and soon they were angling toward the remaining Swarm vessel. "Last call, boys and girls. Let's blow this bastard and then go get drunk and make very irresponsible life decisions."

"Too late," said Spacechamp. "We're already space jocks."

Ballsy smirked. "I'll have you know I'm an upstandin', law-abidin' citizen, ma'am." He pulled the trigger and picked off a stray Swarm bogey. On his sensor screen he noticed another fighter squad nearby getting raked over the coals by a cloud of enemy craft. "On me, boys. Let's spring Stryker Squad outta trouble there."

They veered toward the melee, and Ballsy recognized the voice as soon as it spoke.

"Thank you kindly, Ballsy," said Dogtown, his old squadmate. The voice brought back searing memories of the former squad. Dogtown, Hotbox, Fishtail, Ballsy—two were dead, and two had death's number.

"Hang tight, Dogtown, we're nearly there—"

An explosion cut him off. A Stryker Squad fighter erupted in a fiery cloud as Swarm fighters strafed it in crossfire. Ballsy swore, even as his own squad plunged into the fight, and ten seconds later it was over. He looked around at the field of battle, and at his sensor screen. The last enemy carrier had been neutralized, and was being pummeled by the IDF cruisers bearing down on it. A few dozen Swarm fighters still flew around the cruisers and among their own fighters, but the operation was quickly becoming a mop-up.

He noticed the *Warrior* had returned from chasing down a Swarm carrier, and soon Commander Pierce's voice came over his headset.

"Well done, people. All craft, return to fighter bay. Dogtown and Ballsy, your two squads will bring in the rear and watch for strays."

Strays. It had become a common post-battle Swarm strategy. Inevitably there would be a handful of enemy fighters that would manage to elude them in the mop-up operation, only to reappear as they were returning to the *Warrior*'s fighter bay, harassing them and occasionally making suicide runs at the bay itself.

"Ballsy," came Dogtown's voice, "you and your squad take aft and we'll take fore. When everyone else is in the bay I'll escort my two boys, and you follow in with yours."

"Roger. Taking position now."

He guided his team toward the fighter bay, patrolling the aft side of the entrance as the surviving squads made their landings. Ballsy was thorough, peering around every nook and corner for hidden Swarm craft while scanning his sensor board for any contact. The Swarm somehow were able to turn off all power and reduce all EM emissions to an undetectable level when in hiding, and the *Warrior* was a big ship with many places to hide, especially with so much debris floating around.

"That's it, folks. We're heading in," declared Dogtown. Ballsy watched as he and his two surviving squadmates made their landing.

"Spacechamp, head in. Fodder, follow her. Pew Pew, can you even make a controlled landing with only one wing?"

"I guess we'll find out, man," said Pew Pew.

Ballsy watched with baited breath as Pew Pew made his final, wobbly approach, lurching and tilting as the pilot tried to maintain a straight course on landing. With a jolt and a shower of sparks, he made it, skidding to a stop one hundred meters into the vast bay, nearly crashing into Fodder's craft and only stopping at the last second.

He pulled the controls to guide his fighter into the bay.

"Ballsy! Bogey on your tail!" Spacechamp screamed into his ear.

On instinct, he pulled up and looped around in a tight curve, nearly passing out from the extreme g-force pushing him into his seat. But it was worth it—with a flick of his thumb he pelted the trailing bogey with a stream of fire, and it exploded into a satisfying, muted fireball.

Spacechamp yelled in his ear again. "There's two!"

Twisting his head around, he saw it. It had been hiding behind a large piece of debris from one of the destroyed IDF cruisers, and was now making a full-speed run for the fighter bay. Ballsy was way off course, having been distracted by the first.

"Dammit!" He pulled hard on the controls and wheeled the fighter around, pointing it at the bogey descending full-bore on the fighter bay entrance. His thumb unleashed a storm of fire on the craft.

Mini-explosions ripped through the bogey and it was knocked somewhat off course, but moments later it managed to pull itself aright, and with what Volz supposed must have sounded like a horrific crunch and the shriek of metal on metal, it clipped the side of the fighter bay entrance and spun out of control, passing through the EM shield and tumbling onto the floor, colliding with people and fighters alike before it came to rest, smoldering and steaming.

CHAPTER THIRTEEN

New Dublin, Eyre Sector
Planetary Command Center

PROCTOR HAD NO SOONER listened to Fleet Admiral Zingano dismiss Admiral Azbill when he'd fixed a cold glare on her and said, "Get. Out." Several minutes later she was back on her shuttle, climbing up into the atmosphere toward the distant dot that was the *ISS Warrior*.

From her vantage point it looked like the battle was just a mop-up operation now, as all the Swarm carriers were destroyed and all that remained were a few dozen fighters. By the time the *Warrior* was large enough to fill her window, it seemed all the Swarm fighters had been rounded up and neutralized.

Except one. She watched in horror as a stray bogey fired up its engines from behind a piece of debris and raced toward the fighter bay. One of their own pelted it with fire, but the enemy craft smashed into the fighter bay, leaving fire and destruction in its wake.

"Abort landing in shuttle bay. Get us in there," she said to the shuttle pilot, pointing at the fighter bay. There was still plenty of room for them to land there, and she knew she'd be needed.

Moments later, before the hatch had completely opened and angled down to the deck she jumped off and ran toward the chaos. Broken bodies lay against a wrecked fighter and blood was everywhere. From their uniforms she saw one was a tech, the other a pilot. Other fighter deck crew techs were running with fire suppressants, as others dragged the injured away from the smoldering Swarm fighter.

"Stay clear of it! All non-essential personnel *out!*" She reached down to check the pulse of a tech, but there was no hope for this one. Her forehead was caved in from where the crashing fighter had struck it.

Colonel Hanrahan and his rapid response force arrived, along with a hazmat team, all of them helping to clear the space around the Swarm craft. The characteristic green sludge was dripping out of holes and fissures. The colonel and two pilots assisted a third pilot—Dogtown, one of the few original space jocks they brought over from the *Constitution*. He'd been knocked over, but was at least standing with assistance.

"Came out of nowhere," said a voice behind her. She turned to see Lieutenant Volz. Ballsy, if she remembered right. "Damn cumrat just came out of nowhere. I—I tried to stop it ... but...."

She grabbed his shoulders. He looked shell-shocked—this war was getting to him. It was getting to them all. "Lieutenant. You did everything you could. I was out there—I saw. If it weren't for you, more would be dead."

He was vaguely shaking his head—the young man was clearly still in shock. "If I had have stayed a little closer to the bay. Or if I'd targeted its thrusters instead of its power plant. Or if I'd—"

"Ballsy," she began, looking him in the eye, "listen to me. This is not your fault. Nobody here is at fault. When a killer pulls the trigger, we don't blame the victim for getting in the way. You did your duty, and you did it brilliantly. Look at you! You're still here, two months later. I think that shows that you're one of the best. The best we have."

He shook his head. "Not good enough. Not good enough. Not good enough to save *her*." Before she could ask what he was talking about, he continued: "They're not killers, Commander. They're a force of nature. They're a hurricane. A tornado. An infestation. Calling them killers only grants them humanity, and they are anything but human."

He was rambling of course, but she conceded—internally—that it was a good point. She *had* to get to the bottom of this. IDF and United Earth were losing. Sure, they were racking up victories, but they were ultimately pyrrhic victories. Hundreds of millions were dead already, and millions joined them every week.

And the Swarm were endless. They *were* a hurricane. A force of nature. Volz nailed it.

"Go get some sleep, Ballsy." She let go of his shoulders and turned him toward the exit.

But before she could guide him toward the doors, the shuttle bay exploded again.

She was knocked down by the force of a blast from behind. When she opened her eyes and looked around, several things stood out to her. The explosion wasn't nearly as destructive as she feared. It was only some minor blast coming from the Swarm fighter—probably an overloaded power cap going critical.

But the other thing she noticed was far more disturbing. Colonel Hanrahan, Dogtown, and the two pilots helping him had been much closer to the fighter, and were laying motionless nearby. And worse—green sludge was smeared all around them. Swarm matter had blasted out from the fighter and had sprayed out onto them.

"Hazmat! Get them isolated and cleaned! Now!" She beckoned to the suited hazmat crew, who rushed to the fallen crew members. Thankfully, she saw all of the men move, so at least they weren't dead.

But they might be far worse than dead.

CHAPTER FOURTEEN

Boulder, Colorado, Earth
Office of the Vice President, Tertiary Presidential Bunker

Vice President Isaacson knew many things, but the thing he was most sure about was that the office of Vice President was the most useless office in the world.

"Sir, President Avery would like to talk to you privately in her chambers." The aide called the news in lazily from his office, which was literally just a closet next to Isaacson's own office, which itself barely qualified as a room.

He'd been moved out of his old sprawling office building, and god he missed that place. Lavish, finely decorated, right next to the fountains in the courtyard at the old North American presidential mansion just outside the border of D.C., and far more private than his current setup.

They'd moved him at President Avery's orders. Ever since that day over two months ago when the Swarm attacked Earth, Avery would not permit him to be in the same room—or the same city—as her.

Not out of any loathing or ill feelings she may have born him, though he supposed she didn't hold him in

66

any particularly high esteem. But there was security to consider. If a Swarm singularity bomb were to hit the main presidential compound with Avery in it, at least the government would still have continuity of leadership.

He was the fallback. The contingency plan. The back-up. But until that time he was needed, he was utterly useless. Troop inspections and morale parades were about all he was allowed to do.

"Now?"

The aide sipped his coffee before responding. "The message says to be there in two hours."

"So basically, now. It takes nearly two hours to get there." He glanced at his watch, then wistfully at the stack of reports and briefings piled high on his desk. He was not born for paperwork. He was born for hookers and tequila. And there was a disturbing lack of both in his new bunker of an office here buried underneath a mountain outside Denver.

"One hour, forty-five minutes, yes, sir." The aide tapped the comm patch tattoo on his wrist. "I'll arrange for your shuttle. By the time you get up there it should be ready for takeoff."

"Fine. And get my new body man. That new intern. What's his name?"

"Conner?"

"Yeah. I'll need someone to arrange my coffee and accommodations while I'm out there—it's nearly five o'clock, so by the time I get there and meet with the old battle-ax it'll be well past my bedtime. And one does *not* keep little presidents-in-waiting up past their bedtimes," he added with an ironic drawl, mimicking President Avery.

Twenty minutes later he emerged from the last elevator out into the glaring winter sunlight and pulled his coat tight around him. The intern, a young man who'd been drafted only a month prior, was waiting for him, holding a heavier coat. "Brought this for you, sir. Thought you'd need it."

Nice touch. The kid was young, but not stupid. "Thank you, Conner. Shall we?" Isaacson thumbed in the direction of the shuttle waiting on the launch pad, engines whining in the background.

Conner picked up the overnight bag he carried for Isaacson whenever his duties required him to travel. Usually, he'd rely on whatever establishment was hosting him to see to his every need, even cater to his whims. But times had changed. Almost overnight, the world had changed.

Earth, and most other populated worlds, were on a war footing. Not just a casual war involving just the half-percent of the population that ever volunteered for the military. This was total war. Entire industries co-opted by the government and re-geared to produce capital ships and fighters instead of cruise liners, missiles and torpedoes instead of personal vehicles, targeting computers instead of personal entertainment devices. Everything was different. The stakes were high, so Earth—and President Avery—had risen to the occasion.

"Have a seat, son," he said to Conner, and motioned him toward one of the other passenger chairs. Soon, they were in the air, blazing through the upper atmosphere at three kilometers per second. The noise cancellation system seemed to be down, and an unholy roar pierced the cabin.

"Sorry, sir, we're having maintenance issues," shouted the captain of the shuttle, a squat man with a mustache buckled firmly into his cockpit seat. Isaacson noticed no such restraints on the passenger seats.

"Delightful," Isaacson drawled. "Are we going to make it in one piece, or shall I alert the speaker of the house that he's next in line? I'm sure Mr. LaPierre will be overjoyed."

A gruff laugh. "Sit down, sir, and enjoy the ride. Be there in an hour. Less if we can get through D.C. secure airspace faster than a turd through clogged pipes."

Blue collar workers. He rolled his eyes and focused on the data pad that Conner had pulled out of his overnight bag for him. "Thank you, son."

Conner nodded a brief smile, then closed his eyes, gripping his armrests tightly and apparently making a good play at relaxing.

"You nervous, son?"

The boy opened his eyes with a start. "Sir?"

"Nervous?"

"Oh, it's just ... I hate flying, sir."

"Understandable. You're young, and ... what are you, eighteen? Play sports? You look like a football player."

Conner shrugged. "Nineteen, and yeah, I played my freshman year of college. No, sir, I've never had problems flying. Not until ... well, you know."

Isaacson knew. The smoking craters were still smoldering from the heat of the blasts. Except for Miami. The Gulf of Mexico had flooded into that particular crater. And most of New Orleans as well. But Houston, Phoenix, San Bernardino, and Riverside ... they were desolate, craggy pits.

"Body like that, you should be in the Marines, son. Or at least the Marine's football team." Isaacson settled in to read through the latest casualty reports coming in from the day's skirmishes. It had been a busy week—over a dozen different Swarm incursions.

But each one repelled. Half of them by Captain Granger himself. Gods, the man was practically a legend in his own time. Even half the admiralty was eating out of his goddamned hand.

And for what? It's not like the man was a god. He was no superhero. He was just particularly skilled at using his people and ships as cannon fodder. The brick-layer. He rolled his eyes at the latest report: thirteen state-of-the-art heavy cruisers used as battering rams. Wasted. Thrown away just so Granger could claim another stunning victory.

Conner shrugged again. "Yeah, I guess I could have been drafted into the Marines. But they sent me to the administrative corps instead. Don't know why. Studied political science in college, but only for a year. And bad grades at that—too busy playing football. I figured someone was...."

He trailed off. Isaacson glanced up. "Was what?"

"Never mind. Need anything else, sir? I could use a nap. Stayed up half the night."

"Gotta get your sleep, son. Can't stay up watching football games."

The young man clenched his jaw. Apparently he'd touched a nerve. "Just waiting for your call last night, sir. They told me to stay by my phone in case you needed me for the base readiness tour you were supposed to—"

"Ah, yes. Sorry about that. I cancelled at the last minute. There's too many of those damn things. They do nothing but parade me around like a mascot, supposedly to build troop morale or some shit."

Conner scowled, but closed his eyes and gripped the armrests again. "Yes, sir."

They travelled in silence the rest of the way, and true to the captain's word they managed to fly straight through the controlled airspace above D.C. without any problems. The airspace commission bureaucrats had apparently finally coordinated with the bureaucrats down in the executive office, and *they'd* coordinated with the space force pencil pushers—one big happy administrative circle-jerk. It was a wonder Earth was still standing.

It is still standing because the Swarm failed. And they almost didn't fail because of you.

He shuddered, and pushed the thought aside. It wasn't supposed to be this way. He was supposed to be president by now. Avery was supposed to be dead, and the Swarm pushed back to their own territory. Ambassador Volodin had assured him that was the case.

But Volodin had been recalled to St. Petersburg. Isaacson hadn't seen his old friend in two months. Heh—*friend*. Erstwhile co-conspirator was more accurate. He looked out the window and saw the familiar, sprawling D.C. skyline extending to the horizon in all directions. Now approximately ten times its original boundaries, it was half the size of Maryland. With great galactic republics came great administrative responsibilities.

The ship lurched. He glanced out the window again and saw their course had changed. "Hey. What's up, Captain?"

"Change of plans."

Isaacson stood up. Conner looked to be asleep so he moved past taking care not to brush up against him.

"What do you mean, *change of plans?*" he demanded.

"Sorry, sir, we've been given a new destination. There's been an explosion at the executive mansion."

Isaacson's stomach lurched. Russians again? Were they still at it? He'd explicitly told Volodin right after the invasion that the plans were off. He was out of the assassination game. There was no time for shit like that with Earth's existence on the line. "President Avery?"

"No idea, sir. They just tell me where to fly, and I go there. Order came from her chief of staff himself."

Why didn't they tell him directly? Just like the president's staff to keep Isaacson in the dark. Her chief of staff was prickly, efficient, and had never liked Avery's veep.

"Where are we going?"

71

The pilot pointed to a spot on the map. Isaacson blinked. "Not possible."

"Regardless, sir, that's where we're going. I triple confirmed—thought my earwax had built up too much."

The pilot's finger returned to the navigational controls, but Isaacson was still fixed upon the location on the map the man had pointed to. He sighed—Avery had apparently kept a lot of things from him.

Including secret bases in the middle of the Atlantic Ocean.

CHAPTER FIFTEEN

Atlantic Ocean, Earth
Subsurface Presidential Bunker Eight

IT ONLY TOOK THEM another forty-five minutes to re-enter the upper atmosphere and shuttle out to the coordinates in the middle of the Atlantic. By then it was dark, and all Isaacson could see out his window was the top of a sea of clouds illuminated by the nearly full moon.

The captain's voice called from the cockpit. "We're here, sir. Descending now. Hold tight—I've been told to make the descent quick-like. Leaf on the wind and all that."

Isaacson had no idea what the captain was talking about, but without waiting for a reply he sent the shuttle into a steep dive. The craft only had light-duty momentum cancelers, and so both Isaacson and Conner were forcefully thrown forward and nearly ended up on the floor as the front of the shuttle pointed down sharply; just as abruptly they were then thrust back into their seats as the craft accelerated.

Isaacson noticed Conner's white knuckles gripping the armrests and his wide eyes darting from the window to the cockpit and back again.

Poor kid. "Nearly there, son."

Conner nodded quickly.

Dammit, the kid was probably going to pass out from the g-forces pressing them back into their seats. Isaacson was a little unnerved himself, but at least he wasn't about to vomit—Conner's face, meanwhile, had turned an unmistakable hue of green.

"Tell me about yourself, son. Where are you from? Where's your family?"

The green face turned red. "Miami, sir."

Isaacson's stomach clenched. *Aw, shit.* "I see. I'm so sorry."

Conner nodded his acknowledgment of the sympathy. "I was at college up in Massachusetts at the time. Kingsford college. They sent us to a bunker that morning, and since it was after finals we decided to throw a little party. We had no idea it was a real invasion—thought it was a drill. Got pretty plastered. I ... I felt the shaking, but I thought it was just the beer messing with my balance. Shit, sir—I felt Miami explode from over a thousand miles away."

Isaacson glanced out the window—they'd descended below the clouds and all was pitch black. He hoped the captain knew what he was doing.

"I'm sorry, son. Yeah, I remember that night. I was in the Omaha command center—wasn't dark yet there, but—"

Conner interrupted, the memories apparently making him forget his manners. "It was night up there, and I came out of the bunker at one point and looked up. South, toward the horizon. Saw flashing lights way, way up there. Saw something explode with a flash so bright I had to shut my eyes. Then something like a real slow meteor flying away from the flash. I ... I think I saw the *Congress* go down.

It was heading out toward the east, at least, so I think it was the *Congress*. Crashed out in the ocean, didn't it?"

Isaacson nodded. Dammit, if they were going to give him a neurotic basket case for an intern, couldn't they have at least made it some hot young thing in a miniskirt?

"And ... and, your family? They were in Miami at the time?" said Isaacson almost absentmindedly as he stared out the window toward what he assumed was the surface of the ocean just a kilometer or two below. Where the hell was this secret base of hers?

He immediately wished he hadn't asked. Conner's face screwed up. Contorted with a valiant effort to stave off tears. But within a few seconds, to the boy's credit, he'd pulled it together. Good kid.

"Yeah. My brother was away at school out in L.A., but my mom, dad, two little sisters ... yeah. Gone."

Isaacson had nothing to say, so he kept quiet. Soon, the captain called back, "Here we go. Hold on—"

They both held firmly to their armrests as the craft decelerated at a stomach-lurching rate. Isaacson glanced out the window again, just in time to see a giant tube extend upward out of the water. Since the running lights of the shuttle were not powered—he supposed as a stealth measure—the only illumination came from several tiny red lights circling the rim of the tube.

It opened. Like a giant maw that grew frighteningly large as they approached, it swallowed them up as they passed below the level of the water, but he soon realized that the tube was water-free, and extended deep into the ocean. They plunged straight down for several minutes, the walls of the tube now illuminated by the shuttle's internal cabin light.

They stopped. Below them another iris-shaped door opened, admitting them to a large bay. Several other ships were parked on pads, but no one waited to greet them.

"Follow me," said the captain after the ship had come to rest. He opened the door and led them into the giant bay, passing a ship Isaacson recognized as Interstellar One, the president's personal star-liner. The lights were off, but the underside of the craft still radiated a substantial amount of heat, so he assumed she had only just arrived, too.

"This way, Mr. Vice President." The captain waved a hand slowly past an ID scanner and the bay door heaved open with a mechanical sigh. Odd—he assumed the man was just a simple taxi pilot—a self-styled captain of his own personal shuttle. But, clearly, his security credentials were of the highest caliber.

They walked down a long, stark, poorly-lit hallway, wet with condensation, and soon entered what would have looked like a highly sophisticated command center were it not for all the cots and cooler chests littering the room. It had apparently been lived in by a small army of presidential staffers.

And there she was, right in the middle of her usual entourage: Chief of Staff Miller, a few ever-present aides, Congresswoman Sparks (her direct contact and hand in Congress), General Norton, (the chairman of the Joint Chiefs of Staff), and of course, her poodle, held by what he assumed was a bodyguard, judging by the sidearms strapped to the well-built man's waist.

"Eamon. Good—you're here." President Avery strode over, abruptly cutting off General Norton and extending a firm hand for Isaacson to shake. A large turquoise ring bulged out from one of her fingers—the one piece of jewelry she ever wore. "How's your bunker? Ha! Look at us. Hiding like little girls while our enemies make plans behind our backs. You heard, didn't you?"

"What's that, Madam President?" he asked, falling into step with her as she pulled him by the arm toward a small office off of the main floor. When they'd all filed in and General Norton pulled the door shut behind him, she put her hands on her hips and regarded them all.

"All right, all of you out. Just Eamon. Give us a moment."

Her entourage dutifully stood up and left. Isaacson glanced at Conner, who looked like he didn't quite know what to do with himself, and motioned with his head toward the door. When it was closed she grabbed his arm again and pulled him in close.

"Someone is trying to kill me, Eamon. Someone on the inside. And they very nearly succeeded today."

He tried to look shocked, but before he could say anything, she pulled him in closer and whispered. "And I think they're trying to kill you, too."

CHAPTER SIXTEEN

Atlantic Ocean, Earth
Subsurface Presidential Bunker Eight

AVERY LOOKED HIM UP and down, apparently watching for his reaction. After a moment she repeated herself. "Did you hear me? Someone is trying to kill me. *And* you."

You don't say? Isaacson though with a slight inward smile. If Volodin was behind it, he supposed the other man would try to make it look like he was trying to take out both of them. Less suspicious that way.

He tried to look serious. And concerned—she'd want to see him concerned.

"But why bring me here? I thought it was wisest to keep us apart. You know ... for the sake of leadership continuity in case...." He trailed off.

"In case the bastards shove a stick of dynamite up my ass? Ha!" She turned and grabbed a chair, spun it around and sat on it backward. She was full of swagger—just like during her campaign, but the recent months seemed to have given her a rougher edge.

"Somehow I doubt—" he began, circling the room.

"That someone is trying to kill me?"

That someone would use dynamite, he thought. He knew perfectly well there were plenty of people that wanted her dead. Himself included. At least, he did two months ago. He had to admit that with the national emergency she'd risen to the occasion rather dramatically.

She'd been smirking, but her face turned serious and she pulled out a flask from her jacket. "Look, Eamon, I've made a lot of enemies. You should know. I only chose you as veep to get the Federalist Party out of my hair and appease half the people calling for my head—oh, don't give me that look, we both knew that. Let's cut the shit."

Avery offered the flask to him, and after hesitating a split second, he accepted it and drank. Bourbon.

"Very well," Isaacson said. "And I only accepted because I thought you'd be ousted in the first vote of no-confidence within a year of the election and I'd be fast tracked for the presidency."

"Ha! Now we're getting somewhere." She grabbed the flask back and swigged. "You bet your fat ass you were fast tracked. Probably more than you know. I knew there were rumblings for the vote, but I also knew I had the votes. The next one, though ... who knows?" She stopped the flask and tucked it away. "But it's in the past. Times change. We woke up in a completely different world, you and I, two months ago."

He nodded his approval. "And you've done a singularly remarkable job, ma'am."

"Not good enough." She pulled the flask out, despite having just tucked it away, drank again, and coughed. "I appreciate the sentiment. But the truth is that we need to work together to survive. Not just my life. Not just your life. But all our lives." She looked up at him, and he finally noticed the deep bags under her eyes. In spite of the no-nonsense tough-as-nails commander-in-chief persona she'd cultivated, she looked deadly tired. "They're coming, Eamon. All these skirmishes are just feints. There's no reason they can't just send two hundred carriers to Earth tomorrow and wipe us out of existence."

He drummed his fingers on his cheek. Isaacson remembered the message the Swarm had sent Ambassador Volodin during their brief flight on the *Winchester* during the battle of Earth. *You die.* Terse, but to the point.

And yet two months later, they hadn't come. At least, not in force, and not to Earth.

Volodin knew something. He knew a lot of somethings, none of which he'd told Isaacson, who decided right then he'd force it out of the ambassador. Beat it out of him if he had to. He was almost sure the other man was under the influence of the Swarm, but those last moments in the Omaha command center had convinced him otherwise. And yet there was still something *off* about him. Something out of place. Why be so insistent on assassinating Avery, plot a convoluted scheme with Isaacson and President Malakhov to get rid of her, and then, at the first failure, retreat back to Russia with nary a word, and then supposedly make more attempts on her life without telling him?

It didn't make sense.

"Eamon," she began, "there are Senators. Governors. Congressmen. Many of them hate me, yes, I understand that. It's politics. But there's a group of them plotting my death. For whatever deluded reasoning they've conjured into their vacant brains, they think I'm a threat. Even before the emergency, they wanted me dead. Is it because of my past? My policies? My vagina? You know some of them can't stand seeing an uppity woman grab them by the political balls and squeeze unless they do my bidding. They hate it. They hate me, for whatever reason."

He nodded. He agreed—in fact, he'd been one of them. For months he'd met secretly with over a dozen of them, plotting the overthrow, scheming ways to get her out of office. Only a handful knew of the plans to kill her, but he knew there must have been others that shared the sentiment.

"Will you help me? We need to find them. Root them out, before it's too late. And believe me, Eamon, in a few months—maybe even a few weeks, it could be too late."

He closed his eyes and sighed. "I will help, Madam President. I'm friends with several of the factions, and dozens of senators owe me favors. I have a few thoughts about who it could be, but I'd rather keep that to myself for now. Give me some resources. Secret Service. Intelligence service. With my contacts and their ... methods, I'm sure we can nail a few of these bastards."

She stood up and reached out for his arm with a warm, vulnerable smile. She was so charismatic. Endearing. No wonder she'd won two elections outright, with no runoffs.

"Thank you, Eamon. I knew I could trust you."

He gripped her hand in return. "And I'm honored to have your trust, Madam President."

"Oh, Madam President my hairy ass. Call me Barb."

She laughed again, and pulled the door open, waving her entourage back in. General Norton walked right up to her, about to speak, before glancing uneasily at Isaacson.

"Go on, General. Mr. Isaacson has clearance. What is it?"

The old soldier grumbled. "Madam President, I've just received word from the expeditionary force following up on Granger's most recent lead."

That caught her attention. She grabbed his arm. "And?"

"We found one. A Swarm world."

CHAPTER SEVENTEEN

The first thing he noticed were two blindingly bright lights above him. Was he on the Constitution? *No—the color was off. The lights in sickbay were warmer. Inviting. Healing light.*

These were cold. Almost blue. Harsh. One was bigger than the other.

He tried to move—it was hard. His limbs didn't want to cooperate. It felt like moving through a pool of crystallized honey, but eventually, he managed to lift his head.

He was in a room. Small. A few more tables, some unfamiliar medical or technical instruments scattered on workbenches by the wall.

The strain was too much. He let his head fall back against the table, and just stared at the lights. Hours seemed to pass. Days? But when he lifted his head again he knew there were people in the room. Friendly people? Or enemies? It was all so hazy. The faces indistinct.

He fell asleep again, and when he awoke, he realized he could move his limbs—they were finally mobile. The pain had gone.

But he felt someone in the room behind him. He lifted his head to get a better look.

CHAPTER EIGHTEEN

The Waypoint, Near Sirius
Bridge, ISS Warrior

CAPTAIN GRANGER BOLTED upright in his bed, gasping, hands clutching at his chest. The tumors ... the cancer ... the wilting pain—was it back?

He breathed deeply. Then whirled around to glimpse the person he knew stood behind him.

But the room was empty. It was just his bedroom on the *Warrior*, after all. The nearest people were the two marines standing guard outside his quarters.

It was a dream. Just a dream.

But it seemed like more. It felt so ... real. So immediate and tangible and....

He shook his head. Was it possible? Was he remembering his ordeal? His *vacation*, as gossip on board called it? The dreams were occurring with increasing regularity. Always the same. Always hazy and incomplete and distant, like he was watching a film through blurred glass.

But they were becoming clearer. They were becoming memory, not dream. Dammit, he *had* to remember what happened to him. He felt like their lives depended on it.

"Sir, just a few more q-jumps away from the coordinates," said Ensign Prucha over the comm.

He shook his head again to clear it. "I'll be there in a minute, Ensign. Thank you."

There'd been no reason to change out of his uniform when he slept at night—there was never the need. The Swarm incursions happened with such regularity that he found it far more convenient to only change when he showered. And so minutes later he settled into his chair on the bridge as a yeoman brought him his morning coffee. Was it morning? He glanced at the clock and realized he'd only slept two hours.

The *ISS Warrior* snapped into existence in an unremarkable area of space, just two and a half lightyears away from Sirius. The star shone brightly on the viewscreen, easily the most luminous object visible. Granger cocked his head toward the sensor station.

"Anything?"

Ensign Diamond shook his head. "Nothing yet, sir."

Granger stood up and nodded. "Very well. Looks like we wait."

"Just like Avery. Always keeping people waiting," said Proctor.

Granger eyed her wryly. "You don't like her, do you?"

Proctor shrugged. "She's my commander in chief. Doesn't matter whether I like her or not."

"But you didn't vote for her."

"I ... decline to answer." Proctor tapped her console and changed the subject. "Admiral Zingano should be here momentarily. He was going to make a brief pass through the Proxima System just to review readiness there, but that shouldn't take him long."

"We need all the time we can get to make these repairs." Granger examined the reports on his command console. "How's the hull repair coming?"

"The main hole on the bow has been patched. That blast took out two whole mag rail guns and a laser turret, so we'll have to completely replace them. We've got a dozen of each in storage, but it'll take crews a week to install them. The rest of the hull damage is lighter, but will still take us about a week."

Granger shook his head. "Too long. We need to be on the move. The next engagement could come in a week or it could come tomorrow."

"If we get in a fight tomorrow we may not last long, sir. Especially not if it's thirteen Swarm carriers like today."

She was right, dammit. They'd have to lay low for a bit, or at least choose their engagements more carefully. Nearly three weeks of almost daily skirmishes had taken their toll. In fact, they were due at Churchill Station in the Britannia Sector to pick up replacement fighters and pilots. The losses were harrowing: thirty-five more pilots gone, including their birds, along with some support staff that had been standing in the wrong place when that enemy bogey slammed into the fighter bay.

"We'll try to keep a low profile the next few days. Besides, I think I have an idea about what we'll be doing, and it hopefully won't involve flying into the middle of large formations of Swarm ships."

She nodded, and before she could question further, Ensign Diamond called out. "Sir, the *Victory* just q-jumped in."

Ensign Prucha added, "Admiral Zingano on the horn, sir."

"Patch him through."

The admiral's voice blared over the speakers. "Long time no see, Tim. Avery should be along any minute now. Had a few last minute meetings on Earth. You heard about the latest attempt on her life?"

Granger leaned forward. "No, I hadn't. Who's trying to kill her? Swarm? Do they have agents on Earth?"

"That's what we're trying to get to the bottom of. And that incident with the Dolmasi at New Dublin—well that just confirmed what we suspected. That the Swarm are able to manipulate and control. How the bastards do it as a damn puddle beats me, but Avery's not leaving things to chance. She's left the capital and is running things from a series of secret command centers."

"Is it the Russians? Could they be controlled somehow?"

It was a dangerous question in a way. It reminded everyone that he, too, had been in some sort of mysterious contact with the Russians, during his disappearance. And if the Swarm could control, and if the Russians were under their influence, then he had to tread carefully—what if *he* were under their influence? It was unthinkable, but it was something to consider.

"Don't know, Tim. We've made diplomatic progress recently with Malakhov to get more support with the war effort. At first they tried to pull the neutrality shit, but we reminded them of what happened last time they tried to sit out a war."

Granger shook his head. "I can't believe we're thinking about trusting them."

"Look around you, Tim. We're in a bad place. We can use all the help we can get."

He shrugged. "Yeah, but I don't have to like it."

The arrival of *Interstellar One* and the two escort missile frigates interrupted them. The three ships blinked into place, the stately, sleek presidential ship hovering in between two equally sleek, but deadly-looking military vessels, packed to the teeth with weaponry. Granger knew they were basically mini-*Constitution*s, almost solid blocks of tungsten, but about one hundred times smaller and with a crew of fifty. The hulls were so thick and the mag rails so numerous that there was only room for that many. One captain and forty-nine gunners. The president took her safety seriously.

"Incoming transmission from the president's ship, sir. Conference call to both us and *Victory*. Visual."

"Patch it through." Granger turned to the viewscreen and smiled at the two people who appeared. Fleet Admiral Zingano, and President Avery.

Except she looked odd. A little more haggard. A little different. Had she changed her hair? No, that wasn't it.

"Admiral, Captain," she nodded. "Shall we meet aboard the *Victory*?"

Admiral Zingano grunted. "Not quite finished building the ship yet, Madam President. We've got a hull and weapons and that's about it. We'll come to you."

"Very well, Admiral. See you soon." Her half of the screen blanked out.

Zingano gestured up at the screen. "She looks tired, don't she?"

Granger raised an eyebrow at Zingano. "Tired? More like a different person. She needs to get out into the sunlight more."

"So do we all. You'd look like an albino, Tim, if it weren't for your scruff. Don't you shave anymore?"

Granger grumbled. "Been a busy week. Killing cumrats takes precedent over my grooming."

The admiral chuckled. "Well, when this is all over I'll have time to court martial you." He thumbed to his side. "Come on. Let's get over there."

The image blinked out, replaced by a view of *Interstellar One* and its escorts.

And then the escort ship to the left of President Avery's vessel exploded.

CHAPTER NINETEEN

Atlantic Ocean, Earth
Subsurface Presidential Bunker Eight

AN ACTUAL, LIVE, honest-to-god Swarm world. At least, that was what General Norton had claimed last night. The scout ships had found the impossible. An entire planet, imaged at a distance from the edge of its solar system. No resolution, of course, but spectrographic analysis indicated the definite presence of Swarm matter. Isaacson shuddered—at least that hypothesis was confirmed. The Swarm was in fact, liquid.

"More coffee," he said absent-mindedly.

Conner jumped up and poured out another cup, and Isaacson paged through the stack of security reports his new contacts at the secret service had given him. Reams of paper detailing illegal activities among the staffs of several key senators, a few of which he knew very well from his many meetings with them planning Avery's demise.

His own chief of staff, Hal Levin, sat across from him. Isaacson tossed him a piece of paper. "Look at that. Senator Quimby. The Service caught him embezzling campaign funds."

"So?" Levin asked lazily, glancing over the paper. "Everyone does that."

"Yes, but look at where the money came from. Avery's own fundraising operation donated a sizable chunk toward his reelection. She thought she could sway him over on the Eagleton Commission decision. In return he not only voted against it, but spent her money on a new mansion in Hungary. Idiot."

Levin scanned the paper while absentmindedly holding his mug out to Conner, who refilled it. "Quimby looks like he's hit some hard times. Most of his businesses were folding even prior to the war, and now to add insult to injury they've drafted every single one of his kids. All five of them."

Isaacson snorted. "His fault for having kids." He sipped his coffee. Too hot. No sugar. Dammit, Conner. "Plus, *everyone's* kids have been drafted."

"Yes, but he's a senator. He could've pulled strings."

"True," Isaacson said, spooning sugar into the coffee slowly, looking over the next document. "But they've been clamping down on that. It's total war, Lev. No one's exempt." He stirred. "Where'd they get drafted to?"

Levin scanned the page. "One's in IT production, three in IDF...."

"And the fourth?"

Levin turned the paper over, scanning. "Doesn't say."

"What do you mean it doesn't say?" He snatched the paper from Levin and found the paragraph. Sure enough, it was very clear where four of the five children of Senator Quimby had been drafted to. But the fifth, the oldest, Quimby's daughter that had just graduated ... nothing.

"Maybe she hadn't been assigned yet when they pulled the file?" Levin browsed through another stack of papers. "Tell me again what it is we're looking for?"

"I told you," Isaacson began with a sigh. "Someone's trying to kill Avery. Someone on the inside. She wants me to help track the assholes down."

"But doesn't everyone hate the bitch? I mean, come on, Eamon, it could be just about anyone," Levin said with a wry grin. Isaacson debated telling his chief about his involvement with Volodin and the Senate faction that wanted Avery out, but in spite of how much he trusted the man, that was one bit of information that needed to remain unspoken. Especially with Conner hovering.

He swiped the stack of papers aside in frustration. What the hell was he doing? He had to produce a few culprits for Avery, otherwise she'd suspect him. Which one to finger? Quimby? Senator Smith? Senator Patel? House Speaker LaPierre? Hell, he should just expose all of them and then start from scratch.

But in the background, underneath it all, Isaacson knew where to look: there was Volodin. What the hell was the man up to?

Damn. Damm*it*. "Conner," he said, looking up. "We're leaving. Pack my bags. Get yourself ready."

The kid nodded. "When?"

"Now."

Levin clucked his tongue. "Prison break? And just where do you think you're going without Avery's permission? She wants you in this bunker twenty-four seven. You're only to be let out for the occasional troop inspection."

"No, she just wants my location to remain unknown. The easiest way to do that is, of course, to stay here. But I can go wherever the hell I want."

"And where do you think you're going, Eamon?"

Isaacson stood up and pointed to the stack of papers, then motioned at his aide sitting over by the wall so that she'd put them away in the classified cabinet. She sprang to her feet.

"Moscow," he said, halfway out the door.

CHAPTER TWENTY

The Waypoint, Near Sirius
Bridge, ISS Warrior

GRANGER COULDN'T BELIEVE his eyes. "Hard about! Get us clear of the blast!" He couldn't tell what type of explosion it was—power plant failure, or capacitor bank overload. But if it was an anti-matter leak they needed to move. It looked bright enough for it.

The ship lurched as it accelerated away, and lurched again as the blast front washed over them. Granger bolted toward the tactical station and gripped Ensign Diamond's shoulder. "What the hell was that?"

"Looking over sensor logs now, sir." The man swiped through data and radiation image maps before glancing up. "Anti-matter leak in the engines. There was a gamma emission spike at reactor four right before the blast. Somehow all their anti-matter was injected all at once."

Granger spun toward the comm station. "Get them back."

A moment later Zingano and Avery reappeared on the screen, the admiral with a face of shocked anger and the president with her mouth still hanging open.

Only it wasn't the president. It made sense now. He pointed at her. "You're not Avery, are you?"

The woman slowly shook her head, still speechless.

Zingano punched his console, sending plastic shards flying, composite pieces cutting into his fist. "Shit!"

"I'm one of her doubles," said the woman, who, on further inspection, looked less and less like Avery.

"Then where is the president?" Granger asked, knowing exactly what she'd say, but he still had to ask. It couldn't be. How?

Their troubles were far deeper than he'd imagined.

"She was ... she was on that ship, Captain...."

One of the president's aides came on the screen, stepping in front of the double. Congresswoman Sparks. Avery had decided that having one of her aides be a member of congress would get her better access, contacts, and results in the petulant legislative body. "Captain, Admiral, can you explain this?"

"No, ma'am." Zingano was picking pieces of the console out of his fist, still swearing.

Sparks buried her face in her palms. "Shit," she said. Words seemed to be failing them all.

She looked back up. "Get over here. Both of you. It looks as though we have even more to discuss."

CHAPTER TWENTY-ONE

Moscow, Russia
Yuri Volodin's Office, Diplomatic Complex

THE FLIGHT OVER the Atlantic went quickly, and Conner seemed to have overcome his fear of flying—at least temporarily. Isaacson kept him busy with menial tasks and busywork. Something to occupy his mind so he wouldn't focus on the clouds rushing by dozens of kilometers below at over ten times the speed of sound.

Landing in Moscow, half his secret service detail exited first, securing the path he'd take to the United Earth embassy. The last minute nature of his trip precluded finding any secure hotels or official government residences, and besides, he wanted to stay in a place where he knew not only that he was being bugged, but exactly where the bugs were and who was doing the bugging.

"Take my things to the room, and get the usual ready for me."

Conner nodded. "The usual?"

"Coffee, masseuse, some good Russian porn, and maybe a girl or two. Clean—I don't want to catch anything. Go to Marco's place—tell him I sent you. He has the best ones. Oh, and feel free to grab one for your-self—it's on me."

"Coffee?"

Isaacson rolled his eyes. "Right. The coffee's on me. Go on, see you in a few hours."

The secret service escorted him to the embassy just a short walk away, and from there he got in an embassy ground car that would take him to Volodin's office downtown.

Moscow had changed since he'd started meeting with Volodin a year ago. Gone were all the western shops and vendors. Anti-United Earth hysteria had gripped the entire Russian Confederation during the past two months, or so his sources told him. Anyone who was not a Confederate citizen was not allowed to work, and many had been expelled. Why Confederate society was shunning United Earth citizens was beyond him. Maybe they felt that by distancing themselves from the west the Swarm might take it easier on them when they returned to Earth.

Fat chance.

The ground car pulled up to Volodin's office, and the ambassador stood outside to receive him. "You've come back, my friend, my friend," he said, greeting him with a firm handshake.

"Hello, Yuri. How've you been?" He let the ambassador lead him into the building. The three secret service officers followed close behind.

"Oh, you know. Just assisting President Malakhov with the war effort. While we've kept more of our freedoms than you people out west—no draft, for example—we're still doing our part. Entire industries have been retooled and we're even selling our surplus off to IDF to help out."

Isaacson flashed a wry grin. "For a tidy profit, no doubt."

"Is that wrong?" Volodin laughed. "It was your people that taught us capitalism centuries ago."

"And then you taught it back to us."

"And the circle of life continues." Volodin gestured toward the living room, lined by plush, luxurious sofas and alcohol cabinets. "Can I offer you something?"

"Do you have to ask?"

Two secret service men stood near the doors while one left the room to stand outside. Volodin pulled a small bottle from a cabinet which Isaacson accepted gratefully. "So, no draft? How does your military manage?"

"We are a patriotic people, Eamon. We don't need to be compelled to defend our freedoms like you people do. Young men are volunteering in droves."

"Spurred, no doubt, by the incredibly low attrition rate your military suffers compared to ours. A consequence of sitting all the major battles out, I suppose," Isaacson retorted.

Volodin smiled and sat on a sofa, swishing a drink. "So, why are you here, Eamon? What's the problem?"

After a few swallows, Isaacson motioned to the men at the door. "Give us a moment, guys."

When the security detail had left he stood back up. "Yuri, what the hell is going on? Why did you leave?"

"I told you. Malakhov recalled me."

"Why? Right in the middle of the war? Doesn't make sense. Are you still—" Isaacson paused, and glanced at the door, before lowering his voice. "Are you still targeting Avery?"

"Do you want us to?"

Isaacson glowered at him. "It's wartime. Total war. Changes in leadership aren't ... prudent, during times like this."

Yuri guffawed. "Ha! You've fallen under her sway, haven't you? She's charmed your balls right off with her chest-thumping, dick-waving show she's putting on, playing at being a general when she belongs in the kitchen. My friend, are you getting soft on me?"

Isaacson rolled his eyes. "Please, Yuri, you sound like someone out of the twenty-first century. I wanted her dead so I could be president, not because she's got a vagina."

Yuri finished off his drink. "So why don't you? Hmm?"

"Do what?"

"Kill her?"

"I told you."

"Because of stability during wartime? Nonsense. The people need the best leader during wartime, not the most convenient one. They clearly need *you*, Eamon. Malakhov stands by his pledge of support for you. Even in all the commotion these days, I'm sure we can make something work."

Isaacson drummed his fingers nervously on his cheek and paced the room. "No."

Yuri snorted. "She *has* gotten to you. Taken you in with her act. What, did she say how much she needs you and how much she trusts you? Tell you how important you are? Did she promise to campaign for you next election? Or did she just promise you a good BJ for every thousand ships you christen?"

He would not give Volodin the satisfaction, but Isaacson grimaced inwardly at himself—it was all true. Well, mostly.

"Eamon, think. You've been planning her assassination for months. Surely you've been thinking about it for years, if I know you—you're a man of action, a man of decision, someone who makes the hard choices, come what may. But think. Someone has just made an attempt on her life. A sloppy one, from what my sources say. Do you honestly think that she *doesn't* suspect you?"

Isaacson hesitated. "Who knows what she thinks—she's a loose cannon right now, ever since the war—"

"Exactly. A loose cannon. She's acting on instinct right now. And remember, she's a natural politician. She's drawn you in just as she's drawn in the billions of rubes that voted for her. If I were her, do you know what I would do?" He paused, then continued without waiting for his answer. "I'd bring you in close, get you in my confidences, make you comfortable, then," he raised a hand and made a gun motion, firing it at Isaacson's head. "Bam."

"And why would she suspect me? I've only ever been polite and encouraging to her."

"Why wouldn't she? Who will take the presidency when she dies?"

"Me."

"Exactly."

Volodin was annoying him, so he changed the subject. "Will you tell me how to detect Swarm-influenced people?"

Yuri's eyes narrowed at the question. He poured himself another drink. "Why? Do you suspect someone in your government or military?"

"Possibly. You said that some of those soldiers that went aboard the Swarm ships came out *changed*. Smarter. Faster. Better. Is that the only way to tell if someone's been compromised?"

Volodin swished his drink. "There are many ways. I will not tell you all of them. For classified reasons," he added, noticing Isaacson's eye-roll. "But I will tell you this. Ever wonder how the Swarm communicate with each other? I'm sure you've noticed during all the pitched battles over the past few months that your fleets never detect any transmissions between Swarm ships. It's like they coordinate their attacks perfectly, all from prior plans they worked out before the battle."

Isaacson nodded. "I *have* heard the admirals discuss the matter."

"But it's nonsense. Of course they communicate with each other. You witnessed *me* talking to them, remember? They're not wordy folk, but they do talk. And their coordination amongst themselves is ... effective, wouldn't you say? How many ships have you lost the past two months? How many people?"

Isaacson shrugged. "Too many. Five hundred ships? Maybe more."

"And the Cadiz System. And almost a dozen other worlds. A shame. Truly a great human tragedy."

Isaacson nodded again, hoping the other man would get to the point.

"Think about it. If we talk to them using meta-space signals, it might make sense that they talk to each other with meta-space signals, correct?"

"Right," said Isaacson, leading him on.

"And if they talk to each other using meta-space signals, you'd think they would have figured out a way to talk to those they control with meta-space signals."

But back in the Omaha command center, he'd scanned the entire room for meta-space signals. Not one of the stations registered even so much as a blip.

Unless....

"Are you saying that they've figured out a way to transmit and receive meta-space signals with—" he fumbled for words—he was no scientist or technologist, "—with bodies?

Yuri raised an eyebrow. "Now *that* would be something, wouldn't it? Being able to talk to each other without electronics, without devices, without antennae. Just you, and me ... and our thoughts."

"So you've detected this among those men that came back from the Swarm carrier?"

"Oh," Volodin began, standing up and putting the bottle back into the cabinet. "Hard to tell what was going on in the military back then. I was just a junior member of the diplomatic corps at the time."

So he was going to play coy. Fine. But at least Isaacson learned what he came for.

He was absolutely sure Volodin was not involved in the recent attempt on Avery's life. The ambassador was not a humble man—the fact of his involvement would have been flaunted for Isaacson like a badge of honor.

"I need to get back to Washington." Isaacson stood up. "It's been a pleasure, Yuri, as always. Do keep in touch."

Volodin nodded, and after more small talk, he led Isaacson out where his security detail was waiting for him. They shook hands, and Volodin slipped back into the building as Isaacson allowed the guards to lead him back to their vehicle on the street.

He almost ducked into the car when he heard Volodin call out to him, waving something from the doorway. Grumbling about walking more than he needed to, Isaacson motioned to the guards to get in the car as he went back to the office.

The ambassador held a new bottle of the vodka they'd been drinking. "For tonight. I do know how you love your Russian beverages after your Russian girls."

Isaacson smiled. "Thank you, Yuri. How very thoughtful."

He turned to walk back to the street, examining the bottle. Caspian Black Label—Russia's finest. He suspected most of it would be gone before he left in the morning. Maybe Conner might want the rest.

Moments later, he was thrown backward. The ground car exploded in a massive fireball as he flew through the air, landing on the grass behind him.

CHAPTER TWENTY-TWO

The Waypoint, Near Sirius
Main Conference Room, Interstellar One

INTERSTELLAR ONE WAS IN A STATE of somber pandemo-nium. Aides, department chiefs, interns, all grim-faced and arguing, still not quite believing what had happened, scurried in shock. Zingano and Granger both arrived in the shuttle bay at the same time and followed Sparks and some advisors into a conference room.

"What the *hell* is going on?" Zingano yelled. "Where's the secret service? Are your security protocols really this shoddy? Where's the chief of staff? Where's General Norton? He's her military advisor. Doesn't he personally handle fleet protection for the president? Where's—"

Sparks held up a hand and cut him off. "Admiral, please. We're trying to figure out what went wrong. Could be as simple as an engine overload, for all we know. Right now we have to worry about continuity of government. We need to send a meta-space signal back to Earth and get Vice President Isaacson to a secure location before word leaks out. We can't have this happen again."

"Isaacson? That dipshit?" Zingano tossed his hands up. "Unbelievable."

The door opened again and General Norton ran into the room, along with three armed men. "I've got her secret service detail."

Zingano pointed at one of them, an older man that looked like their commander. "What the hell happened? Why was she on that ship, and how did they know she was there?"

"And who is *they*?" Granger added.

The secret service agent shook his head. He was obviously troubled, his face red. His fist looked bloody. He'd apparently had the same reaction to Avery's death as Zingano. "That's standard protocol these days. She's never to travel on *Interstellar One*. We've got three body doubles for that. One's on Earth, the other's on *Verso.*"

Zingano shot him a look. "*Verso?*"

"The other escort ship. The one that didn't explode— that one was *Recto.*" He sighed. "The third double is here on *Interstellar One.*"

Silence. The enormity of the situation began to weigh on them all. They'd need to make an announcement. Isaacson would need to be sworn in, and then read in to all the top-secret programs, some of which Granger didn't even know about, he supposed. The Earth, and dozens of other United Earth worlds, would be shocked. Demoralized. If the Swarm could not only invade with fleets, but infiltrate this deeply into Earth's elected government with impunity, what hope could they have of winning?

There was shouting out in the corridor. *Shit. What now?*

Granger couldn't believe his eyes. The door opened. President Avery stepped through, flanked by her chief of staff and another secret service agent. She held a small, glittering handbag, a mug of coffee, and a fierce frown.

She strode straight up to Congresswoman Sparks. The other woman's mouth still hung open. "Madam President! You're ... you're alive."

Avery smiled and handed her coffee to the chief of staff. "Yes. And you're not." In one fluid, swift motion she reached into her handbag and pulled out a sidearm, pointed it straight at Sparks's forehead, and fired.

CHAPTER TWENTY-THREE

Moscow, Russia
Yuri Volodin's Office, Diplomatic Complex

ISAACSON FELT HIMSELF being dragged across grass, then pavement. Looking around he saw people running and screaming, but he couldn't hear them. His head felt like it was underwater and his ears stuffed with gauze.

He looked up. Volodin was pulling him toward his offices, his large face red from the effort. Soon, first responder vehicles swarmed the street, lights flashing, sirens blaring—he supposed. He could just barely hear them, as if from a distance.

Someone was calling his name. He looked back at Volodin, who was yelling in his ear. The ambassador pointed to Isaacson's legs, then made a rising motion.

Isaacson nodded, and let the other man pull him to his feet. He immediately felt light headed, and leaned into Volodin for support. The two hobbled to the front door of the office and stepped inside, Isaacson falling onto one of the sofas.

Volodin bolted back out the door and Isaacson closed his eyes. Moments later he opened them to find the ambassador standing overhead with a few paramedics. They examined him, scanned his head with a device and read his vitals, feeling his limbs and torso for wounds.

"He's fine, Ambassador," said one of the men. "Just in shock, and his hearing is slightly damaged. But both will pass."

Isaacson nodded. Good—he could hear again. "Who?"

"No idea, Eamon. Intelligence services are already here, combing for evidence," he said, pausing, "I'm afraid your men did not survive."

Isaacson waved the comment aside. "*I* almost didn't survive, Yuri!"

Volodin nodded to the paramedics and signaled for them to go. When they were alone Volodin sat on the sofa next to him. "Eamon, this is a troubling development."

Isaacson scowled. "You think?"

"Someone just tried to kill you. And this was a far more sophisticated attack than the one on Avery last week. You only survived by chance."

Isaacson closed his eyes and rubbed his head, running through his ancient first aid training. What do you do for shock victims? Blankets? Feet? Something about feet. He propped his feet up on the sofa. "The question is, who would have the audacity to do this? And so publicly?"

Volodin shot him a look. "Do you really have to ask? There's only one person both capable and willing to do this."

It couldn't be. Why would she do it now? Here? Why not just stab him in the back in her mid-Atlantic bunker? "I don't know, Yuri." He opened his eyes and tried to stand up. "But I'm going to find out. I'm heading back to Washington. Right now."

The room spun around him, picking up speed; he fell back onto the sofa holding his head.

CHAPTER TWENTY-FOUR

The Waypoint, Near Sirius
Weight Room, ISS Warrior

BALLSY GRUNTED AGAINST the weights. He pushed the bar away, then let it fall down to his chest, stopping just short of his pectoral muscles. The IDF fleet training program emphasized core and leg strength over arms and shoulders given their frequent use in space flight, but his ego emphasized all of it.

"One more, Ballsy, give me one more," said Lieutenant Yamato. *Spacechamp*, Volz mentally reminded himself. It was just simpler to think of them in terms of their callsign—helped dull the pain when they died if any actual names were tucked safely away.

He yelled out, pushing against the bar until it reached the top, and she pulled the weights away and onto the supports.

They swapped positions after adjusting the weights for Spacechamp.

"How's Dogtown?" she asked.

Ballsy shook his head. "They're in quarantine. All of them—Dogtown, Clownface, and Hotshot. But they're fine. Dogtown broke his ankle, old bastard. But Clown-face and Hotshot just got bruised up. And of course the Swarm shit all over them."

She pressed the bar up a few times. "And that Han-rahan—lucky bastard. Managed to not get a fleck on him. Jumped away at the last second. Pretty spry for an old soldier."

Ballsy nodded. Colonel Hanrahan was something of a *Constitution*—and now a *Warrior*—institution. He was like old Commander Haws, but sober, gruffer, fitter, and of course, more alive. And the old soldier held court off-duty down at New Afterburner's—the reincarnation of the old make-shift bar they'd had on the Old Bird—where he drank ice water instead of alcohol, regaling the crew members who sat nearby with old stories from the last Swarm war. He hadn't even been born yet, of course, but he talked about it like he was there, and made up for the lack of direct experience with creative vulgarity.

"How long will they be in quarantine?"

He shook his head. "Until Doc Wyatt is sure the Swarm matter didn't get into them somehow. I suppose they think contact with the stuff can infect you or kill you or something. Probably aren't sure if it can spread, hence the quarantine. They're just being careful."

"Can't be too careful these days," she said, pushing the bar up a final time and resting it against the supports. She stood up. "What about you, Ballsy? You ok?"

He glowered at her. "And why wouldn't I be?"

She shrugged, and led the way to the squat bench. "I dunno. You've just seemed really distracted the past few weeks."

"It's war, Spacechamp. We signed up for it, but we never imagined it would actually happen." He bent over to lift the bar onto his shoulders. "Besides. I'm not distracted. Just ... I worry about you guys, is all."

"What, me and Fodder and Pew Pew? Aw, you old softie."

"I mean it. You're my squad. The longest I've ever had a squad together in two and a half months. Before you guys came along I was losing squadmates at least once or twice per week. I hate to say it, but I'm getting a little attached to you all, ya' know?"

She steadied him as he bent forward to set the bar back down. "I'm touched." They switched places. "Dogtown was on your squad before, right?"

"Yeah."

"What happened? Why'd Pierce split you up?"

He didn't want to tell her the truth. That Dogtown reminded him of *her*. Hell, he'd lost nearly half a dozen squadmates since then.

But none of them had disappeared into a singularity. He hadn't been the one to deliver the news to all those families. Just to hers.

And none of them had a kid that would insist on sending him drawings. Drawings of fighters, or of his mom and dad. Little scrawled messages that were only gibberish but what the grandparents translated to say things like, "thank you," or, "I'm going to be a pilot too," or, "when can you see Zack Zack?"

He had half a mind to tell the grandparents to put a stop to it. It was distracting. But he couldn't let the kid down. He'd lost his parents. Hell—they'd *all* lost someone close. But he couldn't do it—the kid had latched onto him. Thought of Volz as some sort of hero or some bull like that, so he let the messages come, and would occasionally send him a note too, or a picture of him in his fighter.

"They wanted experienced pilots as squad command-ers, and Dogtown is as experienced as they come."

She nodded. "Yeah, he's ok, I guess. Me? I'm just glad I'm in the Untouchables."

He glanced sidelong at her as they switched places again and he lifted the bar onto his shoulders. "Untouchables?"

She snorted. "Yeah, it's what the other jocks are calling our squad. Between your death-defying stunts, and Fodder and Pew Pew's propensity to not die even in the center of a fiery firestorm of fire, we've gotten quite a rep."

"Give yourself some credit, Spacechamp. You're not so bad yourself. I've never seen better."

It was partially a lie. He *had* seen better. Fishtail had that natural talent. She was new, of course, but she would have grown into one of the best fighter pilot he'd ever seen. Had things been different, that is. *Dammit.*

"Aw shucks, sir."

They finished up and showered. Fodder and Pew Pew were busy in the pilots' lounge recounting their most re-cent death-defying stunts to some of the pilots-in-train-ing, each talking over the other and finishing each other's sentences.

"Call for you, sir," said a yeoman who caught up to him, slightly huffing from the run. "From Earth."

"Who is it?"

"Lady says her little boy wanted to talk to you. Says he's inconsolable. I told her it was against protocol but she wouldn't—"

He sighed and held up a hand. "For good reason, yeoman. Pilots can't answer every single fan-comm that comes their way."

The yeoman's face blanched. "Uh ... I'm sorry, sir. I'll go tell the grandma that you'll call next time we come to Earth."

"You do that."

The yeoman scurried away and Ballsy grabbed a standard non-alcoholic beverage from the fridge—pilots weren't allowed to drink after or before potential engagements when the ship's status was still elevated. He glanced at the alert indicator above the door. Still orange. He grumbled and cracked open the bottle.

The kid wanted a hero. He sighed again.

All the real heroes are dead.

CHAPTER TWENTY-FIVE

The Waypoint, Near Sirius
Main Conference Room, Interstellar One

THE BODY SLUMPED TO the floor with a thud as blood sprayed out onto the conference table from the rear of Sparks's head.

Avery spit on the body. "Looks like Ohio will be having a special election." She thrust the gun back into her handbag and zipped it, and grabbed her coffee back from the chief of staff and took a sip before calmly sitting down.

The rest of them, too shocked to speak, followed her lead, lowering themselves slowly back into their chairs. Two of the secret service officers dragged the body away and the other two stepped out into the corridor to stand guard. Avery broke the silence. "There's a contingent in the government that is trying to kill me. Also, the Russians want me dead. Also, the Swarm. Also—" She paused. "Are you boys sure you want to be sitting next to me?" A dark chuckle, and she sipped her coffee again. "The good news is my ex-husband is too much of an air-headed fool to try something like this, so at least we're all safe on that front. Ha!"

"You were here all along? On *Interstellar One*?" asked General Norton.

"Of course."

Granger looked down at the body in revulsion. Sparks's eyes were still open and a track of blood led to where the secret service officers had dragged her. "And the congresswoman? You're sure she was the assassin?"

Avery shot him a look. "I just put a bullet in her brain. You bet your ass I'm sure she was the assassin." She opened up her handbag and pulled out a data pad. "I'd finally tracked down the leak to my own office, and decided to conduct a little test. At least for my aides."

The president's other aide seated at the table stiffened in his chair.

"Don't worry, Johnson, you check out," she said with a wink. "Based on some other details I won't go into here, I'd narrowed it down to one of you two. So, I told you I'd be aboard the *Verso*, and I told *that*," she indicated the body, "that I'd travel aboard the *Recto*." She sipped her coffee.

"And you stayed here," said Zingano.

"And I stayed here. Poor souls on the *Recto*, though. Captain Newman was a good woman. Frightfully loyal. A patriot. Such a shame."

A brief silence. In spite of the relief that the president was very much alive, there was still death all around them. Fifty aboard the *Recto*. The congresswoman laying the corner. The war touched everyone.

"So. Gentleman. We're here for a reason."

"Several reasons," said Zingano.

"You've tracked another Swarm vessel, and you're sure that it headed toward the Polaris System, and in fact have detected a world near Polaris with Swarm spectrographic signatures." It was a statement, not a question. "And you've made contact with another alien species. My god, to think that I've lived to see days like this. Discovering whole new civilizations. Only for them to come at us with guns cocked and alliances already made with our mortal enemy."

She sipped her coffee again. Granger marveled at how remarkably calm she was, even after an attempt on her life. "You know, in a different life, when I was young and naive and full of optimism and happy sunny thoughts, I worked at a publishing house. Fulbright Press. Most prestigious literary organization in the world. They only published the cream of the cream of the crop. The best of the best. Most people—outside the house—thought that meant the best writers. The most brilliant minds. The most celebrated literary artists."

Another sip.

"Bullshit. You know who we published? The ones who made us the most money, and the ones who *paid* us the most money. One day at work, when I blundered my way into a deal gone south with one of the authors— former senator, nobel prize winner, all that shit—the editor takes me aside into his office, pushes me up against his desk, threatens me with firing, and pulls my pants down, then his. His magnificent, elitist, Ivy-league manhood pressed right up against my leg.

"You know what I did?" She tipped the mug back and downed the rest of the coffee. "I grabbed his swollen dick, knelt down, head bowed, like I was some good, obedient, submissive whore, then grabbed the pen above my ear and stabbed him in the scrotum." She laughed. "Oh, how he howled. Swore up and down he'd have me arrested, swore he'd expose me for seducing him. That

I'd be ruined. But it was all bluster. I stood up and told him: go ahead. Tell everyone that lil' old me stabbed him in the balls. Tell everyone that you let yourself get taken down by a five foot tall, one hundred ten pound stick of a twenty-year-old girl. The southern belle he hired for her pretty face and tight ass."

She set the mug down and dabbed at her lips with a finger. "The next day, I got a promotion. And the month after that, another promotion. And within a year, I had his job. Sorry boys, I'm rambling, so I'll get to the point. The names of my escort ships. *Verso* and *Recto*. Those are the right and left facing pages of a printed book. And what's in the middle?"

Silence around the table.

Zingano offered, "A book?"

"*Interstellar One*?" said Norton.

"A SPINE," she yelled, banging the table with a fist for emphasis. "A goddamned spine. Lesson number one. Show your spine, or they'll eat you up and shit you out like the little turds you are." She waved a hand apologetically. "Not *you* you, but general you. You all have spines. You're no-nonsense badasses that take no prisoners and eat nails for breakfast, I'm sure." She started to sip her coffee again before remembering the cup was dry. "Well? Go on. Brief me."

Zingano cleared his throat. "Madam President, as you know we've tracked the Swarm ship to the Polaris Sector. We sent several scout ships out that way and they confirm: there are various planets out there that might be likely candidates. They detected Swarm activity around several before coming back—we didn't want to tip our hand that we know where their base is."

"We *don't* know where it is. It may not even be in that sector," interrupted Avery.

116

"True, ma'am. But this is the first time we've detected Swarm activity that wasn't in our own systems during an attack. We've explored all these regions of space for decades, and never found anything but ruins of old civilizations. Never any life."

She snorted. "But we never explored out toward Polaris. No, no. Of course not. Russian Confederation territory lies between us and Polaris. Heaven forbid they actually honor their treaties and give us passage through their space. Bastards."

Zingano continued. "All told, there were at least three candidate planets that we detected—mass, atmosphere, gravity, solar irradiance all similar to Earth's. Planets most likely to support Swarm anatomy."

"Anatomy that we know nothing about," Avery interjected. "But you say one of those planets has a bunch of liquid Swarm shit smeared all over it?"

"Yes, ma'am. The scout didn't stick around to get a good look, but telescopic spectroscopy confirms Swarm matter on the surface. Reflectivity, spectral curves—matches all the data from the tests we've run."

Avery cocked her head. "But it's alive? Do we know that?"

"No, ma'am. We've never—knowingly at least—tested a live specimen."

She pointed at Zingano. "Get a live specimen. Capture a fighter. Do what it takes. I can't believe it's taken us seventy-five years and we still have never seen a live specimen."

Zingano nodded. "I'll order one of our task forces to make it their priority."

The President crossed her legs. "And there's also the issue of our new friends. The Dalmatians? What the hell did they call themselves?"

Zingano kept nodding. "The Dolmasi, yes. I'll let Granger talk about them—he made first contact."

Avery turned to regard him. "You're responsible for quite a few firsts, Captain Granger."

"Yes, ma'am."

"Well let's hope you can give us our first total victory over these bastards. I don't want a situation like last time where they just up and disappear for decades, building their strength and advancing their technology while we just sit with our thumbs up our asses getting basket-weaving girl scout merit badges."

Granger chuckled. She was starting to grow on him. In spite of the fact that she was responsible for much of the basket-weaving over the past decade. "Yes, ma'am."

"Go on, then. Dolmasi me."

"Well, we we're chasing down the last escaping Swarm carrier—"

Avery interrupted. "Chasing down? What about Operation Battle-ax?"

"Admiral Azbill was determined to not let any Swarm get away alive. I had to intervene with the *Warrior*."

Zingano chimed in. "I've had Azbill reassigned, ma'am."

"Asshole," she muttered. "Good. Go on." She waved a hand.

"And right as the Swarm carrier was about to be overwhelmed, the Dolmasi q-jumped in out of nowhere. Fifteen ships. From our sensors it looked as if they were more than a match for us. At least, just the *Warrior* and the New Dublin task force that was chasing down the carrier."

"So how did they know to come right *then*?" Avery asked.

"That's our line of thinking, ma'am," replied Zingano. "The Swarm must have sent out a meta-space distress signal that summoned the Dolmasi. Either that or it was previously planned. But that's too much of a coincidence."

"And we detected nothing?"

Granger shook his head. "Nothing above our detection limits."

She nodded. "So, either the signal was below our detection limits, or it was otherwise a type of signal undetectable to us. Some new tech?"

"Could be," said Granger. No one spoke up so he continued. "Anyway, the Dolmasi showed up and demanded we leave."

He recounted the entire exchange, and they watched the recorded conversation on the view panel on the wall. "Interesting. Almost reptilian," said Avery, watching Vishgane Kharsa with vague wonder.

"That was my thought, ma'am. Probably evolved from some sort of species related to our reptiles. At least, the skin looks remarkably scaly, even though it's almost a human skin tone. Proctor said she wouldn't be surprised if they were cold blooded."

Zingano nodded. "This speculation is all well and good, but what do we do? How does this affect our strategic thinking? Do we move forward with Operation Battle-ax?"

Granger scratched his stubble. "What choice do we have? We've got to strike at them before they just pick us apart, regardless of who their friends are."

General Norton shook his head. "Unless all those friends are as powerful as the Swarm. They claim there are six other separate species that are their allies? Even subject to them? If that's true, then we're up against not just overwhelming force, but seven overwhelming forces. There's no way we can win this militarily."

Avery looked down at her hands folded on her lap. "And you're proposing what, General? Surrender? Diplomacy? All our overtures are met with static."

"I've heard rumors the Russians have found a way to communicate with them."

Everyone stared at him.

"My son serves on the *ISS Winchester*. One of the comm officers. Back during the initial invasion it was carrying Vice President Isaacson and the congressional delegation from Lunar Base back to Earth. Turns out that there was an unauthorized use of the meta-space transmitter. Had all the proper security codes, but no-one on that ship has any memory of transmitting that particular signal."

"What was the signal?"

"Gibberish. But the Russian Ambassador Volodin *was* on board," continued Norton. "My son tells me he and Isaacson were quite close during that trip. Holed up in the Captain's quarters. Maybe you should ask him."

Avery nodded. "I will. So the question remains, what do we do about the Polaris Sector. I'm afraid the Mars Project is not quite ready. And besides, we need more information before execution of Operation Battle-ax."

Granger nodded. On hearing about the Mars Project, he swelled with a bit of pride in his XO. Proctor had suggested the name for the Mars Project for the same reason the ancient Manhattan Project to develop the first atomic bomb was named the way it was. It had nothing to do with Manhattan, and the Mars Project had nothing to do with Mars. Though both had everything to do with developing frighteningly powerful weaponry.

Zingano pointed up at the star map on the view panel showing all the star systems in the Polaris Sector. "There are just too many variables out there. Thousands of stars. Tens of thousands of planets. And we're not even sure the Polaris Sector is the right place. We could spend months sending scout ship after scout ship, and still be no closer to learning the whereabouts of the homeworld. No. We need to trace more ships. Lure them into a dozen more raids, and track the last escaping ship like we've been doing. That way we can triangulate their source with more resolution. This," he waved to the star map, "is too much."

Avery nodded. Everyone around the table looked as if the conversation were over.

Granger cleared his throat. "I want to lead a task force out there and take the fight to the enemy."

Zingano's eyes opened wide. "Granger—"

"Hear me out, sir. We've been on the run for months. We completely lost the Cadiz Sector a few weeks ago. Xinhua almost fell a week after that. Nearly one hundred million dead in both. And every engagement costs us dozens of ships and thousands of crew members and pilots. We can't keep throwing our soldiers through the meat grinder."

General Norton snorted. "That would sound very noble if it wasn't coming from you, Granger. What's the tally, huh? How many ships have you sent kamikaze? Full-on, brand new heavy cruisers you just throw against them like bricks? What do they call you? The brick-layer?"

Granger nailed the general with an icy look. "And their sacrifices have given us a fighting chance, General Norton. Let's keep in mind that they'd die anyway, but this way they die and we actually win a few battles."

Norton stood up and pointed down at Granger. "Why, you little piece of shit. Tell that to all the families back on Earth and throughout all the sectors and planets that won't be getting their kids home next shore leave. And all for a man who we can't even trust—one likely under either Russian or Swarm influence. Ever remember where you went, Granger? Memory still hazy? How convenient."

Avery slapped the table. "Sit down, General." She glanced at Granger. "He's got a point, Captain. Our entire society is on a war footing. Every factory and every able-bodied person is churning out ships and shit for our fleets, and here you are burning through them at an alarming rate. Let's get it under control, please."

Granger bit his tongue, and nodded. If they only knew what it was like out there. Under fire. Death all around you. Zingano knew, which was why he'd allowed Granger such wide latitude on his unorthodox tactics. But General Norton? Supreme allied paper pusher. Avery? Tough as nails, but still naive.

"Point taken. But *my* point stands. We're running. Running from one emergency to the next. One invasion to the next. There's a massive dam here with a billion metric tons of water behind it, breaking out with a thousand gaping cracks, and here we are sticking our fingers and toes in the tiny holes. Morale is sinking. And our resources are finite."

Zingano eyed him. "What exactly are you proposing, Tim?"

"I'll lead a task force out there. A hundred ships. Maybe more. Put the Swarm on the run. Where they stand and fight with overwhelming force, we withdraw. We target them ship by ship, system by system. Run a scorched earth campaign behind their lines. Distract them. Make them focus on me and my ships, and give our systems and worlds a breather. And while I'm at it, I'll be deep in their space, sending out scouts and investigating as many leads as I can to locate their homeworld in preparation for Operation Battle-ax."

General Norton shook his head. "I don't like it."

Zingano sighed. "It sounds noble, Tim. But foolhardy. The most likely outcome is that all your ships burn. You'll die within a week without the support of our bases and resupply ships."

Silence. All eyes turned to Avery, whose eyes were closed and hands steepled in front of her face.

"Do it."

She opened her eyes and stood up. "You've got spine, Granger, and so does your plan." She shook his hand. "Go destroy them." She glanced down at the body laying the corner. "Bring back some trophies as proof."

CHAPTER TWENTY-SIX

Washington D.C., Earth
IDF Administration Building

THE SECRET SERVICE DOUBLED his security detail. Isaacson thought that having an entourage of fifteen people as he stepped out of his shuttle onto the launch pad at the capitol made the whole process a bit awkward, but he'd get over it. Hal Levin, his chief of staff, pushed through and whispered in his ear, "Just got a note from Avery's aide. President wants to see you when you get the chance."

"She'll have to get in line." Isaacson was feeling less charitable toward Avery these days, if it were possible. "I've got some actual work to do—troop inspections can wait."

They'd landed at the capitol, but his real destination was the military administration building that lay underneath in the vast underground complex that had been excavated and built during the previous decades—a relic of the post-Swarm-war years. Military planners thought that the further underground they were, they safer they'd be.

Events of the past two months had proven how short-sighted that was. The Swarm's singularity weapon seemed to be able to penetrate farther into the Earth's crust than anyone had thought to dig.

"Does General Norton know I'm coming?"

Levin nodded. "I spoke to him two hours ago. Just returned from off-planet. He suggested he take you on a tour of one of the military's ordnance production buildings down underground—thought it might be more interesting than sitting in his office."

Isaacson rubbed his forehead—he was still off-balance from the explosion. A tour? Sitting in a comfy admin office chair sounded about right at the moment. "Fine."

Conner caught up to him from the rear of the entourage. "Sir, will you be needing anything while you're down there?"

Isaacson shook his head. "Not now, son. Go enjoy the day. Should snow later—get home before the streets clog up." Conner turned to go. "Just go drop off my things at my residence—I think I'll be staying a few days. And later," he lowered his voice, "see if you can't get all those, uh ... things, you were going to gather for me in Moscow."

"The coffee?"

Damn. The kid was either very savvy, or very stupid. Guess he'd find out later that night. "Right. The coffee."

General Norton met the entourage at an entrance to the subterranean military complex a few blocks from the capitol. "Mr. Vice President," he said, eyeing the crowd. "Quite the group you travel with these days."

"Targets of political assassinations can't be too careful now, can we?" he said in as ironic a voice as possible.

"No, sir. Prudent." He waved an arm to the door. It was a tiny building, housing just a security office and checkpoint, and an elevator. The guard nodded and saluted as they passed. "I've been looking for an opportunity to get you down here. Been so busy lately I haven't had the chance."

"Wars are busy affairs, aren't they?" Isaacson motioned to half his secret service detail to wait at the checkpoint while he went down into the building proper. "Actually, all of you wait here. You too, Hal."

The chief of staff started to protest, but grudgingly complied. "I'm used to running a mobile office for you, anyway. We'll just run it out of the waiting room for the next few hours."

Isaacson rolled his eyes at the sarcasm. He'd meant to find a new chief of staff the previous year, but Levin was good, if cranky. "After you, General."

He followed Norton into the elevator shaft. "Munitions," said the general.

"You're going to show me your bombs? Really, General, we've got more important things to talk about."

Norton glanced at him askance. "Not just the bombs. I'm giving you the full tour. If you ever—god forbid—become president, you need to know your shit. Especially in war-time." The lift stopped, and the doors opened, revealing a vast, sprawling space filled with equipment, people, assembly lines, and offices filled with whiteboards and books and arguing engineers. "Now, while we walk, what is it you wanted to talk to me about?"

Isaacson peered down the aisles as they wandered. The expansive room was filled with hundreds of people, all working, assembling, talking, and discussing. Several dozen looked to be assembling small devices, but he couldn't see what they were building.

"Several things. Progress on the war effort, for one."

"Don't the President's advisors keep you updated? They should be giving you the same daily briefings my team and I put together for her."

"Oh, of course they do. But we both know that all the information doesn't make it into the daily briefings."

General Norton smiled as they progressed down the aisle. When they reached a quiet corner he nodded. "Sure. The truth is, the war is going badly."

"Pft," Isaacson scoffed. "I knew that."

"Badly enough that the President is willing to pursue ... desperate measures."

"How desperate?" Isaacson stroked his chin. Desperate enough to kill? To bring him in close and then stab him in the back?

"Desperate enough to order new research on anti-matter." General Norton waved an arm around the room, indicating the benches full of equipment and teams of people.

Of course. "Anti-matter research was banned centuries ago. Too dangerous. Weren't there millions of deaths back in the twenty-second century from anti-matter accidents?"

Norton nodded. "All in the name of progress, of course. And look what it bought us. Anti-matter power plants. A million times more powerful than fusion. But once we reached that point, research stopped. Too dangerous to go any farther."

They kept walking, coming near a team of engineers huddled over a work station full of equipment that looked utterly foreign to Isaacson. Of course, he was never much for science. "Too dangerous, until now."

"Exactly." Norton smiled at a passing manager, a uniformed lieutenant in a lab coat. She nodded back a salute.

Isaacson stopped next to a young woman on the engineering team—one that looked like she couldn't be a day over sixteen. "And what's your name, miss?"

Her eyes met his and she looked like a deer in the headlights. Apparently VIP visitors were not expected that day. She stood at attention. "Sergeant first class, Lisa Gall, sir!"

"How old are you, Sergeant?" He put on his politician's smile and lightly touched her elbow. He could put on the charm better than the old hag, Avery.

"Nineteen, sir!"

"And what's your specialty, Sergeant? What are you doing here?"

"Drafted two months ago, sir. Was an electrical engineering major at Yale. Drafted into the electrical materials team here at MUNCENT."

"Munitions Central," General Norton clarified. "We only picked the finest to work down here with us in MUNCENT. Sergeant Gall was on track to graduate top of her class, if I remember right."

She blushed slightly. "Yes, sir."

"And what are you working on, Sergeant Gall?" Isaacson glanced down at her work station. He recognized a few loose resistors and electrical meters, but that was the extent of his technical knowledge.

She glanced at General Norton nervously, and he nodded. "Designing new electrical containment methods and apparatus for containment of exotic material."

Isaacson raised an eyebrow. "Exotic material, huh? Is that what we're calling anti-matter down here?"

She looked nervous. "Yes, sir. Specifically, anti-neutrons and anti-protons, conglomerated in more massive forms like anti-tungsten, anti-iridium ... that sort of thing."

"And? Any progress?"

She looked down. "Not yet, sir. Electrical containment is ... well, it's problematic. There are better ways to do it, but we've got to explore every method. Just in case."

General Norton saluted; she returned the salute and sat back down to work. They continued walking. Isaacson

NICK WEBB

saw another table full of small spheres with a team of engineers hovering over, picking them up, scanning them, inspecting them, taking notes....

He cocked his head. "General, are those...."

"Bombs?"

"Yes. Are those bombs? Are you actually making bombs down here?"

Norton nodded. "Of course. This is the military's premier research and development facility. What gets deployed in the field gets developed here."

Isaacson felt the color drain from his face. "You're telling me that you're manufacturing anti-matter bombs right here? Under the friggin' capitol building?"

The general laughed. "Mr. Vice President, I assure you, we are all completely safe. There is no actual anti-matter here. The hardware is designed, manufactured, assembled, and tested here. About a thousand per month. The anti-matter is added later. At more ... secure facilities."

Isaacson nodded. "Good. I'd hate to lose D.C. on the eve of victory," he said, with a wry grin.

They kept walking. "And, Mr. Vice President? What else did you want to talk to me about?"

He glanced all around them before continuing. They'd drifted away from any workers, so Isaacson stopped walking and turned to the General. "Does the president have any enemies in the military? Hell, do *I* have any enemies? Is there someone who would want not only her, but me, dead?"

Norton frowned. "Let me make one thing clear, Mr. Vice President. The military is here at the service of the civilian government. We do not involve ourselves in politics. Ever. Period. It's been a strictly guarded tradition in the United Earth government, and in the League of Western Nations before that, and in the

United States before that. We serve, we fight, we protect. Nothing more."

Isaacson rolled his eyes. "Nice speech, General. Now
answer my question."

Norton glared at him. "I just did, Mr. Vice President.
You and your buddies in the senate and congress and over
in the administration are the ones who play your back
room games. My focus is on Earth's safety, and the safety
of United Earth and its fifty-five worlds. End of story."

Isaacson held up a hand. "I'm sorry, General, I did
not mean to suggest *you* had anything but the purest of
motivations. But surely, if there were any whisperings of
discontent against Avery within the military, you'd be the
one to hear it?"

The general stared at him. "There are always rumblings. Always discontent. Hell, any young private will
bitch and moan at you about his current assignment. The
boots are too heavy. The paperwork too thick. The red
tape too ridiculous. The quarters too small. The toilets
too smelly. The coffee too bitter. We're military. We complain about shit. It's our birthright. But when the rub-
ber hits the road, we get our asses in gear and defend
our country and our planet and our civilization without
a peep. Are there rumblings against Avery? Of course.
Half the military hates her. Rumblings against you? Bet
your ass there are. The other half hates you. Does that
mean you're going to wake up with a knife in your back?
Well if you do, it won't be from the military. It'll be some
punk-ass politician's knife, and the blade will be poi-
soned. On the other hand, piss someone like me off, and
it will be a bullet. To your face. With me standing square
in front of you, and you'll be armed too."

Isaacson put on his best politician's smile. "Tell me,
where is the anti-matter added?"

The change in subject threw the general for a loop. "Excuse me?"

"The bombs. Where do they add the anti-matter? It's not here, obviously, or anywhere near the capitol. Where?"

"Classified."

Isaacson wiped the smile from his face, replacing it with a cold, calculating politician's glare. "Tell me. Now."

Norton shook his head. "Under a mountain in Wyoming. I'll tell the colonel you're coming."

CHAPTER TWENTY-SEVEN

The cold, bright lights glared overhead. He tried to move, but his wooden limbs were stiff and they fought against his attempts. His chest hurt, but, thankfully, not as much as he remembered. In fact, all the old aches and pains had subsided, though he could barely move.

People were moving behind him, but he was going in and out of consciousness. One moment he could hear people talking in the room and the next he was alone. Everything was so hazy. Surreal.

He lifted his head, and saw the medical equipment all around him. His eyes rested on something he hadn't seen before—a window. Starting near the floor and as tall as a person. And beyond it....

Space. Stars. And if his eyes didn't lie, a planet, far below. He couldn't make out any more detail beyond the fact that it had an atmosphere. He tried to move—to stand, to go to the window and look out to see where he was.

But he was exhausted. And he didn't feel like himself. Not completely. It was like he was still watching himself from a distance, through gauze.

Like he was the spectator and someone else was in his body.

In a sudden burst of panic, he tried moving his hand, and, with relief, saw it rise up in front of his face.

But something was off.

So hazy.

So tired.

CHAPTER TWENTY-EIGHT

Near Churchill Station, Upper Orbit, Britannia
Bridge, ISS Warrior

HE WAS AWAKE, the customary dreams fading, and he sat once again in his chair on the bridge, making the final preparations.

The fleet was ready.

Zingano had been swayed by Granger's bravado and gave him even more than he asked for, so it was with over one hundred and fifty ships that they left Churchill Station over Britannia. Thirty of them were brand new, built on Britannia itself. He stood at the window of his quarters, looking down on the placid green planet. So far, it had not been attacked, but it was inevitable. All the main centers of IDF activity and manufacturing bases had been hit over the past two months, and Britannia was as big as any of them.

Two billion people lived down there. Millions of babies, kids, teenagers, grandparents, newlyweds soon to be parted by the draft; hundreds of thousands of schools, churches, libraries, parks, shops, gardens, farms. A whole, vibrant, living breathing human world.

And it was repeated dozens of times over, all throughout human-settled space. Hundreds of settlements and colonies. An entire galactic civilization hung in the balance, and Granger couldn't shake the feeling that it was all going to come down to him and his performance over the next few weeks.

His spine.

He shuddered as he remembered the president blowing out the brains of the congresswoman. The body shoved ignominiously into the corner. Total war was making brutes of them all. Not just him. Brick-layer indeed.

The comm chimed. "Fleet's ready to leave, sir."

"I'll be there in a moment, Shelby."

He leaned in toward the window to get a better view of the fleet. One hundred and fifty ships. Most brand new—it was astonishing how fast Avery and the top military leadership had managed to shift the majority of the world's industrial base to the production of ships and equipment for the war effort. And not just Earth—the retooling was repeated across every United Earth world with any kind of industrial base. Most of these ships were heavy cruisers, absolutely bristling with guns and laser turrets. The crews were relatively untrained, having only gone through a month of basic, but he'd try to break them in slowly.

Ten minutes later he settled into his chair on the bridge and pointed to the comm station with a nod. Ensign Prucha understood without a word. "You're patched in to the fleet, sir."

Dammit. Speeches.

"This is Captain Granger. Ladies and gentlemen, today we do something remarkable. For months we've been on the run. We've been playing defense, and a pathetic one at that. We may have won a few battles, but we've lost others, and we've lost friends. We've lost family. We've lost whole worlds."

"But today, for the first time, we go on the hunt. Though many of the details of our mission are classified, I can tell you this much: my prime objective is to kill as many cumrat bastards as I can. To put them on the run, and to keep them running all the way back to their latrine of a world."

He took a deep breath, pondering his words. What the hell do you tell a hundred thousand people who probably won't come back alive?

"I will not lie to you. This is a dangerous mission. Many in the top brass were against it. But I believe it is necessary, as does President Avery and Fleet Admiral Zingano. Many of us will die. But the payoff is safety for your families and your worlds. For the next few weeks the Swarm's focus is going to shift rather dramatically. Rather than wreaking havoc across all our worlds they'll turn and find us suddenly behind their backs with a knife at their throats. They will not be happy, and they won't take it lying down."

He stood up. "But goddammit, we have spines, we have pride, and we are strong. Stronger than the Swarm. Stronger than their allies. I swear to you, we will prevail. Do your duty. Do it unflinchingly. Do it soberly. Take your fear and face it and use it to fuel you."

"Look around you. Look at your comrades. They will become your best friends. You will suffer with them. Sweat and bleed with them. Many of you will die with them. They will have your back and you will have theirs. I know most of you are new, and most of you have been drafted. You come from all walks of life. Your parents are rich and poor, politicians and professors, construction workers and overachievers, deadbeats and prisoners,

CEOs, bankers, and crack whores—we've got it all. But your background does not matter. All that matters is that you will fight to survive. You will fight for freedom—"

He glanced over at Proctor, who was beaming at him. "You will fight for your friends, because at the end of the day ... what the hell do any of us have but that? Captains, lock nav computers with *Warrior*. We leave in one minute. Granger out."

The bridge erupted in brief applause before Granger waved an arm. "Knock it off. Proctor?" His XO had come up to his side.

She grinned a lopsided smile. "A bit longer than your usual taste, sir."

"Extraordinary times call for extraordinarily long speeches." He glanced down at his watch. "What was that, nearly two minutes?"

"We'll make a politician out of you yet."

He held his chest. "That was uncalled for, Shelby. Commander Rayna Scott, how are my engines?"

"Purring like kittens, Cap'n," came Scott's voice through the comm.

"Thank you, Commander. Ensign Prince, are the fleet nav computers all linked?"

"Aye, sir."

"Then take us out."

A moment later, he felt the barely perceptible lurch of the q-jump, and a minute after that, the second. Then the third. On and on for hours they jumped, a tenth of a light year at a time, each shift producing a small but noticeable shift in the star pattern on the screen. As they passed near Earth, New Dublin and several other stars merged into the familiar big dipper, but soon skewed apart.

They moved steadily toward Polaris. Granger imagined he was a sea captain of old, using the old star to guide his old ship, navigating unfamiliar waters by the familiar, friendly light of an old friend.

But these waters would not be friendly. In fact, Polaris's own light was now suspect. Did that system harbor the Swarm? Did their mortal enemy originate from the steady, trusted light of the north?

Nonsense, he knew. The scouts had reported the Polaris System itself barren. But hundreds of other stars systems surrounded it, any number of which could house their enemy. The first they would investigate was Epsilon Garibaldi, an unremarkable red dwarf star that nonetheless had a small planet that the scouts reported bore suspicious signs of activity—both electromagnetic and meta-space signatures.

"Two more q-jumps, sir," said Ensign Prince.

Granger nodded. He turned to Proctor. "So? Epsilon Garibaldi. What do you think we'll find?"

Proctor shrugged. "Who knows? This is right on the edge of the sphere of Swarm dominated space I studied for my Ph.D. I doubt it's their homeworld, and the signals the scouts detected could very well be from an unreported Russian colony. Hell, it could even be a smuggler colony for all we know—there must be dozens of those out here."

"True. But we've got to start somewhere. May as well start with something that'll be a good initial test for our green fleet. Don't shock them all at once with the battle of their lives over the Swarm homeworld."

Proctor nodded. "True. There was little evidence that this was any sort of Swarm hub. It will be interesting, though, certainly."

"Last q-jump," noted Ensign Prince.

Granger pointed at the screen, zeroing in on the weak, red sun at the center—Epsilon Garibaldi. "Go ahead, Mr. Prince."

The view shifted. The small red dot was replaced by a large, greenish planet with a blue-tinged atmosphere.

And about a dozen Swarm carriers waiting for them.

Scores of green beams lanced out and smashed into the fleet, the *Warrior* included.

"Shit," Granger muttered. "All hands, battle stations!"

CHAPTER TWENTY-NINE

Epsilon Garibaldi Four, Epsilon Garibaldi System
Bridge, ISS Warrior

THE SHIP LURCHED AS multiple anti-matter beams slammed into the bow.

"Hull breach, decks fourteen and fifteen, forward section," yelled an operations officer.

"The other cruisers in Beta Wing are getting pounded, sir," said Lieutenant Diaz.

Granger swore again. "Capacitor bank status?" He knew the *Warrior* was the slowest ship to recharge the cap banks that powered the q-jump drive. If they could get away now they might avoid a disaster.

"Thirty seconds until full charge, sir."

"Sir, we just lost the *ISS Davenport* and the *Wyoming*." Lieutenant Diaz pointed up at the screen. Granger turned and watched the aftermath of the two explosions—the shells of the two ships boiled with the streaming debris and escaping atmosphere before secondary explosions erupted down their lengths. In the background the waiting Swarm carriers bombarded the other thirty ships of

Beta Wing with anti-matter beam fire. Multiple green columns pierced clean through the ship nearest the *Warrior*.

"There goes the *ISS Alberta*," said Proctor, now standing next to him. "Capacitor banks charged, sir."

Three ships already gone. And they'd only been there a minute. Getting caught with your pants down is a bitch.

Granger grit his teeth and pounded his armrest. "No. We're holding our ground. Commander Pierce, launch all fighter squads. Beta Wing, Gamma Wing, and Alpha Wing captains, launch all fighters. Directly engage the carriers."

A smattering of replies confirmed through the comm, and he glanced at Proctor. "Take Sigma and Omega Wings. Execute maneuver Granger Three."

She nodded and retreated to the XO's station, yelling out instructions to the captains of the two wings of cruisers. Granger returned his attention to the battle. "Beta, Gamma, and Alpha, divide and conquer. My tactical crew will divvy you up, stayed tuned for assignments. Five cruisers per Swarm carrier. Direct all fire toward their main fighter bays and neutralize their fighter capabilities, then focus on weapons."

He strode over to the annex he had added to the tactical station, a small crew of tactical officers who would coordinate battle maneuvers with the fleet. "*Warrior* will lead Alpha wing against these four carriers," he indicated the enemy ship grouped together on the tactical readout. "Make assignments for the other wings. Move."

Granger turned to watch the viewscreen. Thousands of IDF fighters swarmed out of their bays and converged on the enemy carriers, which in turn belched out thousands of fighters of their own. Damn. This was going to be a rough fight. So much for breaking in his green fleet gently.

The *Warrior* shot toward its target and began pelting the Swarm carrier with a barrage of mag rail fire. Alpha Wing followed on its tail, likewise peppering the first target with high velocity slugs. When the first gaping hole opened up he signaled to tactical. "Open fire with lasers. Boil 'em. Signal to Alpha Wing to do the same."

The *Warrior* rumbled. Explosions sounded in the distance as the Swarm vessels pounded them with devastating anti-matter beams, which cut deep gouges in the hull and occasionally blasted off a mag rail or laser turret.

These ships knew we were coming, dammit. Granger watched in dismay as one Alpha Wing cruiser, then another, caught well-placed green beams on their undersides, piercing their power plants and initiating massive explosions that engulfed the ships. Two more down of his thirty. Another one of their carriers was belching debris and fire, and moments later it, too, exploded.

"Proctor, status of maneuver Granger Three?"

The XO glanced up from her station. "Sigma and Gamma Wings have entered high velocity orbits. Sixty ships spread out in a single-file line, accelerating around the planet toward our position."

"ETA?"

"Five minutes."

Granger nodded. It was risky, and they might not even last that long, and if the Swarm moved or changed orbits then the effort was wasted. But if not, they'd never see it coming.

He sat back down in the captain's chair. "Good. Let's dig in and give 'em hell for a few minutes before they get here."

CHAPTER THIRTY

Epsilon Garibaldi Four, Epsilon Garibaldi System
High Orbit

"PULL UP PULL UP PULL UP!" Spacechamp's voice shrieked in his ear. Explosions coursed through the anti-matter turret on the Swarm carrier filling his front viewport, but the damn thing was still firing.

And a cloud of Swarm fighters was raking him with vicious gunfire. Multiple holes in his fuselage spewed gas—he'd lost atmospheric pressure several minutes ago.

"Almost...."

He looped around the turret again, unleashing a storm of gunfire, and finally sending off one last torpedo which caught the lurching cannon in the side and demolished it in a cloud of debris. Finally, the thing's green beam vanished as its base exploded, and Ballsy peeled away with a millisecond to spare as the wreckage spewed outward toward him.

"*Ballsy!*"

He swerved again, dodging more wreckage flying out from the hole where the turret had been, and more explosions behind him made him grin with satisfaction as he saw the debris collide with half a dozen bogeys on his tail.

"Holy sh—" Spacechamp murmured in his ear.

Fodder laughed. "What's the matter, Spacechamp, ain't you ever seen someone with a death wish before?"

She swore again. "Not like Ballsy just there. Think you need a new call sign, bud. How about ... uh ... Stupidsy?"

Volz groaned. "Spacechamp, that's terrible. Just terrible. I expect better out of you."

"Ok," she went on—and he heard the smirk enter her voice—"how about Shit-for-brains?"

"That'll do. Watch your left flank!" He pulled hard on his controls to come to her aid, but he needn't have bothered—Pew Pew swooped in out of nowhere and blasted the tailing bogey in a storm of fire. "Pew Pew to the rescue. Again. Where the hell do you come from, Pew Pew?"

"I am the wind," the space jock deadpanned drily.

Alarm sirens blasted over their comms, and Ballsy swore as he realized what it meant.

Singularities.

Lots of them.

CHAPTER THIRTY-ONE

ONCE AGAIN, ISAACSON found himself in a shuttle, blasting out over the atmosphere, this time, toward Wyoming. Once again, Conner's knuckles were white as he gripped his armrests.

"Find me any coffee?" Isaacson asked, trying to distract the kid.

With his eyes still closed, Conner nodded.

"Good. What kind?"

"Half-Columbian, half-Indonesian. Very sweet. Smooth. And hot."

Isaacson chuckled. The kid was either very good at double-entendre banter, or he was going to have a very boring, caffeinated evening.

He glanced out the window. Far below he could see the plains begin to fall away, replaced by the rugged landscape of the mountain west. A white blanket covered the lower hills and the taller, jagged peaks stuck out dramatically. The engine noise changed subtly. Good—they were landing.

Hal Levin poked his head up from the seat in front of them. "Sir, just received a message from Ambassador Volodin."

"What is it?"

"A report on the blast that took out the embassy ground car."

Isaacson snatched the pad and read.

The words leapt out at him like a blaring, flashing sign.

Anti-matter.

He tapped his comm card, touching a panel that would initiate a call to the ambassador. Moments later, the man's face appeared on the card.

"You got my note, Eamon?"

"Anti-matter? Wasn't that blast a little small for anti-matter?"

Volodin shrugged. "You only need a little bit. In this case, a nanogram, judging from the gamma-ray flux the intelligence service detected. But whether it's a nanogram of anti-matter or a kilogram of C-4, the blast will be the same. Only in anti-matter's case, it was certainly not looked for. Very difficult to find a properly designed anti-matter bomb."

"And how would you know that?" demanded Isaacson.

"That's what our intelligence reports tell me, anyway. There is only one manufacturer of anti-matter devices, and it is not in the Russian Confederation. Gotta go. Talk later." Volodin's faced blinked out.

Interesting. Only one manufacturer of anti-matter devices in the entire world. In *all* the settled worlds.

"Sir, another message," said Levin, popping over the seat again. "It's from the intern office, Eamon."

"The *intern* office?" Isaacson glanced at Conner, who had suddenly opened his eyes.

Levin handed him the pad, and Isaacson read.

Shit. Why now?

He turned to Conner, whose face was still white and green from the flight. "Son, I'm so sorry. Your ... your brother just died."

-

CHAPTER THIRTY-TWO

Epsilon Garibaldi Four, Epsilon Garibaldi System
High Orbit

A SINGULARITY FLARED as an osmium brick flew into it and disappeared. Good. Four down, one to go.

"Fodder, get in there with your brick! Spacechamp, help me back him up!" Ballsy tailed his squadmate, picking off a few bogeys that had strayed too close.

Pew Pew had already launched his, but enemy fighters had swarmed him and knocked the brick off-course, nearly destroying Pew Pew's fighter. As it was, he'd managed to stabilize his craft, but was just drifting motionless among the debris, too battered to move.

Pierce's voice blared over his comm set. "All hands, ready for Maneuver Granger Three."

"Sir, we've still got a singularity out here...." Ballsy glanced at his sensor board, and breathed harder when he saw a new singularity contact. "Make that two."

Pierce hesitated. Ballsy knew the calculus that was running through the CAG's brain—keep the fighters engaged with the singularities and risk getting hit by Maneuver

Granger Three, or pull back and risk letting one of the singularities launch toward the *Warrior*.

Ballsy shook his head—the decision was an obvious choice to him. The good of the many outweighed the good of the stupid. And he felt particularly stupid that day.

"We're going in," he said.

Pierce confirmed. "Get in and get out, Ballsy."

He checked the status of a rarely-used piece of equipment on the tail of his fighter. Operational. Good—if this didn't work they were screwed.

"Fodder, make your run. Spacechamp, you're going solo on his tail. I'll be back in a jiffy."

"Where the hell are you—" she began, but he'd already peeled away toward the other singularity pulsing nearby. The debris field stretched between him and the miniature black hole, but that only made his job slightly easier.

He set his sights on a particularly large piece of debris, roughly double the size of his own fighter. As it loomed large in his view port he readied the equipment. He'd never used a tow cable before, at least, not outside of standard pilot's training, and certainly not in the heat of battle, but there was nothing for it. All the other osmium bricks had either been knocked off course or were too far away. It was up to him and his tow cable.

His fighter blasted past the chuck of debris—he recognized it as a small section of one of the light cruisers they'd lost a few minutes ago—and pressed the launch button. The cable shot out behind him, and with a swell of relief he saw it attach to the steaming piece of hull.

He lurched forward against his restraint as the fighter pulled the line taut, but it, and the connection to the debris, held.

Now for the hard part.

He pulled with his fighter, and the debris accelerated along with him. And like a piece of string luring in a cat, he seemed to catch the attention of a handful of enemy bogeys flying nearby. They descended on him.

"Dammit," he breathed, and looped around as he dodged the enemy fire. His job just went from stupid to impossible. The debris swung around with him, and, serendipitously, yanked him out of the way with its momentum just as a Swarm fighter flew past with its guns blazing. All the shots missed. "Luck is for the stupid, I guess," he mumbled, and pushed the accelerator forward.

Very close now.

He dodged again to veer away from another bogey, then finessed the fighter into an angle that he prayed would send the piece of debris plunging into the singularity.

He pressed the button to release the cable.

It didn't detach.

CHAPTER THIRTY-THREE

Epsilon Garibaldi Four, Epsilon Garibaldi System
Bridge, ISS Warrior

"TWO MINUTES UNTIL maneuver Granger Three," announced Proctor.

Nearly there, thought Granger. Alpha Wing had lost two more cruisers, and the other two wings had lost their share as well, but they'd managed to destroy four of the twelve carriers.

"Captain Connelly, move the *Eddington* to starboard—you're too exposed." Granger traced the lines on his tactical screen. Damn—the *Farragut* was getting flanked by two carriers. "Captain Verish, pull down hard toward the atmosphere. *Jefferson* and *Wallace* move to support."

The battered *Farragut* started dropping down, even as it began belching fire from its top. Ignoring the cover fire provided by the *Jefferson* and *Wallace*, the two Swarm carriers continued piercing the *Farragut* with anti-matter beams until finally it flared into a blinding explosion.

Granger frowned and shook his head. One more down. And Verish was a good captain. One of the best. A glance at his watch told him it was time. "All ships.

Prepare for maneuver Granger Three. Funnel these bastards into a group—stay on the outskirts. All fighters, pull clear until Sigma and Gamma wings pass."

The fighters immediately dropped away, pulling most of the swarm fighters with them, and the heavy cruisers formed a perimeter around the Swarm carriers, who continued pounding away at the IDF ships around them, seemingly unaware of the coming threat.

Ten seconds later, one of the Swarm carriers started erupting in explosions from unseen mag rail slugs and ten seconds after that the first ship of Sigma Wing blazed past in the blink of an eye. Several of the enemy carriers shot anti-matter beams after it, but to no avail—it was hundreds of kilometers away already, circling around for its next pass.

The next Sigma Wing ship flew by, then a third and a fourth in rapid succession. The addition of the cruisers' massive speed to the already-fast mag rail slugs created projectiles with astoundingly high kinetic energy, and the absence of an easy-to-hit target appeared to confound the Swarm.

That was their one failing. For all their overwhelming firepower and speed, the Swarm seemed to lack strategy. He marveled how they could build such advanced spaceships with devastating weaponry like anti-matter beams and the singularity torpedoes, and yet fail in their ability to counter unconventional space warfare tactics. They couldn't seem to think on their feet—or whatever it was they used to move around. Not that he was complaining about that particular defect.

One Swarm carrier exploded, then the next. Soon there were only two left as the final Sigma Wing ship blasted past, visible for only a second or so. The first Gamma Wing ship would be there in five seconds.

Four.

Three.

Two.

On the viewscreen, one hundred kilometers away, the incoming Gamma Wing ship, the *ISS Mayflower*, exploded.

"WHAT?!"

Granger bolted upright and reared upon the tactical station. "What happened?"

"It was hit by something, sir. Examining the blast signature now...."

The next Gamma Wing ship was fast approaching.

Four.

Three.

Another explosion. Another cruiser lost. Most lives snuffed out.

"Sir! I don't know how we missed it, but another fleet q-jumped in right above us. Fifty kilometers higher orbit."

"Swarm?"

Ensign Diamond shook his head. "No, sir. These readings match the Dolmasi ships we encountered before."

Dammit.

A third explosion illuminated the screen. He waved over to Proctor. "Abort Granger Three. Call them off. Change course. All of them are to reassemble and make a run at the Dolmasi."

He turned back to the comm. "All Alpha, Beta, and Gamma Wing ships, let's finish off these last two carriers and join the others. Granger out."

Proctor waved him down. "Tim," she started, lowering her voice once he'd approached the XO's station, "we've got to get out of here. We have no idea how many more are coming. We've made our point—they'll be on the lookout now for attacks in their own space."

"We can't retreat."

She shook her head. "Not retreat. Regroup. This was our plan—hit them hard, then fade away into interstellar space before emerging to hit them again, always avoiding their larger forces. Well *this* counts as a larger force."

She glanced down at her console. "Sigma and Gamma wings are assembled, about to move against the Dolmasi." She looked back up at him. "There's still time. Let's cut our losses and fight another day."

She was right, dammit.

He was about to give the order to leave the system when the sensor officer and comm officer both spoke simultaneously.

"Sir, the Dolmasi—"

"—carriers all ceased fire—"

"—incoming transmission—"

"—all at the same time, sir."

"—they're asking to speak directly to you."

Granger tried to parse both announcements at once. He glanced at his tactical readout and confirmed—both remaining Swarm ships had ceased fire. He turned to Ensign Prucha at comm. "The Dolmasi want to talk to *me*? They named me?"

"Aye, sir. Incoming visual signal."

Bewildered, Granger pointed to the monitor on the wall. "On screen, then."

A familiar sight greeted him.

"Captain Granger. We meet again." Vishgane Kharsa's scaled face appeared on the screen. "And this time, it is you who are in our space."

Granger smirked. "I suppose you're going to ask us politely to leave?"

If the Vishgane had any emotional reaction it certainly didn't show in his expression. "No. This time I ask for a meeting. Face to face. I offer to come aboard your ship that we might talk. As warriors and potential future allies and friends."

CHAPTER THIRTY-FOUR

Epsilon Garibaldi Four, Epsilon Garibaldi System
High Orbit

SHIT.

Ballsy grimaced as he saw the singularity growing larger ahead of him, the brightness filling his viewport.

He veered away to miss the singularity himself, hoping that the trajectory of the debris would carry it into the shimmering hole, disrupt it, and snap the connection to his own fighter at the same time.

Probably wouldn't survive the blast, though. Did this make him a hero? He grunted. He was about to die, and all the heroes were dead anyway, so why not?

His fighter lurched as it caught a few rounds of bogey fire on its wing, and the Swarm fighter flew by, strafing him and the debris both. The starboard thrusters shuddered, and his craft veered to the left, pulling the debris with it, out of the path of the singularity. He groaned as they both flew by it, just meters to spare.

"Dammit."

He'd lost any favorable momentum and approach vector. That was it—he had only one choice.

Go in himself. Sacrifice his fighter, and his life, so that the others could continue the fight.

Hell, maybe he'd even find Fishtail on the other side. In fact, now that the decision seemed to be made for him, he felt an uneasy peace—knowing he was either about to die, or go through and see his old squadmate, or both.

"Yeehaw!"

A voice hollered out of his comm set, and he looked all around, searching for the source.

"Get out of the way, you moron!" Pew Pew's voice called out again, and that's when Ballsy saw it.

And swore again.

Pew Pew, his fighter mostly disabled, was pushed up against another piece of debris, using only his landing thrusters to guide the chunk of metal on a looping, spiraling, semi-chaotic course. With another curse Ballsy pressed on the accelerator and veered out of the way.

And just in time.

The debris connected with the singularity, and the three objects exploded together in a piercing light.

But not before Ballsy saw something shoot out from the fighter, away from the explosion.

When the blast subsided, he breathed easier. The shock wave bowled over him, and more debris caught in the blast front slammed into a few Swarm fighters nearby.

But Pew Pew was gone. Shit—that guy had lived through everything. Always throwing himself at the craziest situations. Always disappearing and being given up for dead, only to reappear at the last—

"Ballsy, you gonna come get me, or what?"

Volt laughed, and shook his head. "You didn't...."

156

"I did. Ejected at the last second. I'm about to run into a mighty big cumrat ship though, and turn into a soupy blob myself, so I reckon you might want to make all available haste in getting your ass over here."

Still laughing at the absurdity of it—making a crazy suicidal run at the singularity, failing, only to be bailed out by a similar suicidal run, and then having to rescue his rescuer—and within a moment he had his friend on the radar.

He swooped past and matched velocity, glancing out his rear to verify at least some length of cable was still there.

It was. Just a few meters, but it was enough.

"All right, Pew Pew, grab on. Don't get roasted in my ion trail—I hear those bastards can get toasty."

The Swarm carrier loomed closer and closer, and he nudged his craft toward his flailing friend, tumbling and twisting out in the vacuum as he careened toward the enemy ship. Only a few seconds left before they both smeared against the hull....

"Got it! Go!"

Ballsy nudged the left wing's thruster to ease them out of the way. Too much acceleration and Pew Pew would fly off the cable and smash into the Swarm hull.

They weren't going to make it.

"Ballsy, punch it! Don't worry, I'll hold on! Got it tied around my waist!"

Swearing again, he pushed more power to the thruster and they sailed out of the way, sending Pew Pew wrapping around him in a wide arc.

But they missed the hull. By only three meters, but a win was a win.

"Yeehaw!" Pew Pew called again. Ballsy puffed air in disbelief—it was a wonder the other man could still breath.

He glanced at his radar and saw, with satisfaction, that Fodder and Spacechamp had managed to knock out the other singularity. And if his readings were correct, they were even still alive.

But his radar showed something else. New contacts. Lots of them.

Dolmasi ships. But they weren't firing yet. No fighters belched out from their bays.

But it was inevitable. They'd come. And with Pew Pew hanging on by a literal thread, they'd both die.

Time for yet another miracle.

CHAPTER THIRTY-FIVE

Wyoming, North America, Earth
Squaretop Mountain Production Facility

"DEAD?" CONNER'S FACE went red. "How? When? But—"

This was just awful. Isaacson never learned how to console anyone, much less a man-child freshly graduated from high school. He'd never wanted kids. Now everyone on the shuttle was probably expecting him to ... well, *do* something.

Sighing, he went into empathetic politician mode. The *I feel your pain* mode. He stood up and sat next to him, putting his arm around the kid's shoulder.

"I'm sorry, Conner. There was an accident. They wouldn't say what exactly happened, but they say he died fast. Painlessly."

Rather than sob, the young man was completely emotionless. "He was the last one. The only family I had. Now I'm it. Alone," he said, his voice dead.

Isaacson did his best to console the kid, but in the end there was little he could do. The shuttle landed, and Isaacson went down the ramp with Levin. A soldier was waiting for them on the launch pad. He spoke in his chief's ear. "Look after the kid. I'll be back in an hour or so."

Levin nodded, and returned to the shuttle. The soldier held up a hand to salute, then to shake Isaacson's. "Mr. Vice President, I'm Colonel Titler. Welcome to the Squaretop Mountain production facility. Allow me to show you inside."

From the launch pad they walked up to what looked like an old shack set against a low hill. Beyond the hill, just a kilometer away, rose a sizable mountain, which, as the name suggested, appeared flat on top. Once inside, he saw that the interior actually spread out and away under the hill, and, like the small building above the military complex in D.C., it served mainly as a checkpoint and security processing station.

"General Norton said you wanted me to show you around. I think you'll be pleasantly surprised by our progress. When the president showed up last month we were still scaling up production. Heh—she wasn't too happy with us. Now you can report back and assure her we've improved our process flow."

Isaacson nodded. Clearly the officer thought he was there on an inspection tour, sent by the administration. He'd get more information out of the colonel by playing along. "Very good, Colonel Titler. President Avery will be most pleased."

The colonel showed him through a few sets of doors, then down an elevator, through more doors, and down yet another elevator, plunging deep into the Earth.

"How long ago did you start this facility up?"

Colonel Titler opened a door for him and led him through into an antechamber. Giant windows looked out onto what looked like a production floor. Dozens of people in full-body hazmat suits roamed the area, some carrying small sample bottles or vials, others pushing grav-lifts of storage containers.

"A few years ago. But we didn't ramp up production until two months ago. You know, when the war started. General Norton called the next day and ever since it's been a madhouse around here. We staffed up, retooled our production chambers where the material is produced, and now we can get through about ten kilos a day."

All the talk was gibberish to him, but one part caught Isaacson's ear. "A few years ago?"

"Yes, sir. Right at the beginning of the first term of Avery's administration."

Interesting. A weaponized anti-matter facility created at the beginning of Avery's tenure, right in the middle of the implementation of the Eagleton Commission, no less.

"Ten kilos, huh? Tell me, what does that translate to? About a thousand bombs a month?" he said, remembering the figure General Norton had quoted him in the MUNCENT facility underneath the capitol.

Colonel Titler chuckled. "More like fifty-thousand, sir. I think President Avery will be quite pleased with our progress, like I said."

Fifty-thousand? What in the world was Avery going to do with fifty-thousand anti-matter bombs per month? She must have one hell of a war strategy up her sleeve.

But what was she originally going to do with all that anti-matter if the Swarm had not invaded?

Isaacson smiled. "She sure will." He watched the production crew wheel a giant pallet onto the floor, and begin unstacking its contents. "You sure had to acquire new staff pretty quickly. Happy with the people?"

Colonel Titler nodded. "Yeah, they're working out. All draftees, of course. Got a crew of about ten thousand that keeps this place running. You wouldn't know it by that shack outside, would ya'?" He laughed. "Actually, we've got other entrances scattered around the local town. Can't have workers without bars, brothels, and restaurants now, can you?"

Isaacson grinned. "Yeah, I know what you mean."

Titler made a slight choking noise. "Yeah, heh. Well I was kidding. These are mostly scientist and engineering types. They wouldn't know a brothel if it bit them in the ass. Mostly recruited from the Ivies and other big tech and science schools. They wanted the best of the best for this operation—brightest minds, and all that. Mistakes can kill. And stupid workers make dead workers."

Scientists and engineers. Total war, indeed. He'd read the statistics. Every single able-bodied person below the age of forty had been drafted, and millions more older than that had volunteered. No one was overlooked. Every profession was represented. In centuries past, the elite classes might have avoided such duties. Not this time. Everyone—especially the ones with a technical background—was fair game.

Conner's brother—he'd been in science, hadn't he? Had things turned out differently, the young man might have been drafted into the anti-matter research and production program, and would be down there on one of the production floors below. Hell, Conner would have been able to go in and harass him for a few minutes while Isaacson talked. If only.

"Ten thousand workers, huh? Need any more? Are your needs met?"

Colonel Titler nodded. "We're just about at capacity, sir. Any more and we'll have to set up more barracks and living facilities. As it is we've got people sleeping in shifts."

"Good. I'll pass the word on to the president. Excellent work here, Colonel."

An hour later, on the shuttle, Conner didn't say a word, and Isaacson didn't try to draw the kid out. He sat ensconced with Levin in the back, thumbing through documents the intelligence and secret services had provided him with, trying to piece the puzzle together.

"I don't get it, Hal. The only source of anti-matter bombs is our own military. I just went and inspected the material production. Colonel Titler runs a tight ship—I don't see how he could let anything slip through his fingers and into the wrong hands."

The national news was playing on a screen in the cabin, and the news anchor announced the results of the previous day's battles with the Swarm: ten ships lost during the last engagement at New Dublin and the Centauri Systems.

Isaacson snorted—the administration's propaganda arm had been busy. He knew the true losses were far higher. He watched as Captain Granger's face flashed on the screen, with images of a giant parade in his hometown of Boise on repeat in the background. Damn. The man was a legend in his own time. It was a wonder they hadn't promoted him to Fleet Admiral already.

Levin shrugged. "Maybe there are other production facilities?"

Isaacson thought about that. "Others? Seems unlikely. Titler told me that they produce enough material for fifty-thousand bombs per month. General Norton told me his facility under D.C. only made a thousand casings per month. So if anything, there must be other manufacturing facilities making casings for all this anti-matter. Maybe forty-nine more, if the layouts are the same. I can't imagine they'd need any more production facilities."

The news continued, playing footage reels of the battle over New Dublin, emphasizing, of course, the destruction of the Swarm vessels. Eventually, the images changed to damaged houses and shots of dusty, barren terrain—the news anchor had switched topics.

And in other news this evening, residents of Wendover, Nevada report feeling a powerful earthquake this morning. Geological survey equipment recorded the quake as registering at seven point one on the Richter scale, an unusually large tremblor this far from the usual fault lines out west. There are several reports of witnesses seeing fireballs out in the Utah salt flats and hearing an explosion at the time of the quake, but those reports are not independently confirmed at this time. We'll have more on this story as it develops.

"Well look at that, Hal." He pointed at the screen. "I wonder if we've found ourselves another anti-matter production facility."

CHAPTER THIRTY-SIX

Epsilon Garibaldi Four, Epsilon Garibaldi System
Bridge, ISS Warrior

GRANGER MUTTERED A PROFANITY. "And why in the hell would I agree to that? You just destroyed three of my ships, and your *allies* just destroyed twenty."

Vishgane Kharsa bowed his head slightly. "Because, Captain Timothy Granger. I have been instructed by the Valarisi to offer you terms of peace."

"Surrender? No thank you."

"Not surrender. A peace treaty."

Peace? Could it be?

No. President Avery herself said that this would only end one way. With the complete and irrevocable destruction of the Swarm. They would not come back. Ever.

But for now, they had a chance to stall, at least. "Very well. You say you will come here? I assume you won't come alone? How many security personnel will be accompanying you?"

A sound came from the Vishgane that Granger could only interpret as a scoff. "Security? Please. You pose me no threat. If you try to take me from this place or otherwise harm me, over five hundred Dolmasi ships stand ready to descend on our current position and subdue you."

Granger nodded slowly. "Understood. I expect you in our main shuttle bay then. We'll send the coordinates over after—"

Kharsa interrupted. "We know where your shuttle bay is, Captain."

"Oh?"

"We know everything about you, Captain Granger. What the Valarisi know, so do their allies." He held up two fists, as if in goodbye.

The screen went blank, replaced by a visual feed of the battlefield, a graveyard of steaming ship hulls and scattered debris. Occasional electrical arcing raced over the dead IDF ships, and steady rivers of goo streamed from the remains of the Swarm carriers.

"Proctor, with me. Alert the marines—I want fifty men lining the walls of the shuttle bay and perched up above on the walkways. And call Doc Wyatt—he might have some insight after talking to Kharsa. Diaz, you have the bridge."

He led the way out the door. Proctor followed.

"Tim, do you really think they want peace?"

"Are you kidding?" Granger shook his head as they strode down the halls, taking a detour when their usual route to the shuttle bay was cut off by extensive battle damage. Injured crew members, supported by comrades, hobbled down the halls toward sickbay. Doc Wyatt flagged them down and fell into step with them.

"An actual Dolmasi is coming aboard the ship?" said Wyatt.

Granger nodded. "Wants to talk peace. Or so he says. We need to find out what they really want. Are they just stalling to save those last two Swarm carriers? Is there something we have that they want?"

"Is there something we know that has made them change tactics? Maybe our new willingness to invade into their space has changed their minds about this war," added Proctor.

Granger stepped over a steel girder that had been knocked loose from the ceiling. "Or at least given them pause. Maybe they're just stalling until more ships show up. We should have the fleet on a hair-trigger—q-jump the hell out of here if anything unexpected shows up."

"Agreed." Proctor called up to the bridge to relay the order and before long the three were standing outside the shuttle bay. Colonel Hanrahan, the marine commander, met them outside.

"I've got forty men on the walls, and ten up above as sharp shooters should the need arise."

"Good. Clear the hallways around the shuttle bay. If we need it, we'll use the conference room down there by the galley. Get twenty more men stationed around the corner, a few in the galley itself, and in each storage compartment on either side of the conference room. Seal off the deck, and have hazmat units ready in case anything ... completely unexpected happens."

"Aye, sir," replied Colonel Hanrahan in his gruff voice.

Granger walked through the door with Proctor and Wyatt in step just as the Dolmasi shuttle was passing through the electromagnetic atmosphere shield. The giant bay door closed slowly behind it and the small craft settled to the floor.

The ramp lowered. Vishgane Kharsa stepped out, alone.

If not for his obviously scaled face and hands, Granger would have thought him human—two arms, two legs, a largish torso, stark militaristic clothing that covered most of his skin. Two feet, though these were bare and more heavily scaled than his hands. Each had five toes, though. A remarkable case of parallel evolution—Granger supposed the exobiologists would have a field day if the war ever concluded and there were any Dolmasi left to study.

Granger stepped forward and held a hand out toward Proctor and Wyatt each. "This is my executive officer, Shelby Proctor." She stepped forward and Kharsa extended his hand—he seemed very well versed in Earth social customs. Proctor shook it after a tentative pause. "And my chief of medicine, Doctor Wyatt." Doc Wyatt stepped forward and shook Kharsa's hand as well.

Vishgane Kharsa stepped forward and offered his hand to Granger, who accepted it.

Instantly, his head began to swim with blurred images, light, and color. He swayed involuntarily. Granger felt himself falling, and within a moment, all went dark.

CHAPTER THIRTY-SEVEN

Epsilon Garibaldi Four, Epsilon Garibaldi System
Shuttle Bay, ISS Warrior

GRANGER BLINKED AND shook his head.

He was dreaming. Looking around, he recognized the recurring dream he'd been having. But this time he was awake. Two lights shone down from above and he smelled the familiar acrid burn. He sat up—he was sitting on a table. *An examination table?* A tube stuck out of his arm. He ripped it off and slid down from the table, glancing around the room.

A window. There was a window on the wall of the room—a small space that looked like a medical examination room. He hobbled over—his legs hurt—and peered out the thick glass.

Space.

Unfamiliar stars peered back as he looked all around the starscape.

A green planet rotated far below. Speckled with scant clouds and a surface dappled with occasional giant lakes and channels, the sight looked familiar. Almost. He was struck by how welcoming the globe appeared. He yearned for it. He needed to get there, desperately. It looked so close, yet he was far above in orbit, aboard some sort of station. As his eyes grew accustomed to the scene, he noticed shimmering lights—not stars—set against the distant star field. Ships?

With a roar, the world snapped back into view. Kharsa. The handshake. He stumbled forward and released his grip. Proctor reached out to steady him, and half a dozen marines nearby raised their weapons suddenly.

Vishgane Kharsa peered down at him—he was at least two meters tall. "Are you well, Captain?"

The memory was fading fast, just like his dreams. But he'd never progressed this far before. Had contact with the Dolmasi somehow stirred his memories of his disappearance? He waved the marines off. Slowly, they lowered their assault rifles.

"Fine." He stood taller. "Just fine."

Proctor let go of Granger and gave him a look that said, *Are you really ok?*

He nodded slightly to her and looked back at Kharsa. "How do you know so much about us? You know our language. You know our customs. How?"

"I told you, Captain, what our allies know, we know."

"The Swarm taught you our language?"

Kharsa bowed his head slightly. "The Valarisi have been aware of humanity for hundreds of years."

"And they determined we were a threat? That we had resources they wanted? Or do they just attack everyone?"

Kharsa looked confused. "The Valarisi desire all to be their allies."

"Do they control their allies?"

"Are you asking if we are slaves? No." Kharsa made a choking sound that Granger recognized as the laugh. "But the Valarisi are ... very persuasive."

Right. Most conquerers tend to be persuasive with the people they rule, Granger thought.

"Very well. Why have you come? You want peace? Then tell the Swarm to stop invading our space. Stop attacking our worlds. Leave us alone, and we will leave them alone."

Kharsa cocked his head, as if thinking hard. After several moments he finally said, "No."

"Excuse me? That's it? No? Then our business here is finished. Get off my ship."

"My apologies, Captain, I'm merely passing along the will of the Valarisi. Think of me as their conduit. Their mouthpiece."

Interesting. Could they be in constant communication? He gave Proctor a knowing glance, and she looked back, steadily. She turned to the alien and bowed slightly. "Excuse me, Captain, Vishgane, I have duties to attend to. If you'll excuse me."

Good. She understood.

"Captain," she said, nodding to him.

"Commander."

She reached out a hand to him. Odd. They rarely shook hands. As he clasped hers she pressed something into his. Aware that she was giving something to him that she didn't want the alien to see, he closed his fist around it and hooked his hands behind his back.

Proctor left. He turned around to make a show of watching her go, and with his back turned to Kharsa he glanced down at what was resting in his palm.

The tiny earpiece receiver that Proctor wore in her duties as XO.

Her purpose was clear. He was to wear the earpiece. She would help him guide the conversation with the Vishgane. It was obvious what she was going to attempt:

171

Listen in on the Dolmasi's conversation with the Swarm. Crack the code.

Now to keep Vishgane Kharsa talking. Granger turned back to him and smiled.

CHAPTER THIRTY-EIGHT

North American Airspace, Earth
Vice President's Shuttle

ISAACSON SCROLLED THOUGH file after file, directory after directory, searching for the relevant information, but either he just didn't know where to look, or he didn't possess a high enough security clearance. He could find nothing on the anti-matter processing program. Nothing on the bomb casings. Nothing on the Squaretop Mountain Wyoming site. He couldn't even find Sergeant Gall's service record—the young scientist he'd met in MUN-CENT—only her draft record.

Interesting. Perhaps that meant....

He glanced up at Conner. The young man had obviously been crying, but kept it silent. "What was your brother's name?"

The kid sighed and closed his eyes. "Preston."

Isaacson nodded, and discretely entered the brother's name into the draft database he'd brought up on his data interface pad. "A good name. Preston Davenport? Tell me about him. What was he like?"

"Well, sir, he was taller than me, for one. Way smarter. Always scoring higher on tests—"

"He was close to your age? You were in school together?" Isaacson asked absentmindedly, feigning close attention.

He nodded. "Just a year older. He was the smarter one, but I was always more athletic. I could always squish him at wrestling or basketball or whatever we did." Conner droned on. It seemed therapeutic for him to talk about his brother. Isaacson nodded at appropriate points, asking vague questions that induced reminiscent and nostalgic answers.

But mostly he was focused on the data coming across his screen. Or rather, the lack of it. Very, very interesting. There was hardly any information on Preston Davenport either. Nothing besides the draft record, like Sergeant Gall. No assignment. No current location. His current status hadn't even updated to reflect the boy's recent death.

Both Preston and Sergeant Gall simply did not fit anywhere in the government logbooks, beyond the basic record of their existence.

Conner had stopped talking. He'd apparently just told a humorous story about his brother and a pained smile showed on his face. "Sounds like a wonderful young man, Conner. You should be proud," said Isaacson. "Proud of his service. He died defending United Earth. Speaking of which, did he ever mention where he was posted?"

Conner shook his head. "Said it was classified. But it was on Earth, out west somewhere. At least, that was what I guessed from things he said. Something about the heat and the dry air. Made his skin crack."

An idea struck him. Preston was stationed somewhere near Wendover, Nevada. Somewhere he might have been killed by, say, a massive explosion that locals would have felt as an earthquake. An explosion underground. It was too coincidental to be unrelated.

"Well, when we get back to D.C., let's have a drink in his honor. And maybe, when you're feeling up to it, I'll treat you to some, ahem ... coffee." He winked at the young man. Nothing better for the soul than busting a nut.

"Sorry, sir, I'm not a big coffee fan. It's the caffeine. Headaches."

Isaacson almost sighed from the disappointment—that probably meant there was a big can of instant coffee waiting for him at his D.C. residence rather than an exotic half-Columbian, half-Sumatran woman.

But before he could react, the shuttle lurched.

And dove.

"Strap belts, NOW!" the captain yelled into the cabin comm. Everyone around him immediately latched their seatbelt, but Isaacson fumbled with his—he rarely wore it. He fastened it a split second before the entire cabin turned upside down.

The shuttle rolled several times, and lurched into a new direction.

"Captain, what the hell are you doing?" Isaacson screamed toward the cockpit.

Something caught his eye outside his window. He understood.

Two fighters, guns blazing, closing in on them fast.

CHAPTER THIRTY-NINE

Epsilon Garibaldi Four, Epsilon Garibaldi System
Conference Room Three, ISS Warrior

"VISHGANE, WE HAVE MUCH to discuss. You seem to know so much about me and my ship. Would you like a very brief tour before we continue?"

Granger held out his hand toward the doors to the shuttle bay. Colonel Hanrahan stepped forward. "Sir, I don't believe that is prudent at this point."

"I understand your concerns, Colonel," Granger eyed the Vishgane. "But if our guest had nefarious purposes he would have ordered his fleet to directly engage with ours."

"Yes, sir, but he may be here to gather intel. A tour of the ship would not be the wisest course of action, at least from my perspective."

Good man, he thought. But he had no intention of showing the Vishgane anything of importance. He was just stalling. Granger nodded. "Very well, Colonel. We will steer clear of engineering, weapons platforms, and all areas of the ship which may contain technology unfamiliar to our guest."

Vishgane Kharsa made his choking noise, indicating he found the remark humorous. "Captain Timothy Granger, there is very little that we do not know about you or your ship. Let us dispense with your ... *tour*, and speak of more important things."

He needed to get his earpiece in without the alien seeing. "Very well, Vishgane. Please accompany me to a conference room. Just down the hallway. At least there we can sit and talk in a more private setting."

"I assent to your wishes, Captain."

Granger indicated the door. "This way, then. Colonel Hanrahan, please lead the way."

The colonel grunted his acknowledgement, shouldered his assault rifle, and walked out the door. "If you'll follow me, sirs."

Vishgane Kharsa stepped away from his shuttle, and the ramp retracted into its receptacle as the small craft sealed up tight. "I will know if it has been entered, Captain. Do not betray my trust."

Granger smiled inwardly at the remark. An odd request, especially when juxtaposed against the unprovoked aggression displayed by both the Swarm and the Dolmasi, and by the fact that he was about to attempt an intel op far more risky and with a higher reward than simply breaking into the alien's shuttle. They were about to eavesdrop on the Swarm's mysterious communications link, one that allowed for apparently near-instantaneous communication with each other, and with, apparently, the Dolmasi.

"Of course not, Vishgane Kharsa. This way."

Hanrahan led the way, the Vishgane followed, and Granger brought up the rear, discretely pushing the tiny receiver into his ear. Doc Wyatt fell into step with him.

"What do you expect they'll say? What could we possibly give them or do that will make them pull back?"

"I guess we'll find out, Doc. Just keep an eye on us. This is the first time we've ever encountered a non-human face-to-face before. Your observations will be of utmost value, no doubt."

The conference room door was flanked by two marines, and as they all stepped through Proctor's voice came through the earpiece.

"You hear me, sir? If you can, clear your throat."

Granger cleared his throat, and indicated a chair near the table, which he hoped was big enough for the Vishgane. "Please have a seat." He turned to Hanrahan, who'd been accompanied by the two marines. "That will be all, gentlemen."

Hanrahan stood his ground. "Sir, I can't leave you here alone with the alien."

Granger glanced at the heavily armed marines, and back at the Vishgane, who'd sat down. "You may stay, Colonel. Your men will stand guard outside the door."

"Aye aye, sir."

Granger sat. Proctor's voice came through again. "I hope that throat-clear was for me. Sir, we're not reading any EM signals originating from the conference room. Scanning for neutrino-based, graviton, and meta-space signals next."

Vishgane Kharsa broke the silence. "Captain Granger. On behalf of the Valarisi, I offer peace. These are the terms: first, that you withdraw all your ships of war to the Sol System, to your former Lunar Base, where they will await assimilation into the Valarisi defense force."

Defense force? Is that what they called their invasion fleets? Granger held a steady gaze on the alien.

"Next, you will prepare for the arrival of the Valarisi on all your worlds by first confiscating all weaponry from every citizen, and then ordering them to report for conditioning."

"Excuse me, conditioning?"

Kharsa nodded. "The process by which an ally of the Valarisi becomes integrated into the alliance. We all become allies of the Valarisi as individuals, Captain, not only as civilizations. We are more secure this way."

"And what does conditioning entail?"

The Vishgane shrugged. "It is a simple process. Painless, and quick."

"Painless? That implies some sort of contact."

"To come into physical contact with the Valarisi is to come into communion with them. All they desire is to commune with their friends. To ... *bring everyone into the family*, as you might say."

Granger mulled over the implications. *Interesting. To touch the Swarm is to be controlled by it. Shit, did I touch anything while I was out of it?*

"And? Anything else?"

"You will begin preparations for the evacuation of your homeworld at once."

Granger raised an eyebrow. That was ... brash. "Might I ask why?"

"The Valarisi require it."

"Might I ask for what?"

"They require the homeworlds of all their allies. In return, the Valarisi will generously give the people of your world a new planet that they may call home."

"*All* their allies?"

Kharsa nodded. "All their allies. It is an honorable sacrifice that we make to call ourselves friends of the Valarisi."

Granger stroked his chin. In his ear came Proctor's voice. "Sir, we've been scanning every conceivable communication band, but nothing. Perhaps they only contact the Swarm when there is information to be passed, or a decision to be made. Maybe try negotiating? He might have to ask for instruction when you respond to his demands, which we might detect in one of these bands."

"The evacuation of Earth is an extremely unlikely scenario, Vishgane. The logistics involved in something like that would be ... considerable."

"And yet, those are the terms, Captain. How badly do you want peace?"

Not that badly.

"I propose an alternative, then," said Granger, searching for something to say. Anything to both keep the alien talking, and to prompt him to contact the Swarm for guidance. "We relocate a certain percentage of our population to a world controlled by the Swarm, and give the Swarm a designated location on Earth that they can do with as they please."

Kharsa paused. "An interesting proposal, Captain."

"And what does the Swarm think about it?"

Another pause. "They want the planet. The entire planet."

"Again, why?"

"Because, Captain, that is the only way to ensure friends remain ... friends. I believe your word for it might be ... collateral."

Granger snorted. "Where I come from, Vishgane, friends do not require collateral on their relationship."

His earpiece vibrated. "Tim, they clearly communicated there—at least from what he said, they must have—but on our end we detected nothing. Damn. We've tried everything. There must be something else going on. I mean, clearly, he's not wearing any transmission device...."

Her voice trailed off, and Kharsa had begun speaking again.

"—because you are weak, Granger. You and your entire species. Trust is a weakness. Honor is a weakness. All that matters is the power you hold, whether over your circumstances, your enemies, or, as in the Valarisi's case, your friends."

Granger needed to keep him talking. Keep him communicating with his overlords. "Fine. Have Earth. Take it. But it'll take time. And resources that we do not have. Will the Swarm assist with our relocation? How many ships will they provide for the transfer of so many people?"

Another pause. "The Valarisi know more than you think they do, Captain. They know how many ships your species has, and how many it is capable of producing. Even now, this very week, two hundred of your new heavy cruisers are coming online."

Damn, they do know a lot.

"And each cruiser can conceivably fit fifty-thousand human bodies inside. So even with just this week's production of new ships, and assuming a one week loading and travel time, that is ten million people moved per week. Now include your entire fleet, and another six months of ship production, and you will see that Earth does, in fact, possess the ability to move its entire population quite easily."

Proctor swore in his ear. "I'm sorry, sir, I've got nothing. This just isn't working. Either they're operating at some frequency or energy outside our detection limits, or they've got a prearranged negotiation plan—the Swarm may have already instructed him in what terms are acceptable or not."

Granger looked at the creases on his hands. Sixty-five years were taking their toll on his skin, if not his mind. Dammit, he was not going to be outmaneuvered by some alien puppet.

"Let's be honest, Vishgane. There is no way in hell humanity will ever give up Earth. You claim to know us—you think you know everything about us. If you did, you would know that. Humans don't just roll over and give up. So tell me, what's your real angle? What are you *really* trying to get us to do?"

"I assure you, Captain, the Valarisi are quite serious in their demands. I recommend you—"

"To hell with them and their demands. Tell me, Vishgane, how long has it been since the Swarm ripped *your* people away from your homeworld? How long have *you* been their puppets, with your world held hostage and hanging over your head to ensure you remain obedient slaves?"

A pause. "Two thousand of your years."

A little yelp in his ear nearly made him jump. "Sir! We've got something. Just a blip, but it's something."

Granger smiled.

CHAPTER FORTY

Epsilon Garibaldi Four, Epsilon Garibaldi System
Conference Room Three, ISS Warrior

"TWO THOUSAND YEARS? The Swarm have occupied your homeworld for *two thousand years*?" Granger said dramatically. "Are you the most push-over, passive, loser of a species or what?"

Maybe if he provoked him, Kharsa would do something to elicit another triumphant yelp from Proctor. Another blip.

"Captain," Proctor began, "we saw something on the meta-space detector. But it was very strange. Gibberish, for starters, but it was also like it bled over from a parallel band. Like the exact frequency itself was randomized and encoded. Which is extraordinary given that the band itself is only operating at twenty-something hertz. But it's the phase of the gravitons themselves that seem to be anomalous. Keep him talking, sir."

Granger looked the alien in the eye. "Tell me, Kharsa, does it anger you? Does it ever piss you off knowing your enemy walks free on your planet while they've relegated your people to some rock in space? Don't tell me they relocated you to prime real-estate. Don't tell me they gave you beachfront property somewhere. It's a glorified asteroid, or some dead moon, isn't it? Or maybe they didn't even give you the choice you're giving me? Maybe they just wiped out your civilians. The innocent men, women, children—they just were minding their own business one day when they realized their leaders sold them out, not knowing anything was wrong until fire started raining from the sky. Tell me, Kharsa, does that anger you?"

The Vishgane had begun to rise, and out of the corner of his eye Granger saw Colonel Hanrahan's stance shift ever so slightly, his assault rifle angling upward. Kharsa choked out a laugh. "You do yourself a disservice, Captain Granger. Your attempts to alienate us from our friends is laughable, and misplaced. No, none of what you said has happened. We gave our world freely, and count it as a privilege, for the Valarisi now consider us the most trusted of their friends. We are first in the great family of the Valarisi. The second of the Concordat of Seven, subject only to the first—the Valarisi themselves."

Concordat of Seven? How many species had the Swarm conquered, anyway?

Granger waved Hanrahan off—Kharsa had sat down again. Whatever the alien said, Granger had obviously touched a nerve. "Vishgane Kharsa. We are men of reason, but also men of war. We both know that humanity is not just going to roll over and let the Swarm take what is ours. We may ultimately fail, but the price for the Swarm will be steep, even with you on their side. Surely there is something else we can agree to? Perhaps an interim step to peace? Something to give both sides time to consider their options? It may very well be that our leaders on

Earth take the Swarm's offer seriously, but to reach that step from square one is highly unlikely, I assure you."

Vishgane Kharsa nodded slowly. "You will find yourselves craving the friendship of the Valarisi before long, Captain. Find friendship or face total destruction. But your words are sound. Your leaders will come around to the Valarisi's terms, eventually. They need time. And more evidence to convince them of what is best for your world. Very well. I offer these amended terms."

Granger leaned forward. If there was any communication happening, it was now. "Withdraw all your forces from the Cadiz Sector, the Xinhua Sector, and the Lincoln Sector. Your worlds there are forfeit. The Valarisi promise the surviving settlers there will not be harmed, but they will be conditioned and made friends. Do this, and the Valarisi will give humanity six more Terran months to agree to the original terms."

A voice in his ear. "We've got it, Captain. I was right—the gravitons that initiate the meta-space transmission are polarized in a pretty unusual way. We just weren't looking for it before since it's such an oddball arrangement. But we read that transmission pretty clearly. The pattern is almost ... organic. Random, but in a way that's ... well, like I said. Organic."

Granger nodded. "I have no authority to decide on such matters. Allow me to take this proposal to Earth's leaders."

Another pause.

"Agreed, Captain. You will proceed to Earth with reasonable speed, and the Valarisi expects your answer within the week."

Granger stood up. "Very well. I will see what President Avery says. But she is not the only leader in United Earth we have to convince. Besides President Malakhov of the Russian Confederation, there are at least a dozen other leaders and whole worlds who don't fall under our nation's umbrella. And President Avery is democratically elected. The majority of the people on fifty-five worlds voted for her. If the people disapprove of such a momentous decision, she would not survive."

"Survive?" Kharsa eyed him with a look that almost looked like disbelief. Or was it envy? "You kill your leaders when you disagree with them, Captain?"

"Kill? No. We are not so base as that. But they are removed from power if their decisions no longer reflect the will of the people who elected them."

Vishgane Kharsa shook his head. "Such an odd arrangement of power, Captain. In our society, the way *we* survive is to have those with the most power lead us. To go against their wishes is dangerous for our very survival as a people."

"Then we shall agree to disagree, sir," said Granger. "But we've shown now that our people are at least capable of talking, and not just destroying each other. Come." He motioned to the door. "Unless there was anything else you wish to discuss?"

Vishgane Kharsa held up two closed fists, like he had an hour ago on the viewscreen, and Granger took it to mean that the conversation was over.

Proctor's voice blared over his earpiece.

"Captain, as you were finishing, we read an almost continual stream of meta-space signals coming out of that room. But that's not all. It wasn't just one meta-space signal."

Her voice hesitated. "There were two."

CHAPTER FORTY-ONE

North American Airspace, Earth
Vice President's Shuttle

ISAACSON WINCED AS THE shuttle bucked and rolled, miraculously managing to avoid all the weapon fire streaking toward it. The captain was either a former fighter pilot himself, or absolutely insane.

"Hold on, people. Going to hit the booster engines." The captain swore as a round hit a wing, blasting a small hole in it. "Just hold on!" he repeated.

Moments later, the shuttle shot forward and they all sunk further back into their seats as the craft accelerated at a dizzying rate. Several seats away, Conner gripped an armrest with one white-knuckled hand and his mouth with the other. Then he vomited all over his lap.

The booster engines put some distance in between them and the fighters chasing them, but before long they too hit their accelerators. "You called anyone for help yet, Captain?" yelled Isaacson toward the cockpit.

"Yeah, but by all means ask them to hurry!"

Isaacson yanked his comm card out and tapped it furiously. "Emergency. Get me North American CONOPS Command."

The card beeped once to confirm, and moments later a soldier's face appeared on the screen. "Yes, Mr. Vice President?"

"We're under attack! Scramble fighters! Get them now!"

The soldier nodded. "We're aware, sir. Friendlies on their way now from Joint Base Standiford. Stand by."

"Who the hell are they?"

The ship lurched again as the shuttle dove straight down in a desperate maneuver to avoid the advancing fighters. Seconds later, the ceiling became the floor as the shuttle completed the loop, reversing course and now flying westward, upside down. Another barrel roll and a few loops later and they were flying straight down again.

"Unknown, sir. Those are IDF fighters, but the transponders are off, and the identity of the pilots unknown."

The shuttle had mostly re-entered the atmosphere, and the craft contorted as it lurched around through the endless high-speed aerial acrobatics. Such maneuvers were usually reserved for spaceflight, or upper atmospheric engagements. Not down in the lower atmosphere, just ten kilometers from the ground.

Several more rounds rained down on the shuttle, mostly hitting in the rear and the left wing. Isaacson wondered how many holes the little ship could have and still fly. He frantically looked out the window again, searching for the fighters.

There was one. Far to the left of the shuttle, but approaching fast. Craning his neck he could see the other one was right on their tail. *Shit. I'm not getting out of this one.*

The fighter to their left bore down on them fast, showering them with high-caliber bullets. One pierced the cabin and the air started to swoosh out the hole. Death was coming.

With a bright flash, the fighter exploded. The shuttle dove, and Isaacson watched as the second fighter burst into flames behind them, flanked by three other fighters that showered it with continual gunfire.

The rushing of air stopped as the automatic emergency systems covered the hole with a high-powered electromagnetic shield, and the shuttle blasted higher, moving out of the atmosphere. The captain's voice, obviously relieved, came over the comm. "Everyone all right? Rising back into the stratosphere. Be at D.C. in less than ten minutes."

For the first time, Isaacson noticed his heart was beating so fast he was pretty sure he'd have to have a heart attack just to slow it back down. He closed his eyes and focused on his breathing. A few minutes later he looked over at Conner. His lap and seat were wet with vomit, and his face was red. Damn—the kid had had a terrible day.

They landed, finally. Isaacson, accompanied by his security detail, bolted off the plane, intending to go straight to the executive mansion. But to his surprise, before he could get into his waiting ground car, another car pulled up, escorted by a dozen armored military vehicles. A window dropped down, revealing President Avery's frowning face.

"Get in," she said, thumbing toward the other door.

He hesitated. The Moscow car bombing. The anti-matter. She didn't seem like the assassinating type. But, at least politically, she *was* ruthless.

She read his mind. "Get in Eamon. I'm not trying to kill you." She looked over his shoulder and around the

car before waving him closer. He leaned in and she whispered in his ear.

"But I do know who wants both of us dead."

CHAPTER FORTY-TWO

Epsilon Garibaldi Four, Epsilon Garibaldi System
Conference Room Three, ISS Warrior

GRANGER PAUSED AT the door. *Two* meta-space signals? He eyed the Vishgane, and noticed Doc Wyatt behind him—he'd followed them to the door. The doctor had remained silent during the entire negotiation, which was prudent since his friend was there to observe, not to contribute. He eyed Hanrahan. Had *he* been compromised by the Swarm? He *had* handled the disposal of the crashed fighter the week before.

"Something wrong, Tim?" said Doc Wyatt, nearly bumping into him at the door.

Shit. What if it was *him*? Granger himself? The dreams. The strange episode he'd had when he shook Vishgane Kharsa's hand. There was no telling what happened to him during those three days he was missing. Three days ... or was it twenty seconds ... damn. There was a lot he didn't know. And now he knew there was a very good chance he was either under the Swarm's influence, or at the very least that his mind could be completely open to them, to be viewed and read at their pleasure.

"Nothing. I was just thinking, Kharsa—" He turned to the other two men. "A moment alone, gentlemen?" He noticed the look of consternation on Hanrahan's face and added, "just for a moment, Colonel. I assure you, I am quite safe."

Wyatt and Hanrahan eyed each other nervously, but stepped outside. The door closed with a shuddering whine behind them—reminding Granger the *Warrior* was just as old as the Old Bird.

And now that he was alone with Kharsa, maybe that would allow Proctor to narrow down the source of the signal.

"I was thinking, Kharsa: perhaps if we were allowed to take a delegation to your homeworld on a fact-finding mission. And perhaps to a few worlds where your people have been relocated. To verify the claims the Swarm makes. Perhaps it would set our people's minds at ease knowing how the Swarm have treated you as their friends."

A pause, as Kharsa considered his words. Or communicated with the Swarm. Or both. "A wise request, Captain. I believe that will be of immense benefit. There is one problem with what you propose, however."

Of course, he thought. *It would require revealing how the Swarm have treated you like slaves rather than friends.*

"What is that?"

"The location of our homeworld is a tightly guarded secret by the Valarisi. Each homeworld of the Concordat of Seven is kept hidden. It is part of our contract with the Valarisi. It is how they keep our homeworlds safe from external threats."

"But *you* know the location of your homeworld, I assume."

"As I said, it is kept hidden. From all. Two thousand years ago we made our pact with the Valarisi, and since that time knowledge of its location has been ... discouraged."

Very interesting.

"Well, then perhaps we can be allowed to see the worlds you've been relocated to."

Kharsa inclined his head. "That is acceptable, Captain. We will make arrangements when you return from Earth."

Granger smiled and led the way back to the shuttle bay, nodding to Hanrahan and Wyatt where they'd waited outside the door.

Proctor sighed in his ear. "Sorry, sir. Didn't work. Meta-space signals are notoriously tricky to nail down. They have very poor spatial resolution. I still read the two signals, but it was impossible to tell their exact point of origin. In fact, the second ceased just a few moments ago."

Oh well. They'd have plenty of time over the coming days to track it down.

CHAPTER FORTY-THREE

Epsilon Garibaldi Four, Epsilon Garibaldi System
Sickbay, ISS Warrior

"PEW PEW, YOU'RE the luckiest son-of-a-bitch I've ever met."

Ballsy grinned down at his friend on the table. Sickbay was overflowing with wounded and medical staff, but he, Spacechamp, and Fodder had managed to squeeze in around their squadmate.

"Lucky? You're calling me lucky? Have you *seen* my ouchie? Look!" He pulled down the sheet covering him, nearly exposing his crotch—but thankfully stopping just in time—and pointed to the gash in his waist where the cable and his own momentum had dug into him. "Doc was shocked that I survived since it ruptured the suit. But thankfully, only my bottom half was exposed to vacuum since that bitch of a cable held the top half of my suit against my skin."

Fodder's face broke out into a sly grin. "Bro, are you telling me ... your—"

Pew pew nodded. "Yep. You won't believe how bad pulling a vacuum on your dick hurts. Imagine the biggest erection in your life, then swallowing a handful of erection pills, then pricking it with a—"

Spacechamp clamped a hand over Pew Pew's still-moving mouth. "Just ... stop."

Fodder howled with laughter. "I told y'all, don't fly like my brother."

Pew Pew made a muffled chuckle under Spacechamp's still-clamped hand. "And remember, don't fly like my brother."

They chatted a few more minutes before a nurse shooed them out, and then they made their way back to the fighter deck—technically they were still on standby, as the battle could resume at any moment, what with the Dolmasi and surviving Swarm ships still out there. They picked their way through some debris that had fallen into the hallway—someone had tried to shove it aside but it still blocked their path.

Ballsy stopped halfway to the lift. "Hey, catch you two later. I'm going to check on Dogtown and his boys. Clownface and Hotshot. They're just down the hall in the sickbay annex."

Spacechamp and Fodder continued on toward the fighter deck as he backtracked to sickbay, passing it, and stood outside the door to the annex. Two marines stood guard outside.

"I'm sorry, sir. This area is quarantined," said a marine, his hands extended.

"It's all right, I know. I won't touch them. Just wanted to say hi. I can do that from the door, right?"

The marines looked at each other, and the other one shrugged. The first one turned back to Volz. "All right, sir. But stay in the doorway. Not a step inside."

The other marine keyed the door open, and Volz stepped up to the doorframe, poking his head through. "Dogtown?"

He peered inside the room.

The empty room.

"*Dogtown?*" he yelled.

He alerted the marines, and moments later, after a quick search of the adjoining bathroom, they confirmed it.

Dogtown, Clownface, and Hotshot were gone.

CHAPTER FORTY-FOUR

Washington D.C., Earth
Presidential Ground Car

PRESIDENT AVERY OFTEN called herself a true southern belle, and at times she looked the part—perfectly coifed hair, no-nonsense in her business suit but with a grace that disarmed and charmed all those around her. But now, she wore what Isaacson could only describe as a uniform. It wasn't military. No IDF insignia graced her shoulders or chest. But it was almost pure white, like an admiral's. She was a commander coming into her own, and she meant to display her intent to the world: she would win this war, even if it meant transforming herself into the military leader her people needed. And she was doing a damn good job of it.

Dammit.

"What in the world were you doing out in Moscow, Eamon? You know relations are tense right now. You put yourself right out in the open for an attack, and sure enough...."

He shrugged. "Just following up on leads. My investigation here hit a brick wall, and I thought that whoever was trying to kill you might have ties to Malakhov. So I talked to Volodin—he's a good friend."

"Too good, if you ask me," she said, eyeing him with what at first looked like suspicion. She shifted to her vulnerable face and rested a hand on his knee. "Eamon, we've got to be careful. You don't know those people like I do. Ruthless. Absolutely ruthless. Bloodthirsty. They'll stop at nothing to get power over us. Nothing. Killing means nothing to them. Manipulation is learned from childhood. They are masters at it. Always have been. Just ... be careful with Volodin."

He nodded. "And? You say you know who's trying to kill you? I mean, us? You're telling me the same people are trying to kill both of us?"

"Yes. Yes, that's what I'm telling you." She sighed. "And, I debated even telling you, mainly because I didn't think you'd believe me. That was my whole plan—let you discover the truth for yourself. I'm sorry, Eamon. I should have trusted you. I should have told you. I'm sorry."

He had never, to his knowledge, heard her apologize to anyone. *Anyone.* "Madam President?"

"Barb, Eamon. Call me Barb."

"You knew this whole time?" Surely she couldn't mean....

"Yes. At least, I know part of the plot. Not the entire thing. Just pieces. Certain players, yes. The whole scheme, no. But I think it's obvious, don't you?"

He wasn't sure how to react. Show agreement? Confusion? Dammit, his head was still spinning from the bombing.

"Malakhov, Eamon. Malakhov is trying to kill me. And you too. He wants nothing more than to throw our government into a tailspin. Stir up strife and confusion. Sow chaos and fear."

"But what does he gain from that? Surely without IDF standing in the way, the Swarm will come and indiscriminately kill all of us, Russians included?"

She nodded. The car turned down into the maze of streets deep inside D.C. "Of course. But he doesn't see it that way. And I'm beginning to suspect why." She turned to him. "Eamon, what I'm about to tell you is classified. Not just top secret. I mean top top secret. Only I know this, and Fleet Admiral Zingano, Captain Granger. Maybe a handful of others. Less than ten."

"I'm all ears."

"The Swarm can control people. I think Malakhov is under their influence. Possibly their entire government—who knows? The point is, when the Swarm comes again, and if IDF can't stand against them, that's it. With enemies out there, and enemies behind our backs, and with the two of us dead ... well, we fall. Earth falls. All the colonies fall. Humanity as we know it ceases to exist."

The car drove through the financial district, and wove its way through a handful of embassies. He wondered where she was driving him. Or were they driving just to drive? To get away from listening ears?

"It doesn't make sense, Barb. It doesn't explain the anti-matter bomb in Moscow."

She looked at him, surprised. "It was anti-matter, was it?"

"Volodin gave me the technical report."

She nodded. "Of course. Two possibilities there. He either fabricated the report and gave it to you to make you suspect *me*—yes, Eamon, I know you've been poking around the fab. Or, more likely, they stole it. Or, even more likely, they have allies within the government that provided the materiel. Allies with friends in the military."

Isaacson nodded, trying to keep up appearances. He still wasn't sure what she was playing at. Was this an act? Was she trying to get him to slip up? Expose himself?

She continued. "That's another reason I gave you your mission—we need to know not only which senators, which people in the government are willing to kill me, but which ones are in bed with Malakhov. We can't have that going on, even if they *don't* kill me."

He shook his head. "I still can't believe that it's the Russians. Volodin and I are—well, we're friends. That he would give the go-ahead to have me killed is ... unthinkable."

She crossed her legs. "Oh? Think about this then. Who else could arrange for your shuttle to be attacked by actual, honest-to-god fighters? That's not something you just go out and hire. Those were military craft that attacked you, Eamon, not some pay-to-play mercenaries." She paused. "And furthermore, I think we won't be surprised when we learn that they were indeed IDF fighters, with IDF pilots."

"What makes you think that?"

She chuckled. "There's no way in hell the Russians could ever get one of their fighters past our airspace command."

"And yet you still believe Malakhov is behind it?"

"Of course," she said. "Who else could pull it off? And it gets back to my point, and in case you weren't listening, then now is the time to perk up. The Swarm can *control* people. They are controlling Malakhov. I'm almost one hundred percent sure. And if the Swarm can control Malakhov, then he is also perfectly capable of putting two innocent IDF fighters under his influence, and directing them to kill you."

Damn. It actually *did* add up. Volodin had confirmed as much—he said the Russian soldiers who went aboard those Swarm carriers came back *changed*. It wasn't a terrible leap to think the Swarm could *control*. If that were true … who could tell how far they'd infiltrated? That would mean disaster not only for IDF, *and* the Russian Confederation, but all of civilization.

She smirked. "I assume from your silence that you're at least entertaining the possibility that I'm right?"

"Of course I'm entertaining it, Barb. But what are we going to do about it?"

"You're going to keep doing what I asked you to do already. It's obvious there are collaborators within the government. It is even more imperative now that we find who they are. All of them. Then, when we're sure we've discovered who's who, we make our move."

His eyes widened. "What, like a purge?"

"What else?"

"You can't be serious."

She snorted. "I am. We simply cannot tolerate subversive behavior and treason during wartime. Oh, don't look at me like that. I'm not saying we blow their brains out. I'm not the type for that. But we take them into custody. At least until the war is over."

The car stopped. He looked out—they were outside his residence. He glanced back at her, confused.

"Get some sleep, Eamon. You've had two attempts on your life within twenty-four hours, and you've flown across the country twice and to Russia once. You're no use to your country as a walking zombie." She smiled and touched his knee again, with what Isaacson could swear was genuine affection.

He nodded. "It *has* been a long few days…."

A secret service agent opened his door. He started to get up. Avery reached out and grabbed his arm before he left. "We're close, Eamon. We'll nail these bastards to the wall, win this war, then get showered in confetti from a ticker tape parade, and then treat ourselves to some well deserved carnal pleasure and hard alcohol." She winked at him. "See you in a few days."

He climbed the steps to his residence, after the security detail performed the standard sweep, and shut the door behind him. It was getting late. Nearly nine. He wondered if Conner's girl had shown up yet. Stepping into the kitchen he noticed something on the table. A canister: a container from a gourmet coffee brand. Columbian-Indonesian blend.

Aw hell, Conner.

CHAPTER FORTY-FIVE

Epsilon Garibaldi Four, Epsilon Garibaldi System
Captain's Ready Room, ISS Warrior

"DAMMIT, SHELBY, HOW can I trust anything that I do? Anything that I think? What if everything that comes out of my mouth is sent straight to my brain by some goddamned meta-space Swarm signal?"

Proctor shifted uncomfortably on her feet. It was readily apparent that no matter what she said to set his mind at ease, she agreed.

"I think the very fact that you're asking that question means you're just fine. If they were making you say certain things, or think certain things, you'd know it. Tell me, have you felt different since your disappearance? Have your thought patterns changed? Has Doc Wyatt done a brain scan? Surely they would have done a complete medical workup after your cancer was cured, and they definitely would have compared the brain scans to the old ones. You'd know, sir, if you were influenced."

He nodded. It made sense. Doc Wyatt *had* done multiple scans. Brain scans. Lung, heart, endocrine, circulatory, nervous system—he'd checked everything. From what Wyatt could tell, he was the picture of sixty-five year old health. Age lines and hemorrhoids and all.

Out the window of his ready room the nameless planet they'd come to in the Epsilon Garibaldi System rotated serenely, oblivious to the showdown happening in high orbit. They were forbidden from going down by the Dolmasi, and in fact were supposed to leave the system as soon as they were able—the heavily-damaged Swarm carriers had left over an hour ago—but it would take time for his fleet to reassemble and make the necessary repairs. He didn't want to leave anyone behind, so they would wait, Dolmasi protests be damned.

But the wreckage of the recent battle still hung in the space about all the ships. Twenty-three heavy cruisers lost. Twenty-three. Nearly fifteen thousand people dead. Just like that. And he hadn't even laid any bricks that day. No suicide runs. Just intense, brutal, conventional space combat.

Was it worth it? What had they gained?

Time. And of course it was worth it. Every minute he could buy Earth was a minute to treasure. A minute closer to the Swarm's final destruction. Whatever lives that cost, whatever blood he had to spill to reach that goal, well, so be it. Sacrifices must be made.

"Maybe you're right. But what a spot I've been put in, Shelby. On one hand I'm trying to eke out another week for Earth to breathe a little bit and get ready for Operation Battle-ax, and on the other I might be the very tool the Swarm is using to destroy humanity. Gets to a man after awhile."

He saw her reflection nod in the window.

"The fleet is nearly ready, sir. Captain Connelly on the *Eddington* reports they are done with repairs to their q-jump drive, and the *Seattle* is nearly there as well. We'll be ready to depart in ten minutes." She sat down in the chair across from his at the desk and sighed. "Do you think Avery will go for something like that? Kharsa's proposal? Everything I know about her says she'll laugh in our faces."

"Oh, of course she will. There's no way in hell that we're giving up those three systems. It's a nonstarter."

She tapped her fingers nervously on the desk. "But it buys us time. Right. Time for what, exactly? If we need the location of the Swarm homeworld for Operation Battle-ax, what the hell is one more week going to buy us?"

"A lot." He eyed the debris out the window. A giant piece of one of their dead ships began to glow, far below them, as it started to enter the atmosphere. He watched as it fell away from them, slowed by the ultra-compressed air heating up its hull. How many bodies were in that ship? How many sons and daughters? He turned to face her. "It buys the Mars Project time to bear fruit. And time for us to find their homeworld out here."

She glanced up in surprise. "Sir?"

"Send a meta-space signal to the Russian Confederation on Kiev Prime. Ask for permission to cross their space on our way back to Earth."

"Sir?" she repeated. Then it dawned on her. "He said to go back to Earth *with reasonable speed.* You're counting on them buying it?"

Granger sat down too, and propped his sore feet up on the desk. "What, that the Russians will turn down our request, like they have for decades, or that Kharsa will buy it?"

"Both."

He chuckled. "I don't care what he thinks. He gave us a week to get back to Earth and send back a reply from Avery. He said to get back there with reasonable speed. It's just not reasonable to cross Russian Confederation space without permission, don't you agree, Commander?"

She smirked. "At least, not twice in one week."

"Exactly. Then, when the Russians say *no*, we'll have to go the long way around. And chances are the long way will take us right through Swarm territory."

"Seems likely," she said.

He stood up. She mirrored him. "Let's find ourselves a homeworld, then," he said, leading the way out the door.

The comm interrupted him. "Sir?" Lieutenant Diaz's voice came over the speakers. "It's Lieutenants Martin and Palmer, sir. The pilots injured in the fighter bay accident—Clownface and Hotshot. And ... now I'm getting word about Dogtown, too."

"What's wrong with them, Commander?"

"They're dead, sir."

CHAPTER FORTY-SIX

GRANGER STOOD OVER the bodies laying on the two tables, Proctor at his side. He had to keep himself from wincing—the injuries were dramatic. And gory. Someone had literally bashed the three pilots' faces in.

"Doc, how did this happen?"

"It was the night shift, Tim. They were alone, asleep. No one saw anyone else come or go. Not even the marines outside. When one of the other pilots checked on them, he discovered they were missing. After a brief search we found two of them stuffed into a utility closet down the hall. We found Dogtown a deck below in another closet—seems all three wouldn't fit in the one."

Proctor's face looked pained as she regarded the bodies. "But aren't we in sickbay? There must be two dozen wounded in here, with at least half your staff. How in the world did no one see them?"

Wyatt swept his arm around, indicating the crew members lying in their beds. "That's just the point, Commander. We keep those actually wounded in here. These men technically had nothing wrong with them—they were only under observation from being in contact with Swarm matter from that crash, so I had them moved to the sickbay annex down the hall to free up space. That's near where their bodies were found. I brought them here to attempt resuscitation, but ... well...." His voice trailed off with a grim look at the soldier's unrecognizable faces.

Something tugged at the back of Granger's mind. Something he couldn't quite remember, but it felt important.

He rested a hand on one of the dead men's shoulders. Another one. He knew he'd just lost fifteen thousand people that day. Fifteen thousand good and honorable men and women. Soldiers all. But these two were up close, personal and bloody. These men should not have died.

"Our problems are multiplying," said Proctor. "We've got a genocidal alien race eager to kill us all, we learn they have friends willing to lend a hand, and now it turns out we have sleeper agents onboard the *Warrior* willing and able to kill crew members."

Granger was still pulling at the stray thread of thought that had crossed his mind. Something was out of place. "And? Have you found anything? Any way to detect if a person is under Swarm influence or not? Any way to detect Swarm matter in the bloodstream or tissues?"

Wyatt shook his head. "I'm sorry, Tim. All my tests come up negative. If they had anything floating around in their blood or taking root in their muscles or lipid tissues, it's undetectable."

The doctor began dabbing at Lieutenant Palmer's face with a wet cloth to clean off the dried blood from his partially caved-in temple.

He remembered. The hand. Doc Wyatt's hand.
Shit.

"Armand, *you* touched Swarm matter a few months ago, didn't you? During the invasion over Earth? You touched that Swarm matter oozing from the fighter."

Wyatt kept dabbing, gingerly cleaning around the man's closed and bruised eyes. "I did."

"Then why haven't we done any tests on you?"

Wyatt laughed. "Oh, believe me, I have. But you're forgetting, Tim, that I'm a doctor."

"So?"

Wyatt tossed the blood-soaked rag into a disposal bin. And held his hands up. "A doctor who follows strict medical protocol. Do you really think I'd touch Swarm matter—or any potentially infectious fluid—without protection? I wear neo-cordrine gloves at all times, Tim. They conform perfectly to my hand so you might not see them, but they provide an absolutely impregnable barrier to any infectious disease or contagion. Acids, bases, corrosives, hell, they even give me some radiation protection. I never take them off because I never know what I'll encounter or when I'll encounter it. Believe me, if I were infected, we've got bigger things to worry about—it would mean that Swarm fluid can traverse neo-cordrine, which, if true, would mean that many, many more people besides myself have been compromised."

Made sense. If Doc Wyatt *had* been compromised, he would have had ample opportunity to infect a lot more people, or kill Granger, or Zingano—hell—he'd even been present during an awards ceremony with President Avery. He could have offed her then and made this whole treaty moot.

"Ok, you've got your alibi, Doc. Don't worry, I don't suspect you."

Doctor Wyatt chuckled. "Like hell you don't. And you should. It's your job. And that's the most important thing I tell my staff."

"What's that?"

Wyatt smirked. "Do your damn job. No matter who you're working on."

Granger stared one last time at the bodies before taking his leave. Proctor followed him out. When the door closed they turned to look at each other. Within a moment of watching her face, he knew they were about to say the same thing.

"We need to be able to detect Swarm influence," she said.

"I agree. IDF scientists have been studying Swarm matter for decades—what else do you think we can do? Wyatt's already tried, and failed, apparently."

Her eyes flicked to the closed doors of sickbay. "For one thing, get Wyatt off the project. First off, he's a doctor with a lot of wounded, and doctors focus on their patients. Secondly, well, let's just say that his alibi wasn't one hundred percent airtight, no pun intended."

Granger nodded. "Right. Who exactly are you suggesting?"

"Tim," she sighed. "I love command. I really do. But what we need right now is a scientist, not a doctor. Not an XO—"

"Bullshit. I need you, Shelby—"

She touched his arm. "And you've got me. I'm not resigning or anything. But Diaz can step up and be XO for awhile. Give me some time to dedicate to this Swarm matter business. There's no one more qualified—I spent nearly a decade studying the Swarm before I switched to command."

He paused, weighing his options. "If we're in a firefight, I need you."

She nodded. "Agreed. I'll put research on hold if slugs start flying."

It made sense. They simply couldn't afford gallivanting around a Swarm-infested galaxy with potentially one or more infected and compromised crew members. They couldn't be negotiating with the Swarm when one of their own was a double agent. And they certainly couldn't plan an invasion of the Swarm homeworld with their enemy knowing exactly when, where, and how IDF would strike.

"Ok. Get to the bottom of this, Shelby. Too much is at stake to ignore this any longer. I'll go talk to Diaz."

She smiled, squeezed his arm one last time, and took off in the opposite direction. Damn—he was going to hate running the ship without her. Diaz was good, but good in an Abraham Haws kind of way, more than a Shelby Proctor kind of way.

Damn. Damn, damn, damn. Abraham Haws. That old bastard. Granger missed the hell out of him. An old warrior taken before his time.

No. It *was* his time. He did his duty. He made his sacrifice. He put himself forward so that others would be safe and paid the price. A price he paid gladly. Abe did his job.

Now it was time for Granger to do his. He strode onto the bridge. "Ensign Prucha, did the Russians get back to us?"

"Yes, sir. They refused passage through their space."

Granger nodded. "Just as they should. Signal the fleet. Ready for q-jumps. We'll be taking the long way around Russian space. First target," he glanced at his tactical readout which displayed a star map of the adjacent sectors, "the Penumbra System. Calculate route and distribute to the rest of the fleet."

A pause, and shortly Ensign Prince nodded. "Should take forty-five minutes, sir. Communicating our flight plan and linking nav computers now."

"Good. Engage when ready."

A moment later the stars shifted. Then again. And again. Nearly an hour later, they arrived on the outskirts of the Penumbra System. The preliminary scout report had indicated electromagnetic activity in the system that would suggest habitation or occupation. One more q-jump and the fleet would be there. A yellow, g-type sun glittered spectacularly against the background stars, only point one light year away.

"Final q-jump, sir," said Prince.

Granger nodded his assent.

The stars onscreen shifted to reveal a blue, cloud-dappled world. The entire surface seemed to be an ocean, and Granger wondered if it was water, or just an icy-cold bath of liquid methane. No—the color was too deep a blue for that.

But what caught his attention more than the blue planet were the ships orbiting it.

The dozens—no—hundreds of ships.

Russian ships.

CHAPTER FORTY-SEVEN

Washington D.C., Earth
Vice President's Residence

ISAACSON COULDN'T SLEEP. He'd been expecting to come home, bust a nut with a prostitute, have a drink, then fall blissfully asleep knowing a doubled secret service detail was keeping watch in the houses next door to and behind his own residence.

But something was nagging at him. Most unusually for him, they were numbers. One thousand bomb casings a week at the MUNCENT fabrications plant. Anti-matter—enough for fifty-thousand bombs—produced weekly at the Squaretop Mountain facility in Wyoming. Obviously, there were other casing production plants. But how many? And why so many?

That explosion near Elko. Conner's brother and his mysterious death. What were the chances they were both related to the anti-matter program? And if they were, what were the chances that he personally knew of someone drafted into the program? Very low, unless, of course, the number of people drafted into that program was higher than he thought.

Throwing his covers off, Isaacson padded down to his office, waving his computer terminal on. Intel services had recently given him access to most records, at Avery's request—part of his behind-the-scenes effort to track down which politicians were behind the assassination attempts. Time to test them out.

He searched. How many drafted? He ran through the records, collating and compiling lists and spreadsheets of draftees and arrived at a number. From Earth alone, among the United Earth nations, there were three billion. A few more billion were not drafted, but worked in related support industries. But all told, nearly a third of humanity on Earth was directly working and fighting in the war effort. Total war. And that was just on Earth. He didn't even bother with the other fifty-five worlds of the broader United Earth.

Very well. Raw numbers aside, how many were in the anti-matter program? He ran a search, and quickly determined that no such program existed. Seems that Avery wasn't giving him access to *all* classified documents. Fine—he'd have to improvise.

He spoke the next few commands—his computer skills were adequate, but certain search parameters would take him too long to figure out. "Cross reference this list of draftees with the list of assignments. Highlight all subjects whose assignment is unclear."

A moment later the result appeared on the screen. A list of people, over ten million records long. Interesting. Either the bureaucrats had yet to enter in the data, or ten million people had been assigned to black ops programs. Programs so sensitive, not even the projects' code names could be mentioned on draft records.

But how many of these were working on anti-matter?

"Cross reference this list with subjects' personal files. Highlight school and career and general interests in science."

Another list popped up on the screen. Nearly nine million. So nearly all the people working in the black ops programs were either scientists, engineers, or college kids with even a passing interest in science. He supposed the other million were support staff. How many of those died at the Elko facility, he wondered.

"Display how many of these are deceased."

The new list appeared. Damn. That was one big facility. Nearly a hundred thousand had perished so far.

No, that couldn't be right. There was no way to hide that many people out in the deserts of Nevada. There were only ten thousand people in the Wyoming plant alone, and *that* facility dwarfed the one at MUNCENT under the capitol.

There had to be others. Many others. And several of those had already had accidents, just like the one in Nevada.

But why so many? How many anti-matter bombs would it take to destroy the Swarm's homeworld—and was that the intended target?

A soft, unexpected beep made him jolt. Someone was calling him. Who the hell wanted to talk to him at this hour? He brought up the call on his screen, and looked for who it was.

It was an unidentifiable-source transmission from Moscow. Frowning, he punched the call through, and Yuri Volodin's face appeared on the screen.

"Eamon," the other man whispered. He sounded worried. Urgent. "Is the channel secure?"

"Reasonably, secure—I *am* the vice president, after all—"

"No, you need to secure it. Turn on your quantum scrambler."

Isaacson glanced around his desk and saw the little box they'd installed on his system. "Ready?"

Volodin nodded. Isaacson pressed a button, and he saw the ambassador do likewise on his end. "Good. We can talk freely now," said the Russian.

"What is it, Yuri?"

"Something has come up, Eamon. I think Avery is planning something. Something big. Something awful."

"Isaacson frowned. "What do you mean? Against the Swarm? Isn't that what we all want?"

"Not against the Swarm. Against *us*! You know she has it in for us. She and the rest of her party. If the entire Russian Confederation ceased to exist tomorrow, she'd pop out a bottle of champagne, jump up on the table and dance an old-lady Irish jig. She hates us."

It was true, of course. It's how half the government felt, and a good chunk of the citizenry. "That's not exactly a secret, Yuri. How—"

"She's planning something. I just got word. In all the engagements with the Swarm, in all the ship movements and troop transfers, she's managed to hide it quite well. A few ship transfers here. A few more there. A fighter squadron supposedly deactivated for repairs but actually sent off to some unknown location. A secret shipyards facility in the Columbia Sector that we just uncovered. Where do its ships go? We've tracked dozens of odd occurrences like these. She's managed to hide them well, yes, but she finally made a mistake, and now we're on to her. Eamon, Avery is going to blow up half a dozen Russian Confederation worlds. Possibly as early as next week."

CHAPTER FORTY-EIGHT

Penumbra Three, Penumbra System
Bridge, ISS Warrior

"WHAT THE HELL are the Russians doing out here?" exclaimed Granger as he bolted to his feet.

Lieutenant Diaz swore. "There's no way they could be out this far and *not* be collaborating with the Swarm. Epsilon Garibaldi was just fourteen lightyears away. If the Swarm and the Dolmasi were *both* there, then they've probably been here too."

"You bet your ass they've been here. Maybe they *are* here." He turned to Prucha at comm. "Coded transmission to the wing captains. Text only. Can't have our *friends* listening in on our conversations."

"Aye, sir. Ready," replied Ensign Prucha, waiting for Granger's message.

He cleared his throat. "Hold positions. Commence inter-ship chatter as if coordinating repairs from a battle. *Warrior* will make contact with friends. Have q-jump coordinates set on hair-trigger. If any friendly makes threatening move, leave immediately."

Prucha nodded. "Sent, sir. Other ships acknowledge receipt."

"Scan Russian transceivers. Hail the flagship."

Granger sat down and looked the planet over. It was a beautiful thing, really. Deep blue—almost bright turquoise where the water was shallow enough to see down through to the sea-floor. If there were any small islands down there they'd probably be tropical paradises. Both poles showed signs of ice, and in the deepest parts of the ocean he could see great systems of flowing clouds. They seemed to originate from particular places on the water's surface, billowing away in great streams, carried around the planet by the wind into great swirling patterns.

"Sir, I'm reading strange gravitational disturbances from the planet."

"What kind of disturbances?"

The science officer frowned. "Anomalies. It's very strange—most planets have an irregular gravitational field due to variations in crust density and mantle thickness. But here, the pattern is ... odd, is all. Nothing terribly remarkable, just a different pattern from anything I've seen. It's as if—"

"Sir, priority message coming in from the Russian flagship. It's—" Prucha looked up, surprised. "They claim it's Russian Vice President Griega himself over there, Captain."

Granger raised an eyebrow. *Now what the hell is the Russian VP doing all the way out here?*

CHAPTER FORTY-NINE

Penumbra Three, Penumbra System
Bridge, ISS Warrior

"PUT HIM ONSCREEN," said Granger.

Moments later, the smiling face of Russian Vice President Griega appeared on the wall, flanked by two aides—both of whom were women in revealing but practical military-style uniforms, and well armed from the looks of it. Side arms hung from their belts and Granger saw what might have been the hilts of daggers under their sleeves.

Vice President Griega's bodyguard preferences were legendary. He purportedly had an entire battalion of lethally-trained and stunningly beautiful female soldiers. The rumor was also that he had many, many children.

"Captain Granger, welcome to Penumbra. Might I ask what you are doing here?"

Granger flashed a thin smile. "I might ask the same of you, sir. Last I checked, this was not Russian Confederation territory."

"No, it is not. For now. Yet I wonder how it is that you've come all this way without crossing into our space. Such a long journey from Earth—you'd have to loop all the way around the Centaurus Cusp and then back your way through unexplored space."

Granger shrugged. No need to admit that they, in fact, already passed right through the middle of Russian territory. Thank god for the finite speed of light—otherwise ships passing though space a lightyear out might actually be detectable.

"It was a very long voyage, sir. But we decided it would be worth it, as we've recently received intelligence that there may be Swarm activity in this sector. Seen any recently?"

Griega smiled broadly. "No. You? Looks like you've seen some action."

Granger stroked his stubble. "Of course. The *Warrior* sees action almost every day. Unlike some allies I know."

Griega held up his hands. "Come now, Granger. I can assure you our efforts against the Swarm are as varied and effective as yours. You just don't always see them."

Right.

"Oh? How many ships have you lost? Any systems? Surely you've lost a planet or two. We lost the entire Cadiz Sector just a few weeks ago."

Griega let his face contort into the best show of empathy Granger supposed he could muster. "Yes, that was most unfortunate. You have our deepest sympathies. President Malakhov has spoken directly to President Avery concerning the matter and extended his sympathies as well."

Granger chuckled ironically. "It would be even better if you extended some of your fleets. Contribute to the war effort. We'd win a whole lot faster that way."

"Extend fleets? To you? And what would you do with them? No, Captain Granger, we are having enough trouble with the Swarm as it is without divvying out our ships to those who throw them away as if they were old, broken toys. Or bricks, from what I hear. How many have you thrown away this week, Brick-layer?"

Granger's eyes shot daggers at the man. Griega's face of sympathy contorted back to a wry smile.

"Now then, Captain. It is time you got on your way. Lots of Swarm out there."

Granger set his jaw defiantly. "What are you doing in this system, Mr. Vice President?"

"Directing the war effort, Captain. And that is all you need to know. Leave immediately."

"As we've already agreed, this is not your territory, Mr. Vice President. We are on an intelligence gathering mission, and it so happens that this system is one of those we want more intelligence on."

Griega frowned. "No. You will leave immediately. Let us not allow this to become a ... diplomatic incident. God knows you've had your share of those, *Captain* Granger."

The emphasis on his rank spoke volumes. He was trying to get under Granger's skin. Remind him of his past. His history with the Russians. The Khorsky incident from a dozen years ago came freshly to his mind.

"Any *incident* that happens will be from Russian recklessness, Mr. Vice President. I assure you our intentions are to surveil the Swarm, and to defeat them. Not to spy on Russian interests."

"It is not your intentions I doubt, Mr. Granger. It is your competence."

The words hung in the air like a shouted challenge, though they were spoken with the cool, arrogant veneer of a career politician.

"Sir," began Lieutenant Diaz. Granger motioned for Ensign Prucha to mute. "We're reading roughly two hundred cruisers changing orbits to intercept us. Another two hundred already in our vicinity."

Damn. They had to get out of there. He was out-gunned, and outmatched. For now.

He motioned to Prucha again to un-mute and turned back to the screen before glancing up at Proctor at the science station. She flashed him a hand with all fingers extended. *Five.* Fine—he could stall for five more minutes, if it meant she could get a more detailed meta-space scan of the vicinity, in the hopes of nailing down possible Swarm-Russian communications. "Very well, Mr. Vice President, we will leave. We've expended our capacitor banks on the voyage here. It will take several minutes to recharge, and then we'll be on our way."

Griega nodded, and the signal terminated. Granger blinked—that was easier than he thought it would be. Clearly the other man knew little about IDF capacitor technology. The *Warrior*'s capacitor banks were already sufficiently recharged within a minute of showing up in the system.

He nearly called up to Proctor to ask for an update on her scans, before remembering that they needed to keep it quiet from the bridge crew. At least until they could figure out who was under Swarm influence, and who was clear. A few minutes later she looked up. "Done, sir."

Granger stepped up to Ensign Prince and tapped his shoulder. "Signal the fleet. Q-jump us out of here on the previously decided heading."

Within moments, the Russian ships and the ocean-ic planet disappeared, and the star pattern changed. He motioned to Proctor and pointed to his ready room. When they'd closed the door, he turned to her. Finally, they'd have their evidence against the Russians. Finally, they could either expose them and shame them into co-operating, or use the knowledge to disrupt their activities, somehow. Sabotage the Swarm-Russian relationship.

Anything to finally put the Swarm off-balance and gain the initiative.

"And?"

"I did a full meta-space scan of all the Russian ships in the vicinity, accounting for the phase shift I discovered while listening to Vishgane Kharsa."

"And?" he repeated.

She sighed. "Nothing. Not one peep."

CHAPTER FIFTY

Washington D.C., Earth
Vice President's Residence

ISAACSON SNORTED. "You actually think Avery is taking forces away from the main fleets, hiding them, and secretly planning to attack Russian targets? Have you lost your mind? We're fighting an existential galactic war here, Yuri. This is no time for petty global politics." Isaacson sat back in his chair, disgusted. He'd known the other man for years now, and had supposed him to be rational and logical. Cold and calculating, sure. But this?

"Global politics?" Volodin sneered. "Try galactic politics. There is far more at stake here than whether humanity wins this war next month versus next year, and Avery knows it. The war has violently disrupted the social order, and Avery, to her credit is using the current climate to advance her political agenda. If there was ever going to be a time to attack us and have the support of the people to do it, it is now. This is not a joke, Eamon. Hundreds of millions of Russian lives are on the line here."

Yuri was leaning in close to the camera, filling its screen with his jowled, pitted face. He sounded genuinely agitated. Almost like he believed what he was saying. Could it be?

"All right. Give me your evidence. Tell me what you know."

Yuri nodded. "I can't tell you everything, of course. We have to keep our methods and sources classified."

"Of course," replied Isaacson with a wink.

"The story goes back to the Eagleton Commission. It was her campaign promise to modernize the military and cut back on unnecessary expenses. Ran on scaling back the military's footprint, making it more efficient, yada yada. She practically ran as a pacifist dove."

The words sounded like an epithet from the sound of Volodin's voice. "And it worked. People across the fifty-five worlds of United Earth were sick of over half a century of massive military spending, with its concurrent waste, fraud, abuse, and with nothing to show for it. You still didn't know where the Swarm came from. You still had no assurances you'd be safe in the event of their return. People were angry. They thought the Swarm had disappeared forever. It was their grandparents' problem. A ghost from the past. And so what did they do? They elected Avery. Kind, no-nonsense, truth-talking grandma. Spoke common sense. Shot from the hip. Called it like she saw it, and all that nonsense. Folksy. Spoke up for the common man. Blah blah blah—you westerners never change. Your folksy, homespun wisdom, common-sense politicians never really work out the way you think they will, do they?"

Isaacson rolled his eyes. "Get on with it, Yuri. What's the intel?"

"Getting there, Eamon." Volodin paused, reached off-screen to pick up a mug, poured something in from a bottle, and took a long draught. "So you got your folksy grandma of a president, and she immediately started fulfilling her promises. Instigated the Eagleton Commission, and began implementation of its recommendations." He took another drink. "Except that was just a front, wasn't it?"

"It was?" Isaacson shook his head. "No it wasn't. I spent five years opposing her at every turn. Nearly a third of my senate career. I was so successful that she eventually chose me as her running mate for her second term to appease my party. If she hadn't, she'd have been a one-termer. Believe me, Yuri, if there was anything she was committed to, it was a reduction in military spending."

"She may have reduced total spending, Eamon. Maybe not—I think you'd be surprised how easy it is to hide money in military budgets. But while she reduced what the public saw, she built up in private. All with the goal of one day striking at us hard. She'd find a way, a pretense, to make it happen. Some conjured-up emergency or incident, that would give her cover to make her move. Do you have any idea how many secret military bases you have, even just within continental North America?"

Isaacson squirmed. Yuri had at least *that* part right. How many more Wendover sites were there? Squaretop Mountains? Were there dozens more? A hundred? Colonel Titler *had* said that his site was built years ago, right near the beginning of Avery's first term. And these were just the ones in North America. What about the rest of the fifty-five United Earth worlds? Britannia? New Dublin? Lahore? Some of what Volodin was saying did make some sense.

"I see I've struck a chord," said Volodin. "The pieces fit together, don't they? I'm beginning to wonder if somehow Avery herself has orchestrated this whole

Swarm invasion, just as a pretense for invading us. You watch—she'll blame it on us. There are already rumblings from representatives in the United Earth council that she is suggesting as much behind our backs."

"But Yuri, didn't *we* instigate the Swarm invasion? You and I? We practically invited them here to Earth as a distraction of our own. To discredit Avery and get rid of her."

Volodin smiled. "Sure. But did you really think that we were the only ones who've been in contact with the Swarm? You'll recall that we only invited them to come as far as the Jupiter outposts. Rough things up a bit, scare everyone into dumping Avery, then leave. You'll also re-call that that was not what happened. Don't you remem-ber their reply to my inquiry? You were there. *You die*—those were the exact words. Sounds to me like Avery got wind of what was happening—possibly because she's got a relationship with the Swarm as well—and decided to use this as her pretense for war. Invite the Swarm in, en-courage them to focus their attacks on the United Earth worlds, basically ignore the Russian Confederation, then use that as an excuse to preemptively strike us."

Isaacson raised an eyebrow. "A false flag attack? You think she's capable of something like that?"

"Of course she'd be willing to order a false flag at-tack. It's practically a United Earth tradition. Don't you remember your history, Eamon? Twentieth century. Cold war. President Kennedy's generals proposed bombing ci-vilian targets in Florida and along the east coast, then fin-ger the Cubans. What a great pretense for war that would have been, no? Twenty-third century. United Earth Pres-ident Veracruz secretly detonated several nuclear devices on Merida Prime. Started the first Interstellar War that way. Believe me, Eamon, she's capable of it."

"Fine," Isaacson held a hand up. "If it's true—and I'm not saying I believe it is—what do we do about it?"

Yuri smiled. "It's clear from our sources on Britannia that there is a buildup of forces around Calais—one of the moons orbiting a gas giant in that system. Britannia is very close to Russian space. We believe she is going to strike many targets at once, and soon. Something called Operation Battle-ax. But we can't move against her without concrete evidence. That is something that you can provide—one of two things."

"So you're going to preemptively strike, Yuri? I may have been willing to get rid of Avery, but I'm not about to sell out my country."

Volodin nodded. "I understand that. Don't worry, we won't strike unless struck. But we will take measures to defend ourselves. And who knows—once she sees that the defenses of her targets are far greater than she supposed, it may scare her off. Make her think twice."

"Sure. Operation Battle-ax," he said, trying to remember if he'd heard the term before. "And the other thing? Assuming this is all not a complete fantasy of yours?"

"The other thing, of course, is to disable her method of attack."

"And what is that?"

"Her new weaponry she's invested in. The anti-matter devices. If we can neutralize that threat, Eamon, we'll save millions of Russian lives. Not to mention the lives of millions of your own citizens, since there won't have to be a war between us, as there surely would be if we were attacked. Think of it—rather than just be responsible for the countless dead in Miami, New Orleans, and Phoenix, instead you would be the savior of tens of millions. Who knows—you could very well be the savior of the entire human race, since if there is war between us right in the middle of this current assault by the Swarm, we may not survive."

Savior. Yuri was right—he *had* to save all those people. He'd spent the last two months privately dealing with the devastating fact that he'd possibly caused needless death among his own people. Isaacson was fine with individual deaths when politically necessary, but it's not like he was some kind of crazy war monger. If it was true that Avery was the one truly responsible for the invasion of Earth, well, *that* changed everything. He knew he was a good man, and this would prove it to everyone. Himself included. Savior—he liked that word. Much better than opportunistic genocidal maniac.

"Ok, Yuri. I'll get your proof. And if it turns out to be true, I'll put a stop to it. And finally get ol' grandma Avery out of the way."

Yuri smiled one last time. "Good. Thank you, Eamon. I always knew you were a great man. And soon, you'll be a great president."

CHAPTER FIFTY-ONE

Near Penumbra System
Bridge, ISS Warrior

GRANGER ORDERED THE fleet to q-jump out a dozen more steps so they'd be sufficiently far away enough from Penumbra to not have to worry about running into either Swarm or Russian ships. Or Dolmasi, for that matter. Their enemies were multiplying at an alarming rate.

The other captains gathered in the conference room just down the hall from the bridge. Granger sat down with them, a star map splayed out on the wall, and everyone stared forlornly at it. They'd sent scout ships discreetly out to a dozen neighboring systems. Most came back empty—no signs of Swarm, Russian, or Dolmasi activity. One came back and reported suspicious activity around one planet in the Volari System. No visible ships, but plenty of electromagnetic activity coming from the planet itself, indicative of civilization.

But it was fifty lightyears deeper into Swarm territory. Or at least, what they supposed was Swarm territory.

"What have we got to lose?" asked Captain Connelly of the *Eddington*, commander of Gamma Wing.

"Our fleet, for one. Not to mention our lives," replied Captain Barnes.

Granger nodded. "It's risky, I agree. But this entire mission was based on the premise that this was an acceptable risk. That it was worth it to the rest of IDF that we put them on the run. That we send them notice that our conflicts won't be limited to our space any longer. If Volari Three really *is* a Swarm planet, I say we hit it, and hit it hard. Rain what anti-matter pods and nukes we have onto the surface. That'll catch their attention all right."

A few of the captains nodded. Several shook their heads. Granger had operational command of the mission, but he wanted unity. He didn't want to force the other captains into something they thought was foolhardy. Not with a decision this big. He'd give the order if he had to, but he knew their chances of success were always greater when all the commanders believed in the mission. He'd have to sell it better.

"Did the scout take any visuals of Volari Three? Did it get close enough?"

Lieutenant Diaz nodded. "They stayed three astronomical units out, but yes, visuals were taken."

"Let's see them."

Diaz fiddled with the controls on the desk and soon the image of their potential target flashed onto the wall.

It was a greenish gray globe, with several large lakes—big enough to be seas, but not quite oceans—dotting the surface.

Granger gasped.

Though it was slightly grainy, the likeness was unmistakable. It couldn't be. It couldn't be, but it was.

"That's it," he whispered.

"Excuse me, Tim?" said Captain Barnes.

"That's it. That's the homeworld. Volari Three." He stared at it. The familiar feelings he'd experience in his dream and during his brief contact with Vishgane Kharsa came flooding back to him.

"What do you mean, that's the homeworld? How can you possibly know that?"

"I just know," he murmured, still staring at the vast lakes peaking up through the sparse white clouds. It matched the image from his persistent dream. And he was certain, absolutely dead certain.

Volari Three: he'd been there before.

CHAPTER FIFTY-TWO

Near Penumbra System
Science Laboratory, ISS Warrior

"TIM, WHAT IF IT really is just a dream?"

"It's not just a dream, Shelby."

The captains had returned to their ships with Granger having argued them to an impasse. It wasn't rational, he knew—there was no reason he could give to convince them that the planet was, truly, the Swarm homeworld.

But he remembered how he felt in that dream—dammit, it wasn't a dream. It was a memory. A memory that was somehow made more intense by the touch of the Dolmasi. And in that memory—yearning. Excitement. He *remembered* feeling those things. Getting up from that examination table and looking down on that planet from that window and knowing, *just knowing*, that he was looking at the homeworld. The point of origin of the Swarm. The source of all their problems.

"Ok. What if it's something the Swarm *wants* you to think?"

He cocked his head at her. They were in a lab she'd appropriated from the ship's science team, she peering down through some type of imaging device at a sample. Some Swarm matter they'd stored in secure, triply-walled and sealed sample vials.

"What do you mean?"

"Well, just suppose for a moment that when you were gone to ... wherever you went, that you *were* put under the influence of the Swarm, or otherwise had something planted in you. A memory. Something to tell you to come to *this* planet. Something to lure you here with a large portion of the IDF fleet. Then, they're waiting for you, and they destroy you, leaving the path clear to take Earth and the rest of humanity."

Granger snorted. "Why go to all the trouble? Seems a convoluted way to get us all in one place. Why not just amass a thousand Swarm ships, let us see them, and then move very slowly towards Earth. *That* would get our attention. We'd be forced to defend with everything we had, again. And when we did, they send in their reserve force, and *pow.*" He thumped the table.

She looked up and glared at his fist. "Careful. Science in progress."

"Sorry," he said, withdrawing his hand from the table.

She shrugged. "I know, it's a stretch, but so is everything else, Tim. So is thinking that this is the actual, honest-to-god Swarm homeworld that we just *happen* to stumble into and it just *happens* to match the world from your dreams—"

"Memories," he interrupted. "Let's call them what they are."

She looked up at him again with a scowl. "We don't know that, Tim. They could be anything. We have no idea where you—"

"I know. Dammit, I know, I know—"

"—went that day or who you talked to or what they did to you—"

"—dammit, I know! I know—"

"—or what, pardon me for bringing it up, they injected you with that got rid of that cancer! Plus the pesky detail that you were gone not for twenty seconds, but for three goddamned days, Tim!"

"I know! Dammit," he said, trailing off, shaking his head. "You have no idea what this is like for me. Second guessing myself. Thinking I might be a Swarm agent one minute, or just a sleeper agent the next, or even—"

"What?" she said, returning to her scope.

"Maybe I did die. Maybe they reanimated my corpse with Swarm matter and I'm just a piece of shit cumrat like the rest of them. I'm a friggin' Dolmasi. A puppet."

"Now you're in fantasyland, Tim. I assure you, you're not a zombie."

He shrugged. "Maybe not. I'm not normal, that's for sure. But whatever I am, I'm sure of one thing." He pointed toward a bulkhead. "That planet out there is what we're looking for. I know it. I feel it deep down, like I've never felt anything before. No—" He paused. "I've felt this before. The Khorsky incident. I knew, I just *knew* there was something going on in that sector, and sure enough, I saw what I saw. Over Vitaly Three. A Swarm ship, right in the middle of a Russian task force. Then, two months ago, I was *sure* that I needed to pilot the Old Bird into that singularity. After you'd all gone and set the ship on autopilot—"

"You were supposed to be in an escape pod, sir, if I remember correctly. Doc Wyatt should be fired for letting you out of his sight."

"Good thing he had better things to do than babysit some cancer-riddled swooning captain who can't stay on his feet in the most critical moment of a battle," he said wryly. "But Shelby, I was sure of that decision. I had singular focus. Vision. Drive. I knew what I had to do. And it's the same now."

A silent pause.

"So? Are you going to order the fleet to attack?" She shifted from the scope to glance at the data readout on the display nearby.

"No. Not yet."

She cocked her head toward him. "No? After all that? You sounded like you were trying to convince me that we should attack right this second."

He stood up. "No. It's time. Time for Operation Battle-ax. Whether the president is ready on her end or not, we've got to do it. We're heading back to Earth. We'll use whatever she's been able to throw together with the Mars Project, but right now we've got the advantage of surprise. There's no way they could know what we're planning, or that we've finally found the right target."

Her face said, "*If* we've found the right target," but she only nodded, and peered back at her screen as the data flashed by.

"What have you found?" he said, looking at the data on her screen.

"Actually, I'm close. Using the phase modulation, I'm probing samples with as highly focused of meta-space beams as I can manage. Mind you, you generally can't focus meta-space gravitons. They're too long of a wavelength to get them even remotely narrowed down to the tiny space I'm interested in," she said, pointing to the tiny sample of Swarm matter.

"But?"

"But I've induced a response."

His jaw just about dropped. "A response?" He wanted to reach out and hug her. Instead, he sidled up to look at the data. "What kind? What did it do?"

"Well, there was a signal response, almost like a meta-space echo. But, even more interestingly, there was a slight transformation. Almost like a secretion."

"A secretion? Like, the goo oozed more goo?"

"No, but part of the goo separated itself—slowly, mind you—and that separated gunk is a little different than the old stuff."

"Fascinating," he said, peering at the images and scans she'd taken. "Is the new material like the old?"

"No. See? Swarm matter is composed of a complex soup of proteins, heavy metals, and lubricating fluid—almost like our blood plasma. We can only guess at the function of most of these proteins—they're just completely alien. Like nothing we've ever seen on Earth. Our proteins don't have stuff like hafnium and vanadium in the chains. This is utterly foreign. But we knew all this decades ago. What's new is that this new fluid I just produced is vastly different from the original Swarm matter."

Dammit. She loved playing coy too much. Especially when she knew something he didn't.

"How so?"

She looked up, and frowned. The creases on her forehead ran deep—she was clearly troubled by what she'd seen.

"It's viral."

CHAPTER FIFTY_THREE

Washington D.C., Earth
IDF Administration Building

"TELL ME AGAIN, SIR, why we're breaking into the IDF Administration Building?" Conner stood next to him outside the elevator of the vast complex. The bureaucratic heart of United Earth's military arm. MUNCENT lay hundreds of meters below them.

"Conner, I'm the vice friggin' president. I don't break into military admin buildings."

"Then where's your secret service detail?"

Lousy kid.

"I told you, I want to be discreet. You can't be discreet with a dozen bulky well-armed men following you around, calling ahead to all your destinations to arrange security and in general making nuisances of themselves."

"Nuisances that prevent more car bombings intended to kill you?"

Damn. The kid was getting mouthy. He wanted to say, *Car bombings that only happen because the president wants to off her second in command and finger the Russians*, but thought better of it.

"Look, you don't have to be here. I just thought it'd be fun for you to do something other than iron my shirts and get me coffee. Lovely *can* you left on my counter last night, by the way. I was hoping for something a little more ... authentic."

Conner shrugged. "Best I could do last minute. We'll see what I can get for tonight."

The lift arrived, and Isaacson keyed in one of the upper floors—General Norton's offices were down there, and he knew the secretary. A little too well. She'd no doubt be able to get him internal computer access.

A minute later the doors opened, and he strode confidently up to the reception desk. General Norton's secretary smiled. And winked. "Mr. Vice President. Fancy meeting you here. Do you have an appointment with the General?"

He smiled back. "Christine, the vice president never needs an appointment to talk to anyone." He took her hand and rubbed it gently between his. "Except you. How have you been?"

"Lonely," she replied. "You never call anymore."

"Been busy. You know, war. Coordinating planetary defenses and fleet readiness and all that." In truth, he hadn't called because she'd developed a strange and sudden case of halitosis, but that would have been shallow of him to leave her over a thing like that. And if he was anything, it wasn't *shallow*, dammit. Just ... picky. "Very busy. You?"

She sighed. "Busy too. It's been a mad house around here. What can I do for you, Eamon?"

"I need access to Norton's files. He said he'd send some stuff over for me but it never showed up. And rather than send classified files over the air, I thought it'd be more prudent to look at them here anyway."

"Did he authorize it?"

He smirked. "Of *course* he authorized it. Do you want me to call him?" He reached in his pocket for his comm card. "He's probably in a meeting with the president right now and won't be too happy to be interrupted like this, but if you insist—"

"No, no, darling, that won't be necessary. Come on." She stood up and led him to a small room nearby, her high heels clicking neatly on the tiled floor. A few computer terminals lined the wall, along with old, decrepit secure filing cabinets, complete with spin dials and faded classification stickers from a bygone era. The general was old-school.

"Thank you, dear. I won't be long." He smiled and squeezed her hand again. "Conner, wait outside, please. Let me know if someone wants to see me," he said with a look that said, *see that I'm not disturbed.*

He shut the door and rushed to open up a computer terminal; soon he was digging through the top-secret classified files. There were folders with titles like *Logistics*, *Production*, *Draft*, *Deployments*, *R&D*, and a host of other one-word descriptions of IDF's activities.

There. There it was—a folder most likely to tell him what he wanted to know. At least about the anti-matter program. *Special Offensive Capabilities.* Such a sterile term for something so menacing. He opened it.

And was disappointed. Just budgets, with only vague descriptions of line items. Something called the Mars Project—what the Mars habitation programs had anything to do with offensive capabilities was beyond him ... ah, except there within the Mars file was a list of material production facilities. And casing fabrication facilities. As he suspected there were dozens of bomb casing plants, not only on Earth but on Britannia as well. But what surprised him was the number of locations involved in anti-matter production. Not just the Wyoming plant. Not just the Wendover plant. There were ten. Scattered throughout North and South America and India.

He followed the production line. Special material was produced at one of the ten production centers. Bomb casings were manufactured at one of the dozens of fabrication facilities. The casings and material were all shipped to a third type of building—integration labs. He supposed it was quite an engineering feat to stabilize the anti-matter within the casings and keep the blasted things from exploding at inopportune times.

From the integration labs, the completed weapons were shipped to ordnance storage. As far as he could tell, there were only two of those. One in Saskatchewan. The other in the Britannia System, several dozen light years away, in a station orbiting Calais, a gas giant near Britannia itself.

Britannia. Calais. Just like Volodin had said.

He opened the files for fleet movements and tried to follow the tracks, but it was hopeless. There was nothing to indicate any type of covert buildup of forces near Britannia. He opened the file labeled *Missions and Operations*, and likewise was met with disappointment. Just standard fleet operations against the Swarm. Files for each engagement to date, describing intelligence leading up to the fight, tactics used, casualties, recommendations for future strategies—somehow the pencil-pushers in the Administration Building had managed to take such a deadly, serious affair and turn it into mind-numbing buzz-word-filled bureaucrat-eese.

"Eamon. How kind of you to drop in. Can I help you find something?"

Isaacson's head snapped around and he felt the blood leave his face. Dammit.

"General Norton, I'm glad you're here. Actually, I think you *can* help me find something." He waved the general over, wondering if his act was convincing.

Norton didn't move. "I know why you're here, Eamon."

Isaacson raised an eyebrow. "You do?"

"I'm not stupid, Eamon. I may not be a politician, but I know how you people operate. You're looking for dirt on Avery. I know. Don't deny it."

"Of course I deny it! How could you suggest such a thing?"

Norton smirked. "Of course. Then, might I ask, what *are* you doing here? In my offices, going through my files, uninvited?"

For once, words failed him. "I...."

"Exactly. Let me help you out then, Mr. Vice President. You're looking in the wrong place."

Interesting. Was the General wanting Avery out as well? "Oh?"

"I'm sure by now you've heard of Sparks's death?"

Congresswoman Sparks. The accident involving the president's escort ship. "Yes. That was unfortunate. She was a friend. You're sure it was Swarm sabotage? Has their reach really extended that far?"

"Farther," said Norton. "But in this case, no. Congresswoman Sparks didn't die in a Swarm sabotage event. That *did* happen—fifty good soldiers lost their lives on board the *Recto*—but that's not how she died." General Norton took a few steps toward him and took a seat nearby. "She died when President Avery put a gun to her head and pulled the trigger. Murdered her in cold blood."

Isaacson couldn't believe it. He didn't want to believe it. He knew she was ruthless, tough as nails, and would do anything she thought was necessary to save Earth. But murder?

And yet it was aligning with the recent picture Volodin had painted. "Why?"

"Why? She thought Sparks was plotting to kill her. Hell, *you* should know all about that." Norton smiled at him—his tone made it sound like he knew a lot more about Isaacson than he thought. He'd been *careful*, dammit. And now the chairman of the joint chiefs was alluding to possible treason on Isaacson's part. What did the man want?

He decided a direct approach was warranted. "What do you want?"

Norton held up his hands. "To save United Earth, of course. And I think you've found in your research that saving Earth may not be President Avery's strong point. My god, just look at what the Eagleton Commission did to us. Caught us with our asses hanging out. And now, with Operation Battle-ax, it may be that Avery leads us right into a trap. Leaves our worlds essentially undefended while she's off on some fool-hardy cleverly-named mission that in reality will gain us nothing."

"Operation Battle-ax?" He remembered Volodin mentioning it.

General Norton eyed him, then scooted his chair closer to the computer terminal Isaacson had open. A few swipes and file folders later, he stood up and walked to the door. "Mr. Vice President, I hope you can do something with this information. Otherwise, I fear the worst."

He opened the door, then paused again. "Also, there is a discreet location, just a dozen light years away, smack in the middle of empty interstellar space, where Ms. Avery confers with her top military advisors. Me, Zingano, Granger—"

"*Captain* Granger? He's a top military advisor?" asked Isaacson.

"Don't tell me you don't watch the news. Avery would be fool not to include him. He's Earth's hero, after all," Norton replied with a derisive snort. "They meet there roughly once a week. I could discreetly arrange for an extra passenger to accompany me on board my frigate. Stay in my state room. Patch you right into the meeting. Given your position, it would be wise for you to be up to date on current events. Should anything ever ... *happen* to the president."

With that, the general stepped out. Isaacson caught a brief glimpse of Conner's apologetic face before the door closed.

He examined the folder. No wonder he hadn't found it—it was categorized under *Meals and Beverage Service*, and subcategorized under *Supplementation, Nutrition, and Additives*. Brilliant. Hide sensitive information in the most bland, unremarkable places imaginable.

The file was called Operation Battle-ax.

It involved transferring large quantities of "special ordnance" to a fleet of IDF vessels in the Britannia System. The fleet had twenty separate attack groups. In a word, it was massive. To Isaacson's untrained eye, it looked big enough to not only take out a few Russian worlds, but the entire Russian confederation. On one hand he appreciated the massive scale of the operation Avery had spearheaded—building a fleet of more than a thousand ships from scratch in two months was impressive, and hiding it for that long was nothing short of miraculous.

Then he remembered. She hadn't been building for only two months. She'd been building for years. From the looks of it, her covert building plans didn't only include secret anti-matter production facilities. They'd apparently included secret shipyards.

And there were soon to be far more than just a few million casualties. This was total war, as Avery understood it: wiping out all of her perceived enemies.

Every single one of them: Swarm, or Russian.

CHAPTER FIFTY-FOUR

Near Penumbra System
Science Laboratory, ISS Warrior

"YOU'RE TELLING ME this stuff can literally infect someone? Is it communicable?" asked Granger.

Proctor shrugged. "No idea. I still need to run a whole gamut of tests—I only just discovered this before you walked in. Usually doing science like this requires protocols and controls and all that shit, but I'm kinda bootstrapping here, flying by the seat of my pants. Science at light speed."

Unbelievable. If the Swarm could not only put someone under their influence, but have that influence spread like a viral infection, then everyone on the ship could be at risk. Hell, everyone on Earth and throughout inhabited space.

But, no. If the Swarm virus were truly communicable, Earth would have been overthrown long ago.

It didn't make sense.

"And one more thing: I'm not sure about this, but the evidence is compelling, based on what we know about Swarm communication. These metallic groups within the proteins ... they're set up in such a configuration that makes graviton-based manipulation possible. It's really ... quite remarkable."

Unbelievable. "You're telling me that the meta-space signal not only has organic patterns, but is organically generated?"

She nodded. "It's incredible. I don't completely understand it yet, but if it's true, that would explain the Vishgane's ability to communicate with the Swarm without any type of comm device."

Interesting. With communication abilities like that, it was no wonder the Swarm was able to coordinate such vast and varied forces from such large distances.

"Keep at it, Shelby. I'll get out of here and leave you to it. Keep me apprised of any breakthroughs."

She raised her eyebrow and returned to look through her scope. "Oh, believe me, you'll hear about it."

He smiled—it was nice to see her absorbed in her work—she'd seem distracted of late. He knew she loved commanding a starship, and longed for a ship of her own. But she just seemed so ... driven. Happy was the wrong word since recent events really did preclude anyone feeling any joy whatsoever, but single-mindedly driven and purposeful seemed appropriate words.

Once on the bridge, he summoned the captains of the main attack wings on conference call. Their faces tiled the screen on the wall, each showing immense relief at the news they'd be going back to Earth.

"We've just got to confirm this first, Tim. Very prudent," said Captain Connelly.

Granger squinted. "We're not returning to Earth to confirm, Connelly. We're going back to summon the rest of the fleet. We're going all in on this."

Captain Barnes shook his head. "If you can convince the president, then yes." The words hung in the air between all of them. The implication was obvious—Barnes, and several of the other captains, judging by the solemn uncomfortable looks on their faces, didn't think the president or Admiral Zingano would go for it.

"I'll convince her. Volari is it. I know it." He debated telling them all the truth. That he was starting to remember his *vacation*, as several of the crew had started calling it. That he could remember looking down on this planet so clearly it was like he could see it with his very eyes.

But they wouldn't understand. That would raise their suspicions even more. If he let on that he was trying to get the whole IDF fleet to this mystery planet based on what they would call nothing more than a hunch and a dream, they'd probably mutiny and take the fleet away from him and haul him back to Earth in the brig for being a Swarm agent.

Hell, *he* didn't even know if he was a Swarm agent or not. *Hurry up, Shelby.*

"We'll depart immediately. Stay tuned for our flight plan—we'll link up nav computers shortly."

"Through Russian space?" asked Captain Connelly.

Granger nodded. "Yes."

"Not going to ask for permission this time, Tim?" said Captain Barnes with a wry grin.

"I think not. I hope they don't mind. And if they do, then they can go shove it up their—"

A blaring klaxon interrupted him. All five captains on the screen simultaneously looked around quickly as they heard the alarms on their own vessels.

"Captain!" Ensign Diamond waved him down. "We've got company!"

CHAPTER FIFTY-FIVE

Near Penumbra System
Bridge, ISS Warrior

"WHO?" GRANGER PUNCHED fingers at his tactical display, seeing the new sensor contacts appear.

Shit. They were all around them. Coming in from every vector. Completely surrounded.

This ought to be an interesting fight.

"Swarm, sir. So far I'm reading thirty carriers. And that's not all, sir. There's Dolmasi ships out there, too."

Granger looked back at the screen, a momentary look of horror on his face. There was no way the Swarm could know they were there. Or the Russians. Or the Dolmasi. That was the point of deep space rendezvouses. You didn't hang around at some random point in deep space because of the scenery. You did it because space was immensely, hugely, massive. The chances of anyone simply stumbling upon you were near zero.

Captain Connelly grumbled. "We've got to go, Tim."

He nodded. "Agreed."

"Send over the coordinates," said Barnes.

Granger shook his head. "No. Split up. Get to Earth on your own vectors. Pick random directions and meet back up there by tomorrow."

"What?" Captain Connelly looked incredulous, as did the others. But it made sense. If the Swarm knew they were here, it meant that someone on the *Warrior* was broadcasting coordinates to them. Dammit—they'd probably been doing that all along. What else could explain the Swarm at Epsilon Garibaldi, or the Dolmasi trap there?

"If we go together it means we're going to be intercepted many more times before we ever get back to Earth." He sighed—the truth would have to come out eventually. No sense hiding it now. "There's a chance we've got a Swarm sleeper cell over here, people."

Silence among the captains. He supposed they were all thinking the same thing. That *Granger* was the sleeper agent. Or the active agent, more likely. Connelly shook his head. "No, Tim. It could be someone on any of our ships."

Granger nodded. "Doesn't matter, does it? Wherever the agent is, they're broadcasting our coordinates. No. Get back to Earth however you can. We'll rendezvous there and discuss our next moves. Go."

The screen flickered off, replaced by the image of a scattering IDF fleet. "Swarm vessels converging, sir. Fifty thousand kilometers and closing."

"And sir," said Ensign Prucha, "the Dolmasi flagship is hailing us. Visual."

"Prepare q-jump coordinates," he said to Ensign Prince before nodding to Ensign Prucha at comm.

The Dolmasi's familiar face flashed onto the screen. "Captain Granger, I can't say I'm happy to see you here, but I also can't say I'm surprised. You were told to proceed directly to Earth to bring our demands to your president. And yet you are still here."

Granger shrugged. "We asked the Russians if we could pass through their space. They denied us passage. Therefore we have to go the long way around."

"And yet you are *still here*," repeated Vishgane Kharsa.

"We've never travelled this region of space before, sir. It is not wise to just q-jump our way through it without stopping on occasion to take scans and make adjustments to our course."

A good bluff, he supposed. Not bad for coming up with it on the fly. The Dolmasi's face did not look convinced, however.

"It is too late for you, Captain Granger. Prepare to be boarded. The Valarisi have had enough of this nonsense—you will all be made allies."

"Fat chance." Granger smirked. He made ready to give the order to q-jump. On his tactical screen he saw that over half his fleet had already left.

Vishgane Kharsa choked on a laugh. "I suppose you think you're going somewhere? Think twice, Captain Granger. You, too, will be made an ally. Again."

CHAPTER FIFTY-SIX

Near Penumbra System
Science Laboratory, ISS Warrior

VIRAL. THE DAMN THING is viral. Proctor had run the scans at least a dozen times, and every single one confirmed it. In spite of random morphologies—she saw any number of vertices, capsomers, and pentons, some with tails, some with no discernible structure at all—it was clear.

This thing was built with one purpose in mind: evade capture and destruction. And probably, she supposed, the ability to control any host it infected. So varied were the morphologies and functional groups, it was obvious this virus had come into contact with dozens, maybe hundreds, of other species.

For another hour she ran a few tests, and, with a burst of inspiration, ran a few experiments. Most of the functional groups seemed to have certain heavy metals in them. Metals that might bind to certain alkali elements if introduced properly.

The problem was, the heavy metals also harbored cyanide-based compounds. Cyanide was deadly. Remarkably so. She supposed it was another defense mechanism—kill too many viruses, and the host will die a painful, cyanide-induced death.

She needed to find out how Swarm-infected blood would respond. The three pilots were dead. That left Hanrahan as the only possible suspect. True, he'd managed to get away from that explosion of the Swarm fighter—Doc Wyatt hadn't found a trace of the stuff on him—but he was her only lead.

With little alternative, she marched down the hall and boarded the lift for the fighter deck. He liked to keep his post near the fighter bay since he often directed security and Hazmat operations during flight ops. She nodded at passing pilots and deck crew as they passed by her with informal salutes. She liked to maintain discipline onboard, but she also wanted a rapport with the officers and crews—no sense making them resent her by insisting on tiny details in protocol.

There he was. Ahead of her, in the hall, talking with some marines, his back toward her. If he was Swarm-infected, he would most likely find some reason not to give her a blood sample. That was his right—no officer or crewman had to submit to any medical procedure they didn't want to. She'd have to find another way besides asking.

She approached from behind, coming in close, then intentionally catching her foot on the deckplate. As she fell with a short cry, she pulled a tiny meta-syringe out of her pocket and pressed it against the back of his calf.

"Commander!" cried one of the marines who started to reach down to help.

Hanrahan pulled the marine back. The next moment, Proctor's vision dazzled as something connected with her forehead. On instinct, she rolled away and sprang to her feet. She risked a glance back as she ran and saw Hanrahan brandishing the butt of his rifle again.

"Arrest her!" he grumbled to his men. They hesitated for a split second, then sprang into action as they advanced on her. Proctor bolted, head still spinning, weaving in and out of the traffic in the hall, literally pushing them aside in order to block the path of her pursuers. Adrenaline surged, and part of her mind noted with mild surprise that it was quite easy to toss people around like that. The other part said only one thing.

Survive.

CHAPTER FIFTY-SEVEN

Washington D.C., Earth
Munitions Center, IDF Administration Building

ISAACSON HAD TO STOP IT. It was genocide, pure and simple. He nearly ran down the steps of the entrance to the IDF administration building, Conner close behind. As he expected, his secret service detail was waiting for him outside.

"Sir, how can you expect us to protect you when you give us the slip like that?"

Isaacson scowled. "I might have more confidence in your ability to protect me if it wasn't so *easy* to give you the slip, mister. How long was it before you'd realized I'd left?"

His head of security shut his mouth in frustration, then motioned his arm toward the waiting car. Isaacson started toward it, then stopped.

No, he had more business inside the administration building. He turned around and walked back up the steps. The security detail fell into step behind him, Conner trailing at the rear. Once in the security checkpoint reception area, he waved off the men. "Stay. I'll be just fine down there—it's IDF administration, for hell's sake," he said, when he saw the chief's scowl.

He got back on the elevator and lifted his head to speak. "Munitions," he said, remembering what Norton had said to get them down to MUNCENT, the casing production facility deep underground.

A few minutes later he was stalking the aisles of the production facility. Once in a while a floor manager or engineer would recognize him, but they kept going about their business, thinking it was an unannounced inspection tour. He scanned the floor, looking for....

Ah, there she was. Sergeant Gall, the Yale scientist. He strode over. "Ms. Gall?"

Her face reddened. "Mr. Isaacson! I ... you ... I—"

He held up a hand and smiled. "Not to worry, Sergeant. I'm just here to follow up on our conversation from the other day. You said something that interested me. You said you were working on containment methods?"

"Yes, sir," she replied, apparently still unsure of what in the world the vice president of United Earth was doing in her workspace, unaccompanied, in the middle of a war.

"You said your particular method was probably not viable, correct?"

She nodded. "That's right, sir. Electric containment is problematic. Well, at least the way I've been trying it."

"Explain." He pulled a chair over and sat down next to her. She nervously sunk down into her seat as well.

"Well, we're working mainly with anti-tungsten. Basically a whole lot of anti-neutrons, some anti-protons, and of course, the positrons."

"Positrons? I'm sorry, I'm not a physicist."

Her face said, *clearly*, but she nodded and added, "Anti-electrons. And that's the problem with electrical containment."

He stroked his chin. "Positrons don't like the electrical containment?"

"Positrons are a lot freer to move around compared to the anti-neutrons and protons. So when you've got an electric field pushing them one way, if *anything* is out of balance, even slightly, just one positron being pushed too far is all it takes to send the whole thing into a cascading chain reaction."

"And that's ... bad."

"Boom," she replied.

He crossed his legs, glancing at the white board nearby, full of incomprehensible equations. He didn't even recognize most of the symbols. An upside down triangle? What the hell was that? All her letter h's had crosses through them. "We want a more controlled reaction."

"Well, not necessarily *controlled*. I mean, when we want the reaction to happen, we *do* want it to happen all at once. Like I said, *boom*. If there's no boom, there's no bomb, uh, so to speak."

"So?" He tried to appear patient. But in truth, he hated talking to scientists. They could never get to the point.

"So we need to precisely control *when* the reaction happens. And furthermore, we need to make sure it doesn't happen accidentally. The default state needs to be *off*. We can't have anti-matter devices sitting around, getting old, and exploding on us. We need them to be safe long-term, and make it impossible for them to go off on their own. It was the same deal with nukes for hundreds of years. We got *really* good at making those things stable long-term. But all this anti-matter business is new, and a few years ago the team here made a breakthrough."

She stood up and went to the whiteboard. Isaacson tried not to let his eyes glaze over as she pointed to a few equations. Shit, didn't she realize it was a friggin' foreign language?

"Look—the Schrödinger equation for a single atom. Dolled up a bit since it's anti-matter we're talking about, and a pretty big atom—tungsten's wave function isn't exactly aesthetic. But for our computers it's no problem to crunch through. Turns out, if you get the electron wave function surrounding it into this configuration," she waved toward another equation nearby, "the anti-tungsten will stay put. And it takes a very precise signal to change this wave function. You can't just throw the bomb at something and hope it explodes. You need to trigger it right at the moment of impact."

He nodded. "And you do that remotely? From a safe distance?"

"Well, no, it's still triggered internally. There's a complicated set of electronics inside the casing that detects whether the bomb has been launched, or is just taking a beating. That way you can't detonate one by just hitting it, or, for example, destroying the ship carrying the bombs. The casing is basically indestructible to any outside force. Nearly solid chunks of reinforced tungsten-iridium composite alloys don't break easily."

He waved his hand repeatedly to move the conversation along. She needed to get to the point. Fast. "So tell me, Sergeant, say a foreign power were trying to sabotage these. Make them inoperable. How would they go about it? What's the easiest way?" He watched her face, looking for any sign of suspicion. Just to be safe, he added, "The president is worried about this, yes. We need to be sure we can count on these devices to work when we deploy them, and therefore we need to know how someone else could conceivably disable them."

She nodded, not the least bit suspiciously. "Oh, that's actually pretty easy. Just adjust the wave function of the surrounding material, such that it doesn't respond to the trigger signal."

"Adjust? How?"

"Any kind of adjustment, really. The wave function is imprinted during manufacture by an external field, but it's easily changed." She pointed to one of the equations. "For example, take the coefficient of the wave function of the surrounding material. Optimal is exactly two-pi. Six point one four yada yada. Change that to six point one five, and, whoops! No boom."

He nodded slowly. "And no *boom* means no bomb."

CHAPTER FIFTY-EIGHT

Near Penumbra System
Bridge, ISS Warrior

AGAIN?

Vishgane Kharsa *had* to be bluffing. But more importantly, what had he meant by *again*? You will be made an ally, *again*?

He nodded to Ensign Prince, indicating he initiate the q-jump.

Nothing.

The Dolmasi's smirking face continued staring out from the screen. "Trouble, Granger?"

"Ensign, have you initiated the drive?"

"Aye, sir. Everything reads normal. But, uh ... nothing happened," Prince shot him an apologetic look.

Granger raised his head. "Commander Scott. Talk to me, Rayna. What's going on?"

Silence.

"Commander Scott, come in." Granger glanced at his ship status board. Everything normal. "Engineering, come in."

A familiar voice came over the comm. "Everyone's here, Captain. Can I help you?"

Hanrahan? "What's up, Colonel? What's wrong with Commander Scott? Why aren't we moving?"

Before the response came he knew the answer. He glanced up at the empty chair at the science station. *Dammit, Shelby, you better be alive or I'm going to kill you.*

The colonel's voice drawled slowly, almost triumphantly. "Captain, we are not going anywhere because I have intervened on behalf of our friends. The crew is fine."

Shit. He should have known. Hanrahan was in the conference room when Proctor had detected *two* Swarm meta-space signals coming from the vicinity. "And Commander Proctor?"

A pause. "She is not fine. Gave her quite the knock."

From the viewscreen the Dolmasi grimaced—probably a smile. "It appears you'll be staying here for the moment, Captain. Prepare to be boarded."

"Like hell," he muttered. He made a cutting motion toward his neck and Ensign Prucha terminated the channel. He glanced at his tactical screen—over seventy-five percent of the fleet had left. But the rest seemed to be staying—either intentionally or not.

The comm came to life. "Granger, this is Captain Barnes. We heard."

Granger growled. "Get out of here. Save yourselves." The sensor status screen showed the armada of Swarm and Dolmasi ships approach. Less than twenty thousand kilometers now.

"Sorry, Granger. The fleet's broken up. You're not in charge anymore. We're staying to protect you, you old bastard." He could almost hear the smirk in the other captain's voice.

"This is a death trap, Barnes. Get the hell out."

"Granger," began Barnes, "you taught us all something over Earth two months ago. Yeah, you went down with the ship, but that's your duty. Any of us would have done the same. But you cling to life like a cranky old bastard and you don't stop fighting. And against all the odds, you came back from death and the void itself to continue the fight. So no, Tim, we're not going anywhere."

Granger sighed. Hero worship was a bitch. Another glance at the tactical screen told him there were nearly thirty-five IDF ships still with the *Warrior*. Not enough to even mount a serious defense, much less win against a nearly equal number of Swarm and Dolmasi carriers. But maybe it would be enough to give him time to get his engines back.

"Captain Barnes, take the lead. Mr. Diaz, my Lieutenant XO, will command the *Warrior* in my absence."

Barnes swore. "Where the hell are you going, Tim?"

He motioned to a marine at the door to hand him his sidearm, and shoved it into his waistband behind his back.

"To get my ship back."

CHAPTER FIFTY-NINE

Near Penumbra System
Science Laboratory, ISS Warrior

PROCTOR STUMBLED ALONG the hallway, blood streaming from her head. Hanrahan had hit her good—the butt of his assault rifle had nearly split her head open and she wondered if her skull was fractured.

But she had the sample. The scenario replayed over and over again in her mind on a continuous a loop— walking up behind him, intentionally falling, extracting the sample. Then the world began to swim. It was a wonder she'd gotten away.

She paused at an intersection, trying to remember where she was going. Several crew members ran past, and a few stopped to try and help. She waved them off— clearly there was an emergency going on—the klaxons were blaring and the red lights flashed. Swarm? Dolmasi? Russians? Some new enemy? Another race from the Concordat of Seven?

She'd come off the lift—she could hardly remember getting on it—and glanced around. Where was she going?

She recognized the hallways to sickbay. Her lab. That's where she was going. And it was just down the hall. She tried to run, but stumbled and nearly blacked out. Damn—she'd lost a lot of blood. A hand grabbed her shoulder and she spun around.

"Commander! What happened? We've got to get you to sick bay."

Doc Wyatt held onto her arm and tried to guide her down the hall. Given Colonel Hanrahan's recent actions outing him as a likely Swarm agent, she was relieved to see Wyatt. He'd been present with the Vishgane when she'd detected two meta-space signals. Hanrahan too—but he was the source, she was sure now. Not Wyatt.

"No," she said, stopping outside the door to her lab. "I need to check on something."

"Come on, Commander, you're in no condition to be on duty."

"No, it's important. Special mission ... I ... special mission. Science. Granger ordered me...." The words were a jumble coming out of her mouth. Thankfully, she could still think. Or could she? The hallway started spinning again.

"Come with me, Commander. We need to stop the bleeding. Come—sickbay is just down the hall."

She wrenched free of his grip and bolted into her lab. Before he could catch up she shoved the needle into the sample chamber and shut it, flipping the power on to the scope. Within moments the sample would be scanned and she would see the viruses infecting Hanrahan's blood.

"Commander! That's enough!" Wyatt dashed into the lab after her, but before he could wrench her free from the scope she peered in.

Red blood cells. T cells. Plasma. Ah. There it was. The virus. Hanrahan had been infected, all right.

Then it was true—they could now detect Swarm-controlled people. She breathed a little easier—at least now they could neutralize one of the Swarm's most potent weapons.

"All right, Doc. I've done what I came for. Let's go." She allowed herself to be led off and out the door before stopping suddenly. "Wait!"

"Oh, what is it now, Commander? If you lose any more blood you'll need a transfusion, and judging by these sirens there's about to be a whole lot more wounded coming down who'll need it more than you."

She pulled free of his grip and returned to one of the lab tables, searching for something. Her vision was hazy, and the room spun violently. Her head ached. Ah, there it was. A tiny micro-syringe. She plucked it from a pile of disheveled lab material and slipped it into her pocket.

"Ok. Sickbay," she said, nearly collapsing into Wyatt's arms.

CHAPTER SIXTY

Near Penumbra System
Engineering, ISS Warrior

"COME WITH ME," Granger said to the marines standing guard at the doors of the bridge. They nodded and readied their assault rifles. "Hopefully you won't need those. Keep them lowered. Do not shoot on sight. Let me talk, but wait for my signal. Be ready for anything."

Granger led them down the hallway toward the lift, and once inside, the ship started bucking and shuddering under the assault that accompanied the arrival of the first Swarm carriers. Dammit, his place was on the bridge leading this battle, and here he was, going to plug another hole in the dam.

But he was the only one that could plug this particular hole. Within a minute the lift doors opened and he strode out into the hallway that led to engineering. The space was almost identical to the hallway outside engineering on the *Constitution*, and he was immediately struck by a memory. Just two months ago, he'd stood outside those doors with two other marines, sending them to their escape pods while he continued on to what he thought would be his death.

The doors did not open. He raised his head. "Colonel Hanrahan, this is the captain. I am outside engineering. Let me in there, *now.*"

The colonel's voice boomed over the speakers in the cramped hallway. "Alone?"

He glanced at the two marines, clutching their assault rifles at the ready. "Just a standard marine escort, Colonel. Three of us here. Let me in there and we can work something out."

The doors slid open. Engineering appeared deserted. Granger stepped forward, signaling for his men to follow him. He felt the bulge in the waistband on his back, but resisted the urge to reach back there and pull the sidearm out.

The central command console was unmanned, so they continued down the vast bay. The power plant looked normal, as did the standard drive. He supposed the q-jump drive looked fine, too, but there was no way to determine its status without an engineer inspecting it. Where the hell were all the engineers?

He rounded the corner to the coolant bay, and stopped. The entire engineering crew was on the floor.

Dead?

One of them moved—a young engineer laying on his front, turning his head to look at Granger. His eyes were wide—the man was terrified.

Hanrahan, flanked by an entire squad of marines with their rifles aimed directly at Granger, stood close to the far wall.

"I didn't think you had the balls to come yourself, Granger. What's that they call you? The brick-layer?

Always sending others to do your dirty work for you. Thanks for proving me wrong. Our friends out there will be delighted that I've got you cornered—you've been betraying us for long enough." He motioned his men forward with his rifle. Were they under the Swarm's influence, too? He noticed that Hanrahan kept his words vague, possibly because he needed his men to think he was apprehending Granger at the behest of one of the other captains.

"Wait," said Granger. He took a step forward. Toward Hanrahan. Vishgane Kharsa's words came back to him. *You, too, will be made an ally, again.*

Again. That confirmed it—Granger had at one point been under their control. Maybe he still was. But at least he still *felt* in control of himself, and while he felt like that he was going to figure out a way out of this.

It also meant he had, at least at one point, been able to communicate through organic meta-space transmission. He had no idea how it worked. How in the world they could generate a meta-space signal with bodies was completely beyond him. Not even Proctor had any idea.

But he had to try. He focused on Hanrahan's face. Locked eyes with him. Tried to connect, to speak, to feel. To shout a word at him with his mind. *STOP*, he said. *STOP. STOP.* He concentrated on that word, and on that face, and on that concept: *STOP.*

Hanrahan cocked his head, looking confused. He motioned for his men to pause, and he walked forward until he stood just steps away from Granger. Hanrahan still had his assault rifle trained on him.

Had it really worked? Regardless, he needed to seize the opportunity. Create enough confusion in the other man that would give Granger the time he needed to act.

"I'm a friend. Just like you," said Granger.

The marines all looked confused, but Hanrahan's eyes narrowed. "A friend? You were a friend, but you were lost. You turned back. The reports say you are no longer an ally."

"Those reports were wrong."

Hanrahan looked perplexed. The rifle still pointed at Granger's chest. "Our friends are never wrong."

"They know about me, you idiot. I'm in deep cover. They're testing you. Seeing if they could trust you with their friendship."

Hanrahan's face looked hopeful. "And?"

Granger grinned. "You've done ... admirably. Our friends are pleased." He concentrated on the man's face and concentrated: *GOOD. GOOD WORK. WELL DONE.*

The assault rifle lowered slightly. Granger smiled more broadly, and extended a hand. Hanrahan let the rifle dangle from the strap and reached for the handshake.

They touched, hands gripping. Hanrahan's eyes went wide with shock, then anger. But before he could lift his rifle, Granger reached around, grabbed the sidearm from his belt, pointed it at the colonel's chest, and fired.

Blood sprayed out from his back.

Hanrahan stumbled backward. He coughed blood. The rifle dropped. He fell to his knees.

But he smiled. "Doesn't matter," he rasped. "They'll get to you, Granger. You will be a friend again. Our greatest ally. Through you, we will claim Earth."

Granger fired again. Blood splattered. The ship rumbled from the battle raging outside. Hanrahan slumped to the ground, still rasping. "How's your XO? Last time I saw her, she didn't look so good."

"Sickbay. Doing just fine," replied Granger.

One last bloody smile. "Good. Wyatt will take good care of her. He's always been a *friend*."

A friend? *Shit.*

Hanrahan's head thudded onto the ground, his eyes cold. Granger looked up at the confused marines. "Put your weapons down. *Now*." One of the marines faltered, and set his rifle on the floor. "*All* of you. Go on. I promise you'll be safe. In case you hadn't noticed there's a battle going on out there. Swarm's banging us up something fierce. Wouldn't you rather have me up there saving our lives than down here dicking around with you sons of bitches? *Now. To the ground!*" He pointed to the floor as he yelled.

The rest of them complied. He waved toward his two marines to pick up the weapons, and scanned the engineering crew on the floor until he found Commander Scott. He knelt down next to her. "You ok, Rayna?"

She seemed shaken and dazed. "Fine, Cap'n, just fine. He ain't hurt no one. Kept telling us he was our friend. Sure, he kept saying that with a rifle pointed at my face, but ... kids these days."

She was rambling. He gripped her shoulders and looked her in the face.

"Rayna, I need the q-jump drive *now*. What did he do to it?"

"Nothing, Cap'n. Just made me disable it. I can fix it up right quick."

"How long?"

"Ten minutes?"

He helped her to stand. "Move."

Commander Scott rounded up a few engineers and they retreated to the command station. "Get them in the brig," he said to his two men, pointing at the rest of the marines. "We'll sort them out later."

The ship lurched and bucked some more. He needed to be up there. But he had one last problem to fix. One more person to rescue. The lift doors closed behind him and he raised his head to speak the destination.

"Sickbay."

CHAPTER SIXTY_ONE

Washington D.C., Earth
Meta-Space Communications Center, IDF Administration
Building

IT TOOK SOME TIME, but finally Isaacson tracked down a colonel that had access to the actual production line. The entire process chain began in the casing production facility and ended with final delivery to storage, or deployment aboard vessels.

The news was not encouraging. "Yes, sir, I can confirm that eighty-two percent of all devices have already been deployed."

"Total number?"

The colonel lazily glanced at his computer readout. "Nearly nine-hundred thousand, sir. Is there a problem?"

Isaacson nodded, but he wasn't sure how much to reveal. Word would surely travel up above the colonel's head if the vice president were poking around. "Just a potential security vulnerability. Tell me, is there a way to alter a bomb's containment wave function while deployed?"

He bunched up his brow. "I suppose so. Each device is linked and addressable by the ship's central computer. Shouldn't be a problem to adjust any parameter on any device. Could even do it remotely, I suppose."

Good. It might just be possible, then. He made his way up to the surface, but stopped one last time at another level. "Meta-space communications," he said to the elevator, trusting there was such a comm center in the admin building. The lift started moving right away, opening its doors just a few floors above where he'd been. He found a station manned by a solitary technician, whose eyes widened when she saw who was exiting the elevator.

"Easy, there. Don't get up," said Isaacson, settling into the seat beside the young woman, who looked as if she were about to hyperventilate. Comm techs didn't often get to hobnob with politicians, he supposed. "What's your name?"

"Private first class Pickurel, sir. Can I help you with something?"

"You can. Look, sweetie, I know this is not protocol, but I have an urgent message I need sent to the Britannia System."

"But, sir, I usually only send messages my supervisor gives me—"

"Good for you, Private. That is excellent security hygiene. But in this case we have a security leak at the highest levels. This message needs to stay between just you and me. Not one word to anyone. You'll erase the fact it's been sent and tell no one but the president or myself."

He could tell by the look on the kid's face that she was skeptical. This was not only out of the ordinary, but extraordinarily so. "Look, sweetie, what I'm going to tell you, you need to keep between you and me. And that's this," he leaned in close, giving his whisper a note of urgency.

"IDF has been compromised by the Swarm. Their spies are everywhere. If this message doesn't get out to the fleet in the Britannia Sector, we may well lose the war within the week. Now, you don't want the deaths of billions hanging over your head, do you, sweetie? I know what that's like, and believe me, kid, it ain't fun."

The private's eyes grew even wider, but to her credit, she nodded. "What's the message, sir?"

CHAPTER SIXTY-TWO

Near Penumbra System
Sickbay, ISS Warrior

PROCTOR TRIED TO FOCUS. She tried to stay conscious. But she'd lost a lot of blood. Doc Wyatt had said so.

She propped herself up on the bed in sickbay—she noticed the doctor had put her in one of the beds in a private alcove, but all the other beds in sickbay were empty. Strange. There had been half a dozen wounded in there earlier that morning, and the ship was rumbling all around them. A battle raged outside, she knew. More wounded would be coming.

And yet the rest of the staff was gone, too. She looked around the room, searching for any other nurse or physician.

"I sent them out to the peripheral decks. Set up temporary triage centers there—much closer to where we'll have wounded."

Doc Wyatt stepped out of his office with a smile. He was holding a tiny syringe, though she couldn't get a good view of what it contained. She rubbed her forehead—a smear of anti-bacterial cream and flesh sealant covered the wound, and it itched terribly.

"Don't touch it, Commander. Our friends want us all in perfect health." He held the syringe up to the light and flicked the tip, working the air bubbles out.

The contents were vaguely green. Swarm matter.

Someone started pounding at the door, yelling. "Shelby! *Shelby!*" It sounded like Granger.

So—he'd figured it out too. Good. If she didn't make it, at least someone knew what was going on. Someone else knew about Wyatt.

Doc Wyatt stood over her bed, looking down at her. "The time is coming quickly, Commander. It's the dawn of a new day for humanity. Our new friends are benevolent and generous and kind."

Her eyes flicked from him to the syringe and back to his face. "Does it hurt?"

Wyatt chuckled. "Of course not! It's like waking up. I've never felt more alive in my life. And now, my life will be much, much longer. That's the thing about our friends—always learning. Always growing. They discovered long ago how to stave off death in life-forms like us. Not forever, of course, but you will be around for a long, long time."

Proctor's eyes narrowed. The pounding at the doors continued. Wyatt glanced up at them, a look of vague concern passing over his face. "Unfortunately, I won't be around to enjoy the new world." He fished around in his pocket with his free hand and extracted a gun.

She saw his plan now. Infect her. Kill himself. She'd be under Swarm control, Wyatt would be dead, and Granger would think that all was well. The Swarm would infiltrate up to the highest levels of IDF command that way, as Granger and Proctor both were deeply involved in the war effort.

A loud *clang* hit the entrance, and she saw something metal protrude from the seam where the sliding doors met. They were trying to force it open.

"Goodbye, Commander. And hello." He reached down with the syringe and held the gun to his head.

Before he could insert it into her arm, she pulled her hand out of her pocket where it had been fingering her own syringe, and jabbed it into his abdomen. With a grunt, she thumbed the entire contents into him, and he jumped backwards in shock.

"What ... what was that?" He stumbled forward toward her, and she rolled off the bed and crouched behind it.

"Oh, just a vial of ... actually, you know what? I'm not going to tell you. Monologuing is more of a super-villain kind of thing."

He held his stomach and dropped his own syringe. He screamed. Froth welled up at the corners of his mouth, and he screamed again. He held the gun up and pointed it at her.

She closed her eyes and bent forward. Gunfire. Multiple shots rang out. Her shoulder exploded in pain, and she instinctively rolled out of the line of fire.

A thud nearby made her risk a glance beyond the edge of the bed.

Wyatt had collapsed, still moaning. She glanced up at the doors and, in addition to the metal spike prying the door open slightly she saw a hand poking through, clutching a sidearm, still pointing at Wyatt's prone, shuddering form. The doctor screamed again.

"Shelby? You ok?" Granger shouted through the partially open door.

Proctor leapt up, ignoring the pain in her shoulder, and dashed toward the doctor, snatching his gun where it had fallen. Wyatt was bleeding from the arm, shoulder, and leg where Granger's bullets had struck him, but he seemed gripped by a pain far worse than bullet wounds.

"Fine." Holding her bleeding shoulder, she backed up to the door and released the lock. The metal spike fell to the floor with a clatter and Granger burst through, advancing on Wyatt, gun pointed at his head.

"No! Sir, stop," she said.

"He's Swarm," said Granger, cocking the sidearm.

"Yes, he is. Just ... wait." She didn't want to say anything out loud yet, not with Wyatt still listening, and capable of communicating her words to the Swarm. He breathed heavily and groaned from her earlier injection—her first attempt at a rudimentary pathogen for the Swarm virus she'd created.

Proctor yanked a drawer open and searched for a tranquilizer. Finding the right vial, she loaded it into a meta-syringe, bent down, and injected it into Wyatt's neck. Within moments, the moaning stopped, and the doctor closed his eyes.

The ship lurched.

"What did you hit him with?" he asked, astounded. "He had a gun trained on you. He fired, and missed." Granger pointed to the wall behind her—the shot had gone wide. Apparently Wyatt was in so much pain that he was in no condition to aim.

"Took him down with science." She glanced up at him. "Don't mess with science." The ship rumbled again. "Look, Tim, I'll explain later, but they need you up there."

He glanced up at her head. "You're wounded."

"Yes. But I'm fine. I can handle him now. On your way back to the bridge order the medical staff back down here—Wyatt said he sent them all over the ship to set up triage centers, probably to get them out of here so he could infect me."

He nodded. On the way out the door he glanced down at the unconscious, bleeding form of Doc Wyatt. "Proctor, I'll say it again."

"What's that?"

He smirked at her. "I'm glad you're on our side."

CHAPTER SIXTY-THREE

Near Penumbra System
Bridge, ISS Warrior

THE BRIDGE WAS A SCENE of mayhem. He'd only been gone for twenty minutes, but even five minutes battling the Swarm was enough to destroy most ships.

But, like the *Constitution*, the *Warrior* was not most ships.

"Status?" he barked, striding toward the center of the bridge. Lieutenant Diaz looked up, relieved. "Captain Barnes has kept us alive. For now."

"How many of us left?"

Diaz winced. "We've lost ten more ships, sir."

Ten ships. Ten ships just for this. He'd been throwing ships around left and right for two months, ordering their sacrifice to obliterate the Swarm carriers' fighter bays and giving the rest of them a fighting chance.

But this time it felt different. These captains all stayed behind to take the bullet for him. For *him*. It was stupid, and irresponsible. One ship and one crew—even *his* ship and *his* crew—was not worth ten others. But he supposed he'd cultivated this. He was an unbeatable legend.

The one who would drive back the Swarm once and for all. At least, that was what he had let his people think. He never made any attempt to squelch the talk. To scuttle the hero-worship. To them, he was essential.

And now it bit him in the ass. His other captains should not be throwing their ships and crews away just for his life, as grateful as he was to, in fact, still be alive.

For now, at least.

"Commander Scott. Please tell me our drive is back?"

From the mayhem of engineering came Scott's voice. "Aye, Cap'n. Just came back online now."

On the screen the camera showed Barnes's ship, the *ISS Nottingham* take a direct hit from a Swarm anti-matter beam, and in the background a Dolmasi ship was pummeling the *Eddington*. "Signal the fleet. We're back online. Get out of here."

"Aye, sir," said Ensign Prucha.

Over the comm Captain Barnes's voice boomed out. "Good to see you back on your feet, Tim. Now, let's blow this joint."

"See you at Earth," Granger said. "And thank you, Captain, for sticking around. We owe you one."

"Hell, Tim, you would have done the same for us."

Would I? He thought it more likely that he would cut his losses in order to fight another day. To win the war, not the battle.

But he felt more at ease, now. He was sure—*almost* sure—that he wasn't controlled by the Swarm anymore. Under their influence? Maybe. Could they track him? Maybe. But controlled? No.

"Ensign Prince, take us home."

A moment later, the view on the screen changed, and a star field replaced the scenes of battle.

He breathed deep and sat down. Glancing at his hand he realized some blood from Colonel Hanrahan had sprayed onto him, and he rubbed at the dried flecks.

"Now let's just hope the rest of them make it."

CHAPTER SIXTY-FOUR

High Orbit, Earth
Bridge, ISS Warrior

EARTH WAS A WELCOME SIGHT, but it had come with a high cost. The fleet had rendezvoused, and the stragglers were still coming in, but it was clear—the mission, at least by the numbers, had been disastrous. That was what he knew the admiralty would tell him. Thirty-three ships. Thirty-three ships and crews gone, and all during the space of less than three days on a mission that he'd claimed would take them weeks as they navigated behind enemy lines, striking Swarm worlds and then fading into deep space just as quickly.

Except Granger knew the truth—the mission was actually a stunning success. He finally knew the location of the Swarm homeworld. He was sure of it.

He glanced over at Lieutenant Diaz. "Commence repair and recovery operations. Ensign Prince," he turned to navigation, "get us to Wellington station. We'll need to restock our supplies and ordnance. Commander Proctor," he said, looking up at the ceiling, wondering if she was awake.

"Yes, Captain?"

"We need to go report to Admiral Zingano. Are you well enough to share your results?"

"Well enough. And they are what they are. I wish I had more for you, Tim."

He shook his head. "You've done more than enough already, Shelby. One hell of a scientist, huh? Careful, or Zingano might take the *Independence* away from you before you even step foot on it, and stick you on a science ship."

She chuckled. "We don't have science vessels anymore, Tim. Remember there's a war on?"

"Not for long. I'll meet him in the shuttle bay and then we'll come to you. Don't get up—stay in sickbay."

He stood up, ready to turn the bridge back over to Lieutenant Diaz. "See that armed marines are posted at the entrance to sickbay at all times. Doc Wyatt is not to be released from his bed restraints until I say so. Do not believe a word that comes out of his mouth—he's been stripped of all rank and authority indefinitely. Do not touch him, or go within ten feet of him. Understood?"

Diaz nodded. "Yes, sir."

Good. The last thing they needed was more Swarm-infected people running around. Proctor had used some sort of agent that attacked the virus itself, unintentionally releasing poisonous pathogens into Wyatt's body as a result—causing him incredible pain—but there was no guarantee the doctor was himself again.

Steps from the door, he was stopped by the comm officer. "Sir?"

"What is it, Ensign?"

"I'm receiving a coded transmission from Admiral Zingano's private channel."

"Decode it."

Ensign Prucha nodded, and a moment later said, "It's marked for your eyes only."

Granger returned to his chair and swiped his console on, presenting his palm for credentials. The message flashed onto the screen.

President Avery missing. Keep it to yourself. After resupply meet me at the waypoint.

CHAPTER SIXTY-FIVE

High Orbit, Earth
Comm Center, ISS Warrior

BALLSY FLICKED THE viewscreen on. They were at Earth, and who knew when they'd come back—their previous mission was supposed to last weeks, not days.

He didn't know when he'd get a chance to talk to the kid again. The kid that needed a hero.

The grandmother's worn, lined face filled the screen. "Oh, Tyler, I'm so glad you called. Hang on, I'll go get him."

He smiled and her face left the screen. In the background he could hear her corral the little kid. Volz heard his name mentioned, and at that the boy shrieked, and moments later his small face lit up the screen.

"BALLSY!"

Volz grinned. When three-year-olds said something, they *said* it. "Hey Zack Zack, how's it goin', little man?"

"GOOD."

He started babbling and showed Volz pictures he'd drawn and explained all the parts in his broken little-kid sentences. Before long he pulled something out of his pocket and held it up to the screen.

"Hey, buddy, you still have it!"

"YEAAAH!"

The little toy was chipped at the edges from extensive play, but the model fighter still gleamed impressively in Zack Zack's hand. "It's FAST!"

Volt chuckled. "Yeah, man, sure is. Fast as lightning."

"Did you fly today, Ballsy?"

It still threw him for a loop that the little kid called him by his semi-vulgar callsign, but it made him grin all the same.

"Not today, little man. But maybe tomorrow. I'll go fast then, ok?"

"OK." Zack held the fighter up as he soared it into the air and made what he supposed were explosive fighter noises. After a moment Zack focused on the screen again, his eyes smoldering, staring at Volz. "Did you find Mommy yet?"

Volz's throat caught. "I ... I ... no, little man. Haven't found her. I don't know if I will. But she's flying fast and fighting hard, buddy."

"You'll find her tomorrow?"

He struggled to talk. *Dammit, why the hell was he doing this? This wasn't his job.* "No, little man. Not tomorrow either."

Zack regarded the viewscreen, then made more explosive noises as he raced the fighter off into the air. "Maybe she's flying too fast. FLY FASTER BALLSY."

Volz half chuckled and half cried. "Yeah, kid. I will. Hey, I gotta go, Zack Zack. Are you doing ok? Are you being happy for your grandma?"

"YEAAAH."

He nodded. "Good, buddy. See you later, little man."

The kid ran off, and the grandmother's face filled the screen again. "Thank you so much, Lieutenant Volz.

This means so much to him. And to us. He asks to talk to you every single day."

He nodded again. "Is he doing ok?"

She sighed. "As well as can be expected. But he'll manage. He has to. And you're an absolute saint for taking him under your wing like this. His ... his uncle just died too. On Cadiz Prime. His father's brother. It's...." She paused and closed her eyes before forcing a smile. "It's been rough. But he's doing well. Thank you."

The transmission terminated. Dinner an hour later felt bland and mushy. His weight sets with Spacechamp and Fodder passed like a blur. The evening training session seemed pointless and repetitive. All he could think about was *her*.

The boy's voice echoed in his ears. *FLY FASTER, BALLSY.*

Kid, if it were only that simple.

CHAPTER SIXTY-SIX

The Waypoint, Near Sirius
Bridge, ISS Warrior

AFTER A BRIEF RESUPPLY at Wellington station, the *Warrior* q-jumped its way toward the point a few light years out from Sirius. The waypoint. Granger immediately recognized Zingano's ship, the *Victory*, waiting for them just a few hundred kilometers away. A moment later, the comm beeped—he nodded to Prucha to patch it through to his station.

"Good to see you, Tim," said Zingano.

"What's going on, Bill? Where's Avery?"

The admiral shook his head. "Late last night I got a cryptic message from her chief of staff. Told me she's nowhere to be found. Just disappeared. Several secret service agents on her detail are missing too, and, well, he fears the worst."

"How in the world can the president of United Earth just disappear?"

Zingano shrugged. "Ever since the invasion, Avery has been meticulous about both her security, and her freedom of movement. Body doubles, unpublished schedules—

hell, even General Norton doesn't know where she's off to half the time, and he's in charge of fleet escort security when she flies out from Earth. She could be visiting her mother on Britannia, for all we know."

Granger shook his head. "And she could be dead."

"And, yes, she could be dead."

Dammit. They were on the verge of victory. The eve of what could be the final and decisive confrontation with the Swarm. And now this.

"We don't have time for this nonsense. Who could be behind it?"

Zingano shrugged. "The way I see it, there are two possibilities. Either she's responsible for her disappearance—say, she's in hiding trying to throw off her attackers, or someone else is responsible for her disappearance. If it's someone else, there are two possibilities there, maybe three. Either it's someone in the government that wants her gone, or it's a Russian actor, or a Swarm-controlled actor. I figure if she turns up dead immediately, it's someone in the government—having a missing president is far more unstable than having a dead president, and a domestic enemy would want a quick change in leadership. Whereas both the Russian and Swarm scenarios would want to maximize chaos and instability by keeping her missing."

Granger kept shaking his head, still in disbelief. "This is ridiculous." He looked up at the admiral's face on the screen. "Bill, we need to make our move anyway. It can't wait."

Zingano tipped his head toward the screen. "You're sure then? You've remembered your ... disappearance? You know where the homeworld is?"

"I do. I'm sure of it. Bill, it's as clear as day to me. I remember laying on an examination table. Like in a hospital clinic. I remember being treated for my injuries. I remember looking out the window—I was in orbit, aboard some sort of space station or ship, and down below was a planet. And the more I try to remember what planet that was, the more I remember it was explained to me that ... well, that it was the source of our troubles. The place we need to be."

He didn't dare finish the line of thought. He'd remembered a little more than that. Ever since Vishgane Kharsa had told him that he'd once been an ally. A friend to the Swarm, and therefore under their control. And with that revelation came the memory that when he was looking down on that planet....

He'd felt pride. A knowledge that he and his allies—his Swarm allies—would overcome. Would subjugate all and make the entire galaxy their friends. God—that need for friendship, that drive to be not alone, that urge to bring all into communion with them—it was powerful. He'd come to understand something—the Swarm was lonely. Genocidal, sure. But, oddly enough, it was murder driven by loneliness.

But Zingano couldn't know that. No one could know that he'd once felt those things. He searched deep inside—he didn't feel them now. He was absolutely sure. He wanted the Swarm destroyed. Wiped from the fabric of the galaxy. But at one point he *was* them. And he looked down on his homeworld with pride.

"I'm sure, Bill. I can't explain it, but I'm sure. You've got to trust me."

Zingano nodded slowly. "Ok. Operation Battle-ax is on. I'll send word to Britannia—the missile frigate fleet is assembled there at Calais. I'll call in the rest of the attack groups and all the planetary defense forces we can spare. If we're going to do this, we go big or we go home. Overwhelming force or none at all. Agreed?"

"Agreed. Let's throw everything we've got at this."

It felt right. In spite of the mystery of the president's disappearance, and the assassination attempts on both her and the vice president, and the discovery of Russian movement out near Swarm space—in spite of all the uncertainty, he knew this was right. Finally.

"Sir! *Interstellar One* and her escorts just q-jumped in!" called Ensign Diamond from the sensor station.

"Put it onscreen," Granger replied, and a moment later the viewscreen split between the admiral's face and the new arrivals. The stately *Interstellar One*, flanked by the *Verso* and another identical ship Granger supposed had been renamed *Recto*, along with another battlecruiser flanked by its own escort frigates.

"President Avery is hailing us, sir."

Granger motioned toward the screen. The image of the ships disappeared, replaced by Avery's lined face.

But before Granger even had a chance to say a word, the signal cut out, her face disappeared, replaced by a screen lit up with fire and debris.

He felt the blood drained from his face.

The vacuum snuffed out the fire, and when the screen cleared, he saw that *Interstellar One*, the *Verso*, and the *Recto*, were all gone.

CHAPTER SIXTY-SEVEN

The Waypoint, Near Sirius
Bridge, ISS Warrior

IT WAS LIKE DÉJÀ VU, only much, much worse. He couldn't believe it. For just a fleeting moment, Granger thought that there had been some sort of confusion. That the president hadn't disappeared, that it was some sort of miscommunication. He *saw* her. She was alive. But the smoldering hulk of *Interstellar One* wiped those hopes away.

Zingano still stared out through the screen. The shock was only now dawning on him. Before either of them could say a word, a new face appeared. General Norton, aboard the battleship.

"Gentleman ... I ... it appears that despite my best efforts to keep her safe out here, the president is dead." He, too, looked shocked. "I'm sorry. I've failed us all. I thought—I thought if she went underground, disappeared for awhile, it would draw her attackers out. Throw them off balance and make them do something that would alert us to who they were. She agreed. It was ... it was supposed to keep her safe. And now...." He shook his head. "I'm sorry. This is all my fault."

The three men sat in heavy silence for nearly a minute.

Finally, Zingano cleared his throat. "Regardless. The plan goes on. General, I've decided now is the time. We have a target confirmed. Operation Battle-ax is a go."

Norton shook his head. "You know my feelings about this, Admiral."

"I do, General. But I disagree. We need to strike. And strike hard."

Norton glanced at Granger, narrowing his eyes. "But on information derived from a compromised source? Really, Bill, we can do better than this."

Zingano nodded. "It's not ideal. But it's what we've got. We need to move now before the government has a chance to reorganize and catch its breath. It'll take time to get the new president up to speed. Where is Isaacson?"

Norton opened his mouth, then closed it.

"General?" said Zingano.

"Well, to tell the truth, Isaacson was part of the reason I even showed up here with Avery—why I encouraged her to go underground. It seems Mr. Isaacson is missing as well. Truly missing."

CHAPTER SIXTY-EIGHT

ISS Lincoln
Executive Stateroom

ISAACSON POUNDED ON the door to his stateroom. Ever since he'd boarded the *Lincoln,* General Norton's battlecruiser—at Norton's behest—to listen in on Avery's planning session with her top military advisers, he hadn't been able to leave his room. No one answered his comm calls. Banging on the door didn't seem to be helping. A pit was growing in his stomach, and he knew something was terribly, terribly wrong.

Why hadn't he listened more to his secret service detail? He'd assured them going with General Norton for a short trip in his battlecruiser was one of the safest things he could be doing in one of the safest places. The secret service chief had assented to sending along only two agents, who were supposedly staying in the room next door.

He was *supposed* to be on the bridge by now. The trip out to the secret location near Sirius, the waypoint, should only take an hour or so.

He slumped down into a chair and tried to turn on the computer terminal. It was disabled. *Dammit.*

Avery was behind this. She must be. Just like Volodin had warned him.

The door opened. General Norton strode in with two MPs, both heavily armed, one holding a pair of handcuffs.

"Mr. Isaacson, you're under arrest for the murder of President Barbara Avery." He nodded to the MPs who moved forward and pushed him against the wall, cuffing his wrists behind his back.

"What is the meaning of this? What do you mean, is she dead? How?"

General Norton turned Isaacson around and faced him, nose to nose. "*Interstellar One* just exploded. Along with the *Verso* and *Recto*, her two escort ships. Somehow, someone knew that she might be aboard any one of those ships, and so targeted all three in their sabotage. Despicable."

He felt the blood drain from his face. "But ... but, someone's been trying to assassinate *me*! Clearly someone is out to get *both* of us!"

Norton shook his head. "A clever ruse, sir. Making it look like someone was targeting you too. I'm sure the Russian Intelligence Service was too kind to oblige. Blowing up your own car in Moscow. Brilliant. Arranging for two plants in our fighter corps to attack your shuttle. Very convincing. You had all of us fooled. Until today."

"But I'm telling the truth! I had nothing to do with this!"

The two MPs pushed him toward the door at a motion from Norton. "And just what was in those meta-space transmissions you sent yesterday, Mr. Isaacson? You gave Private Pickurel quite the exciting day."

Good. At least they hadn't been able to decode his transmission, or determine the intended recipient.

"None of your business." He struggled feebly against the firm grips of the MPs. "You have no authority to do this. I have governmental immunity. If anyone does the arresting here it is the civilian federal police corp—the judiciary, not the military. This is a coup!"

Norton shrugged. "It's only a coup if you're a president. Last time I checked, you weren't. Don't worry, Mr. Isaacson, the government will be in good hands with Speaker LaPierre." He nodded to the men. "Put him in the brig."

Speaker LaPierre? Suddenly it all made sense. It wasn't Avery. It wasn't Volodin. It was the only person who would benefit from the deaths of *both* the president and the vice president. And somehow, he'd swayed some of the top military leadership over to his side. Or at least, General Norton.

The MPs jostled him through the hallway, down several flights of stairs, and through a heavy metal door which slid aside at their approach. Bars lined several cells, and soon he found himself locked into one of them: a space no bigger than a cage with a small, hard bed.

Shit.

CHAPTER SIXTY-NINE

Volari Three, Volari System
Bridge, ISS Warrior

GRANGER HAD NEVER q-jumped with so many ships in such a coordinated fashion before. His short-lived excursion into Swarm space a few days ago was one thing— one hundred and fifty vessels was nothing to sniff at. But this was an entirely new ball game. The largest space fleet ever assembled.

After each jump an accounting had to be made, to slightly adjust all the spacing between each ship in case any had drifted. In all, there were sixty battle groups in three separate task forces. Nearly two thirds of the IDF fleet. On his command console the ships were listed out by type, position, purpose, and name. Over two hundred heavy cruisers, including the *Warrior* and the *Victory*. Four hundred light cruisers. And of course the eight hundred missile frigates with their precious, deadly cargo.

"Jump two hundred and three complete. All attitude adjustments made," said Ensign Prince.

"Very well. Commence two hundred and four."

Granger looked back down at the screen. Each missile frigate was carrying close to one thousand anti-matter torpedoes—the fruits of the Mars Project. With each one coming in at a yield of over ten thousand conventional thermonuclear warheads, the combined firepower would pack no small punch. Whatever world they found at the other end of this journey was not going to ever look the same. It would most likely be uninhabitable for thousands of years.

Small price to pay if it meant the extermination of their enemy.

Twenty more jumps passed. Forty more. And soon they were counting down to the final ten.

He tapped his commlink to Proctor in sickbay. "You ready for this?" She'd taken a breather from her research, at his insistence. Between the concussion and the bullet hole in her shoulder, she needed a break. But she'd set up a small work station in sickbay to stay abreast of what was happening on the bridge—her Swarm expertise would come in handy during the operation, no doubt.

"Ready as we'll ever be. We've prepared for three months. Millions of people working around the clock."

"I just hope we brought enough. They ran through the simulations for weeks, and everyone agrees that, if anything, we're overdoing it."

"Overkill is safer than under-kill, in this case at least," she replied.

Ensign Prince looked back. "Last one, sir. We're at the edge of the Volari System now."

"What do sensors say?" Granger leaned over to the tactical station. His memories of the planet had cleared to the point where he'd even remembered what type of atmosphere surrounded the homeworld. Had he seen a technical readout of the planet? Had he scanned it while still onboard the *Constitution*?

"The third planet matches the description you gave us, sir. Reading high concentrations of oxygen, methane, nitrogen, and an unusually high reading of argon, just like you said it would. Several space stations in orbit. Giants. Each bigger than Wellington station over Earth."

"EM signals?"

"Weak. What we can read from out here, at any rate. Though what we read out here is about six months out of date due to light speed."

Granger nodded. It was time. Now or never.

"Initiate q-jump two hundred and fifty-four."

"Initiating," replied Prince.

And in the blink of an eye, they were there, in high orbit around Volari Three. The Swarm homeworld. The surface looked faintly green, just as he'd remembered, with scattered giant lakes and few clouds.

"Any welcoming committee?"

Ensign Diamond shook his head. "Besides the stations, none that we can detect, sir. Counting five space stations in different orbits. No defensive postures yet. Reading some scattered meta-space transmissions using Commander Proctor's new detection technique, but they're indecipherable."

So definitely Swarm. Granger stroked his chin—he'd neglected to shave that morning. He tapped the link to Proctor. "Are we sure its Swarm? The planet?"

"Yes. High concentrations of organic material on the surface that matches Swarm matter. And these meta-space signals are definitely theirs."

"Incoming transmission from Admiral Zingano, Captain," said Ensign Prucha.

Granger nodded, and the admiral's voice came over the speakers. "Will you do the honors, Tim? Everyone's ready. I think it will mean more coming from you."

Damn hero worship.

"Very well. Patch me through to the fleet."

"You're on, Captain," said Prucha.

"This is Captain Granger." He paused, knowing that this was a momentous occasion. Whatever the outcome, the history books will make note of this day, possibly as a turning point for Earth. The day she finally conquered her most despised enemy. "All vessels, prepare for engagement. Frigates, take your positions previously assigned to you. Task forces, escort them in. We've got one shot at this, people. Let's make our families, our friends, and our civilization proud."

"Sir! Detecting massive energy readouts from the space stations! Several hatches are opening ... sir, I—"

"What is it, Ensign?" Granger snapped.

Diamond blanched. "There's something coming out of the stations. Ships ... carriers ... looks like about fifteen Swarm carriers powering up."

So, they *were* waiting for them. All the better—more Swarm to kill. Fifteen carriers versus two thirds of the entire IDF fleet. Should be a quick fight.

"Task force Granger One, engage Swarm carriers. Task force Granger Two, escort those missile frigates in." He paused and glanced at his status display. Five giant orbital stations, fifteen carriers. It didn't quite add up.

"And Task force Granger Three, stay here with the *Warrior*. Just in case there are any more surprises out there."

CHAPTER SEVENTY

ISS Lincoln
Brig

ISAACSON THUMPED HIS HEAD repeatedly against the hard surface of the bed in his cell. How the hell had he allowed himself to get caught in a situation like this? He supposed Speaker LaPierre had been planning this ever since the invasion—saw it at his prime opportunity to seize the presidency.

A situation caused by Isaacson himself, dammit. Though he knew no one was around to see it, he felt his face flush red. Not only was he responsible for Miami, for Phoenix, hell, for all of it—tens of millions of lives, now he was responsible for his own undoing.

But at least all those Russian cities would be safe. Unless that was a ruse, too. Dammit, his head ached—he had no idea what was real, what was imagined, what lies had been told, what lies were actually true, who his enemy was, who *he* was fighting for. It was all a blur of deception.

He was fighting for himself—he knew *that* at least. But who was on his side? Volodin? Avery? LaPierre? His own party? He had to get word to them somehow. If the people knew what was going on, there'd be a revolution, Swarm invasion or no.

A moan came from the cell next to his. Solid metal interrupted his direct line of sight, but someone was definitely in there. Some young draftee, most likely, who'd gotten homesick and tried to call his parents or girlfriend one too many times.

Another moan. It was a woman.

"You all right in there?" he said.

The moaning stopped. He heard sudden movement, as if someone had sat up quickly. They stood up, whoever they were, and he heard soft footsteps.

"Eamon? Eamon, is that really you?"

Holy shit. He bolted to his feet. "Madam President?"

A chuckle. "I told you to call me Barb, Eamon."

With two steps he crossed the breadth of the cell and held onto the bars, straining to see around and to his left, to the other cell holding Avery. "You're alive? But ... General Norton told me your ship exploded. He accused me of doing it!"

She chuckled again, then sighed. "Well, in his defense, I *did* suspect you. Told him to keep an eye on you. Told him you might try something like this."

"You *did?*"

"Looks like we were both played. Played like a freshman congressman. Here we are, at the top of our games, seasoned politicians, feared or loved by everyone, and we were outdone ... by a soldier."

He shook his head. "He can't be acting alone. Speaker LaPierre must be behind it. Why else go after both of us at once?"

She didn't say anything for a moment, and he heard movement as if she'd sunk down to her knees or sat down on the floor. Moments later, a hand reached out, just visible past the last bar of his cell. The gold band of her turquoise ring flashed in the dim light. It was Avery all right. He knelt down and reached out to it. Holding it. She gripped back tightly.

"Eamon, I'm so sorry. I should have trusted you. This was all my fault. All I wanted was to save Earth, and now I may have doomed it." Her voice sounded small. To his ears, she seemed broken. Her tone sounded like one defeated. Utterly defeated. Had Volodin been wrong about her? He was insistent that she was a Swarm agent. He supposed a Swarm agent knew how to act. But act so completely convincing like this?

"No, Barb. You did good. I should have taken you more seriously. You told me to feel out the opposition and root out the ones trying to kill you. But instead I dallied. I ... should have exposed all of them."

She squeezed his hand again, then let go and pulled back—it sounded like she slumped to the floor from kneeling. "Well, we did our best. What else could we have done? I suppose I could have just rounded them all up and put a bullet through their brains like I did to that bitch Sparks. Ha!"

"So you *did* kill her?"

"Of course I did. I knew she was one of the ring-leaders months ago. That's why I invited her to my inner circle right after the invasion. I mean, true, I did appreciate the quick access to congress I had through her, but really I wanted to keep an eye on them all. Tapped her comm, had her followed when she wasn't with me. Whole nine yards. Traced her to you, too, by the way. I had half a mind to blow *your* head off right after the invasion. But ... you were different. You changed afterwards. You stepped up to the plate, stopped talking to your buddies, did your duty and didn't complain once. I ... I should have trusted you."

The ship rumbled in the distance.

"What the hell was that?" he said, standing up.

He heard her sigh. "That would be the Swarm, most likely. Ever been in a battle, Eamon?"

The ship shuddered again. So did he. "No."

A small chuckle. "Hold on tight, then."

CHAPTER SEVENTY-ONE

Volari Three, Volari System
Bridge, ISS Warrior

"TASK FORCE GRANGER ONE has engaged the Swarm, sir. The *Tel Aviv*, *Poseidon*, and the *Canada* have already taken heavy damage, but three Swarm carriers are already destroyed."

Granger nodded. So far, so good. "Status of the missile frigates?"

"Entering low orbit and dispersing across all longitudes and latitudes. Task Force Granger Two reports minimal response. Several hundred Swarm fighters detached from the main battles and tried to intercept the frigates, but the heavy cruisers made quick work of them."

He examined the tactical readout and watched the battle unfold on video. The space between the twelve remaining Swarm carriers and the cloud of IDF vessels surrounding them was filled with flashes, explosions, streaks, and flares, like a fireworks display on United Earth day. He winced as he watched another heavy cruiser explode, but in response a wing of light cruisers caught one of the carriers in a vicious crossfire, peppering it with tens of thousands of rounds of mag rail slugs. Soon, it too exploded, crashing into its neighbor as it spun out of control.

Admiral Zingano's voice rang out of the speaker nearby—the two had an open commlink for the duration of the battle. "Tim, these carriers are toast. We shouldn't need reinforcements. I recommend you take your task force and go deal with those stations. Careful—they're most likely armed. Keep your distance and hit them with nukes under mag rail escort."

"Aye, aye, sir." He glanced over at Diaz and nodded—he'd get tactical ready. Proctor's research was more or less concluded, but with a gash across her face and a minor concussion, she wasn't quite up to directing a battle. He stood up and pointed to a spot by the nearest orbital station and rested a hand on Ensign Prince's shoulder. "Take us in, son." He tapped his commlink to the rest of fleet. "Task Force Granger Three, converge on the stations. Mag rails and nukes. Forty ships per station. Let's get this over with."

The *Warrior* sailed through the gulf of space between it and the nearest station, accompanied by nearly forty other cruisers. He supposed that this particular station could very well be the one he had memories of. The one where he'd looked out longingly at the planet below, turned into a Swarm agent, compelled to do their bidding. Compelled to feel their feelings and think their thoughts. To be their "friend." There was no way to be sure which of the five it was, but assuming it was *this* one made the approach that much more enjoyable.

"Open fire," he said. And with a surge of pride and unexpected emotion, he watched as thousands of mag rail slugs slammed into the massive station, initiating hundreds of small explosions as they ripped through the armor. Dozens of green anti-matter beams lanced out from the undamaged portions, but gradually they fell quiet as more and more eruptions of fire and debris burst out from the surface.

"Nuclear strike. Fifty warheads."

"Nuclear strike," repeated the nuclear targeting officer, and the woman nodded to her crew. "Arming. Targeting solutions found. Firing."

Granger stood back up. He wanted to soak in the moment. Bask in it. Finally, after months of casualties, blood, horror, sacrifices, lost friends, razed cities, and devastated worlds, he was ready for a win. An utterly convincing and final win.

The anti-matter beams blazed out from the surface of the battered station, searching for the incoming missiles, but the beams were too few and the warheads too many. Within another few seconds the first nuke found its target, then another, then two dozen more. The screen lit up, oversaturated with the intense explosion, and when the glow finally subsided, Granger grinned. The station had broken up into at least five pieces. What was left of it, anyway.

He checked his tactical board to watch the progress of the other four attack wings, and satisfied that the other stations were either destroyed or nearly so, he sat back down. "Diaz, status of missile frigates?"

"All in position, sir."

He tapped the fleet's open commlink. "What are you waiting for, boys? Deliver your packages, and let's get the hell out of here."

On the video feed he watched as each of the eight hundred missile frigates launched their cargos. Thousands of small tungsten spheres blazed through the atmosphere like a meteor storm. He supposed the view from the surface was spectacular. At least, it would be spectacular only for the next minute or so. Soon, the entire continental crust would be a molten, radioactive wasteland.

"Twenty seconds to surface detonation," said Diaz.

Granger tapped the fleet commlink. "This is the beginning of the end, my friends. This is where we break the Swarm's back. We'll mop up the rest of them in the months ahead, but when it's all over, you get to say you were here to witness this moment."

"Ten seconds," said Diaz.

Finally.

"Five seconds."

"Four."

"Three."

"Two."

"One."

Granger crossed his legs and leaned back. Any second now....

Any second now....

"Tactical? Anything detected on the surface? I thought we would have seen them from up here."

The sensor officer shook his head. "Nothing, sir."

Granger leaned forward and hesitantly tapped the all-fleet comm. "What happened?"

The commander of the lead missile frigate answered. "Looks like they ... uh ... looks like they were duds, sir."

"*All* of them?"

"Yes, sir. Looks that way."

Granger punched the line to Admiral Zingano. "Bill?"

"I got nothing, Tim. They've been tested extensively. This ... this is unbelievable."

"Sir!"

Granger recognized the panic in Ensign Diamond's voice. *Dammit.*

He knew what was coming next.

"New sensor contacts! Dozens of them. Q-jumping nearly all the way into orbit. Reading thirty ... no ... forty—" Diamond looked up, his face turning ashen. "One hundred Swarm carriers. More appearing every second."

Granger slumped down into his seat and could only think of one thing to say.

"Shit."

CHAPTER SEVENTY-TWO

ISS Lincoln
Brig

ISAACSON NEARLY JUMPED with the next lurch of the deck-plate. He couldn't imagine why, for the life of him, General Norton had taken the ship into battle, especially with the president and vice president on board. That thought came automatically, before he realized how silly the concern was, really. With the Speaker of the House already dusting off the chair at the Executive Mansion there was really no concern about losing either of their lives at once. They'd most likely be secretly executed once they returned anyway.

"Calm down, Eamon. For hell's sake I can hear you hyperventilate from all the way over here."

He snapped. "Calm down? *Calm down?* We're being held captive by the chairman of the joint chiefs of staff on board a ship that is apparently locked in battle with Earth's mortal enemies all while the Russian Confederation is colluding with members of congress behind our backs and trying to kill us, but they needn't bother because

Speaker LaPierre is most likely going to off us if we get out of here alive, and you're telling me to calm down?"

A strange noise came from the cell next door. A snicker. Then a full-blown laugh. In spite of himself, he started chuckling along with her. It was somewhat humorous, after all. Gallows humor—the only kind those on death row enjoy.

"Oh, Eamon, look at us," she started, before descending into another laughing fit. "Look ... look at us. If we get out of this alive I need to treat us to a long, long weekend at Camp David."

His laughter died down, and he said, still smiling, "What? You and me? Camp David?"

She snorted. "Don't think I haven't seen you look at me. And, now that we're here—now that we're essentially about to die—I'll say it. I admit it. I asked you to be my running mate not only because it would satisfy the opposition, but I found you incredibly sexy. Oh, don't laugh—"

He'd descended into another laughing fit, and she joined in, trying to finish her sentence. "No ... no, seriously. You, the oldest eligible bachelor in D.C., me an old spinster—though I'm only fifty-five, and they call me *ancient*! That chiseled jaw of yours. Those piercing blue eyes. Shit, Eamon, it was everything I could do to keep myself out of your pants that first year of our term."

He wiped an eye and hiccuped. "Our first year was last year!"

"My point exactly." She sighed. "Oh, Eamon. Things could have been so different, without the Swarm. Without this bullshit war." She paused. "Ok, here's another confession. You were right. And Norton was right. Your whole faction was right—I was planning an action against the Russians. I was finally going to expose them, bomb their military industrial centers to hell and back, and finally put them in their place. Payback for the last Swarm war. The Khorsky incident only reminded us: they're not to be trusted. They want us dead, and I was going to be damned if I didn't see them dead first."

He sat up from the wall. "You were actually going to bomb their worlds? Start a war?"

She made a dismissive noise. "No. No war. I was going to finish the war with them before it ever started. They were building up their forces covertly. They were manufacturing ships and weapons on a scale that was starting to dwarf us. They were blocking all our settlement moves in the United Earth council all the while moving out into new territory of their own. They've been openly hostile for years. Threatening us. Humiliating us with our inaction while they built their strength. War? No. I was going to destroy their military bases. Their manufacturing facilities. Their industrial base. Their weapons stores. General Norton told me how he saw you snooping around the anti-matter facilities. Yes, that was how I was going to do it. Shock and awe, the old term was. It was going to be sudden, it was going to be devastating, and it was going to be complete. Minimal civilian casualties, of course, but it would have set their military back for half a century."

Silence. So—Volodin was telling the truth. What else had he told the truth about? What was a lie?

"Ok, your turn!" She laughed again.

"*My* turn?"

"That's right. It's confession time. I told you mine. You tell me yours. And if they give us a moment alone before we're executed I'll give you the best blow job you've ever had."

He snickered. "I don't know, I've been around the track a few times. Done my share of test drives." He

313

paused. "Fine." He stood up and started pacing his cell, which only allowed him four steps before he had to turn around.

The ship rumbled again and Isaacson swayed.

"All of it, Eamon. I want it all." She sighed. "Tell me a good story before I die."

"All of it. Right." He took a breath. "I planned to kill you. I was going to do it. But ... I changed my mind. I'd discredit you first and force you to resign. I arranged a little surprise with Ambassador Volodin—something that would scare the public into thinking you'd betrayed us all with the military cuts."

It felt therapeutic in a way. He in his cell, next to her cell. Like a confessional box from older times. But with bars. And a deposed president instead of a priest.

"A ... surprise?"

What the hell was he doing? Oh well. No turning back now. And if there was a god, if there was anything after he closed his eyes one final time, at least he could check off this box. Insurance.

"The Russians have been in contact with the Swarm for a decade. Volodin claimed they figured out not only how to communicate with them, but to control them. Claimed they made them hollow out an entire asteroid for them and some other shit. So, he was going to arrange a minor Swarm incursion for me. Target a few decrepit old Jupiter System bases. Send a shock to the voters, making them realize what a huge mistake it had been to vote you in and allow you to neuter the military. There would be a recall election. And I would be there in the middle of things and denounce you. Force you to resign."

She sighed. "But the Swarm didn't stop, did they?"

He shook his head. "Volodin swore they could control the Swarm, but it appears he was ... mistaken."

"So that's why they were early. Why their cycle was broken...." She trailed off. "How did the Swarm penetrate so far before they were stopped? Our ships were nearly powerless against them. If it weren't for the *Constitution*—for Granger...."

"I gave Volodin the smart-steel modulation frequencies."

"Ah."

He paused again. "Sorry. It was selfish of me, Barb. I know."

"It was," she said matter-of-factly. He heard her stand up. She'd been sitting on the ground the entire time, apparently. "And I forgive you, Eamon."

"You do?"

"Of course! We all make mistakes. Who knows? I may have done something similar in your place. But that's neither here nor there. Go on. What else?"

He sighed. "When *that* all went down, I got scared. I pulled back. I stopped talking to the faction that wanted you out. Senator Quimby. Speaker LaPierre. Congresswoman Sparks. All of them."

"Holy shit, man, how many were there?"

He shrugged. "Oh, ten or so. Senator Smith was sympathetic to us. Senator Daly reviled you and wanted to pull the trigger herself. Senator Patel wanted you dead, but not if I was taking your place—it was a complicated mess at times. I'm glad I pulled back from them. Disgusting people if you ask me."

The shaking had died down somewhat, but a sudden violent lurch nearly threw Isaacson off the hard bed. His stomach rose up into his throat and he started breathing heavily again. How any IDF soldier could stomach a space battle was beyond him. How long could Norton's ship last against the battle raging outside?

"Tell me more, Eamon. That will keep your mind off of it. That was a pretty big one—Swarm will probably finish us off pretty soon anyway. Let's both go out with clean consciouses."

His hands shaking, his head reeling from the blood pressure, he tried to find words. Dammit, when it came down to it he was as bad as Conner on an airplane. "I ... I ... I had sex with your secretary once."

She made another dismissive noise. "Oh, I new about *that*. I very nearly came in and joined the two of you. Next? Tell me more about Volodin. Have you spoken with Malakhov?"

The rumbling intensified and he searched for words. "Never talked with him. All my back and forth with the Russians was through Volodin. We got pretty close." He paused, thinking. "You know, Barb, I think it's the other way around. The Russians don't control the Swarm. The Swarm controls the Russians. Volodin told me something very interesting. He said when they first met the Swarm in person, they required the Russians send several officers into their ship. A handful of them were ... consumed, I think the word was. But the rest—well, he said they came out ... *changed*."

"What do you mean, *changed*?"

"He said they came out smarter. Better. Their minds were ... faster, he said. It was like they could talk to one another over distances. He mentioned these men had risen through the ranks pretty quickly since then. For all I know they could be colonels by now, or commanders or whatever ranks the bastards use. I don't know about you, but to me that sounds like the Swarm can influence a person. I mean, they are liquid—Volodin confirmed that for me. They're a liquid-based life form. They apparently can enter a person and ... who knows what they do.

And now that I think about it, all their ships from seventy-five years ago were set up inside as if they were built for ... well, bipedal people like us. Organisms with hands and feet. There were handles on the doors. Chairs. The works. Their ships would only require features like that if they occasionally had humanoid crews, right?"

Silence. "Makes sense," she said, after a moment. "Is that all he said?"

A massive explosion ripped through the hallway outside, and Isaacson yelped. He slid off the bed, turned it over, and shoved it between him and the bars of the cell, half-expecting another fireball to erupt through the brig's door and consume them both.

"Eamon, focus. Listen to my voice. We're not dead yet. Focus. We'll get out of this. You're strong. I'm strong. Pull yourself together."

Her steady, confident voice soothed his nerves a bit, even as the thrashing and shaking intensified further. Good god, how much more could the ship take before it ripped apart?

"Keep going, Eamon. Is that all he said? What else did Volodin tell you about the Swarm?"

"He ... I ... he ... I—I can't remember. Sorry, Barb. I just can't focus on—"

Another explosion ripped through the hallway outside. The bright white light of the blast shone through the tiny space under the door.

"Wait," he said. "I remember one more thing."

CHAPTER SEVENTY-THREE

Volari Three, Volari System
Bridge, ISS Warrior

"TOTAL OF ONE HUNDRED and twelve Swarm carriers, sir," said Diamond.

Granger swatted the commlink to Admiral Zingano. "Bill, what do you think?"

"They knew we were coming. And they must have infiltrated the anti-matter supply chain somehow. We've been had, Tim. They may very well have been intentionally steering you to this planet right at this time."

Dammit. Zingano was right. He'd been compromised—he'd been *Swarm*. What in the world had made him think this was prudent?

He watched the viewscreen. The camera had shifted to the incoming fleets. They approached from all directions—a dozen carriers from about ten different vectors. Yeah, they definitely knew Granger was coming.

"Sorry, Admiral. Looks like Norton was right."

"Tim," said Zingano, "this is over two-thirds of our fleet. We've got to get out of here. If we lose here, we lose the war."

It was two thirds of the fleet, yes. But it was also a huge chunk of the Swarm's forces. They'd never have a chance like this again, especially on offense. "Bill, we've got to stay. This is exactly what we wanted, besides the flub with the anti-matter. We've got them here, away from our territory. We won't have to be defending a planet and a civilian population while we fight. This is the best chance we'll have in awhile to hit them and hit them hard."

"I don't know, Tim...."

Granger pounded the console. "Dammit, Bill, you asked me to come back to IDF and I did. You asked me to lead the fleets and I did. You asked me to repel invasion after invasion, and I did. I did it all. Gladly. You called me back into command after my experience with the Swarm because you thought I had some brilliant insight into Swarm behavior or innovative tactics or could be the hero you could hold up to inspire the men. Whatever. It's all bullshit. I survived because I fought to survive. I clawed my way to victory three months ago. Me and the Old Bird. And now here we are. The odds are against us. But if we win, we're one step closer to winning for good. Let's claw our way to victory. One more time."

Silence over the comm.

"Sir, two minutes before the nearest Swarm vessels arrive," said Diamond.

Zingano swore. "All right, Tim. Let's give 'em hell. I'll lead Task Force Granger One. Admiral Tabor can take Task Force Granger Two. You take Three. I'll tell the missile frigates to get the hell out of here—they're sitting ducks."

Granger eyed his tactical readout. Eight hundred missile frigates still orbited the planet below, though they were rapidly pulling up to join the rest of the fleet. Each had around forty officers and crew aboard—just enough to run a medium-sized ship and launch its bombs and missiles.

"No. Keep them here."

"Tim? They're useless. Just another target to defend."

"Exactly. Another target for the Swarm to focus on while we pound them. Plus," he watched the screen as several of the closer Swarm carriers started disgorging hundreds of fighters. "Bill, we need to clog up their fighter bays. These frigates would be perfect for that."

The brick-layer. He could tell Zingano hated the idea by the sound of his voice, but to his credit he only hesitated a moment. "Fine. I'll send the orders to them. You focus on mobilizing your task force. Provide cover for the frigates on their approach. Zingano out."

The comm fell silent, and he bolted to his feet, nodding toward Diaz.

"All hands, prepare for engagement. Mag rail and laser crews stand ready. Arm nukes. Redirect all auxiliary power to laser cap banks." Diaz unleashed into a flurry of orders to the bridge crew while Granger opened up the comm link to the fighter bay.

"Commander Pierce. Launch all fighters. Patrol for singularities and target their fighters and weapons installations at will."

"Aye, aye, sir," came the reply over the speaker.

He turned back to the screen. His task force had reassembled, and they were almost in range of the nearest cluster of incoming Swarm carriers.

But there was something else. Before his eyes saw them, he felt them. The deckplate started quivering slightly, and he recognized the tremor of the imbalance of the spinning engines cause by the gravitational distortion of artificial singularities.

"Detecting twenty-one singularities in this cluster, sir."

Damn. Commander Pierce had his work cut out for him.

CHAPTER SEVENTY-FOUR

Volari Three, Volari System
High Orbit

SPACECHAMP'S FIGHTER WAS spinning out of control, and Ballsy knew he had just moments to pick off every single one of the four enemy fighters tailing her before they finished her off.

"Punch your starboard thruster to max!" She was spinning counterclockwise—what he was telling her to do would make her spin faster and more chaotically and might even make her pass out. But it was her only hope to evade being hit before he could knock out the four bogeys. He pressed the trigger. Make that three bogeys.

"Got it," she said, her speech slurred a bit as her spinning accelerated and she began looping in wild, random patterns. The g forces would knock her out any moment, but it was all he needed. He could order her fighter to right itself remotely. With three more quick bursts he dispatched the remaining fighters who had begun to swarm over her, trying to lock her down.

When it was over he saw her fighter begin to slow down and right itself. "Thanks, Ballsy. I owe you one."

"Four," he corrected. "But that pays you back for last week—we're even now."

The comm set lit up, interrupting their chatter. "All squads, interdict and terminate singularities. Reading twenty-one contacts. We've got our work cut out for us today, people. *Warrior* squadrons will handle singularities at twenty-one mark four, eighteen mark six, and fifteen mark twenty."

Ballsy nodded. "Let's go, Untouchables. We've got a singularity with our name on it. Fodder, you'll deliver the package. Pew Pew, you're up next if he gets a null impact. Move."

He veered away from the Swarm carrier they were flying near, and angled toward the nearest singularity along with two other squads. Each would attempt to deliver an osmium brick simultaneously—as a redundancy, since the likelihood of a single fighter's brick connecting with the singularity were less than fifty fifty. Though so far, the fighters from the *Warrior* had only had two slip through the cracks over the past few months.

"Spacechamp, you good?" He saw her craft struggle to maintain a straight course.

"Yeah, just working out the new calibrations on these thrusters—got hit pretty hard back there."

Red flashing lit up his cabin as enemy bogeys came up from below, but he saw them just in time. Looping up, around, and down, he caught two in his strafing fire, and grinned as he saw Pew Pew pummel his way through three more.

They veered back onto their course, with Fodder still at point and Spacechamp tailing. Less than a kilometer to go—just a few seconds.

"Releasing package," said Fodder. His brick shot away as he pulled up and veered right.

Out of nowhere a Swarm fighter slammed into the brick. The bogey exploded into a million pieces, barely scratching the brick, but the momentum transfer was enough to push it just out of the way of the singularity. Ballsy, with a groan, watched it sail past and clear.

He sighed and shook his head. "All right, Pew Pew, you're up."

CHAPTER SEVENTY-FIVE

ISS Lincoln
Brig

THE SHAKING OF THE CELL intensified—soon, Isaacson's teeth were chattering, though he wasn't sure if it was from the shaking or from fear of imminent death.

"Volodin told me ... he told me the singularities are not a Swarm technology."

"They're not?"

"No," he whispered. "That's one of the Swarm's strengths. They force an exchange of technology with their new allies, he said. They gave the Russians better gravity field emitters, and in exchange, they gave quantum field technology to the Swarm. Somehow the Russians use them in their fusion cores to get better yield, but it looks like they've weaponized it with help from the Swarm. The singularities ... they're not Swarm. They're Russian."

From the other cell he heard Avery whisper a profanity. Then, she spoke. Her voice had changed. She didn't sound vulnerable anymore.

She sounded angry.

"That will be all, General."

And, as if at the touch of a button, the shaking stopped. He heard a clang from nearby, and realized the other cell had opened.

Footsteps.

Avery appeared in front of the bars of his cell. A frown tugged at the corners of her mouth and her eyes were taut with a piercing glare.

She was holding a gun. Pointed straight at his head.

CHAPTER SEVENTY-SIX

Volari Three, Volari System
Bridge, ISS Warrior

THE *WARRIOR* SHIVERED as devastating green beams ripped into her hull. A cloud of Swarm fighters enveloped her, nearly blocking out the view of the rest of the battle, which stretched out into the distance in every direction. Vast capital ships pounded each other while nimble fighters dodged and danced. Weapons fire of every kind blazed like a million crazed fireflies. Debris erupted from exploding ships and showered the vessels around them with their detritus: dead ship and dead men.

"Focus covering fire on the carrier at twelve mark two," Granger called to tactical. "As soon as the *Willow* makes its omega run, shift fire to escort the *Aspen* into its target at twenty-eight mark five."

Granger had seen over a dozen battles in the nearly three months since the invasion.

But none like this. The sheer scale was something that, if he'd been watching it on a theatre screen from the comfort of his retirement home in the Florida panhandle knowing it was a fiction drama, would have delighted him. Broken ships started blazing through the upper atmosphere, creating stunning, glowing tails like comets.

But this was not beautiful. This was death. All around him.

He glanced at the tactical readout. Thankfully, it was also death for the Swarm. They were taking a pounding as well, paying a heavy price for the ambush. Perhaps they hadn't planned on so many IDF ships showing up. Either way, he was encouraged as he saw the count of active Swarm carriers tick down. Fifteen destroyed, five more disabled. And they'd only lost a tenth of their own fleet so far.

"The *Aspen* has destroyed the fighter bay of that carrier, sir. Redirecting fire to the other carrier."

Granger nodded. He watched a shimmering singularity wink out as one of the osmium bricks hurled by a fighter connected with it. *Where in the world are those things going?* he wondered. If *he* came out on the other side of his journey above this very planet, where were all those things coming out?

Before he had a chance to wonder more, one of the larger singularities disappeared, and an instant later the *Palisades*, a heavy cruiser nearby, seemed to contract as if something were sucking it inward, then explode in a dazzlingly white blast. The shock wave hit the *Warrior* and the entire bridge lurched to starboard.

"Pierce!" He hit the comm with his fist. "We need fighter support on those singularities! We just lost the *Palisades* because of one!"

"Sorry, Captain. There's too many of them. I had two squads assigned to the one that blew, but the Swarm fighters managed to catch them in a crossfire. Besides that, we're running out of bricks, sir. Down to just twenty fighters with packages intact."

"Keep at it, Mr. Pierce. If it comes down to it—if we run out of bricks—send fighters in. Granger out."

Damn. They came up with the osmium brick strategy to avoid having to expend the lives of fighters on suicide runs. But if they ran out of bricks ... well, sacrifices must be made. He remembered the very first fighter he'd ordered into a singularity. What was her name? Miller. Jessica Miller. How many more Millers would be required before the end?

He glanced at the tactical readout again. In spite of the loss of the *Palisades* and two dozen or so other cruisers, it was not a rout. In fact, if things continued the way they were, they'd not only win, but with up to half of their force still intact.

Some flickers on the viewscreen caught his eye. More ships.

"Captain—"

Before the sensor officer even said anything, Granger knew. He recognized that design. He'd spent ten years dreaming of the chance to smash a few dozen of them to pieces. And here they were, just like seventy-five years ago, coming right at the tail end of the fight. Right before total victory. Enough time for them to throw in a few token ships and claim they'd helped.

"—Russian ships, sir."

He shook his head. The gall of those people. "How many?"

"Nearly three hundred, sir. Mostly heavy cruisers. A few super carriers."

"Fine. Let's see what kind of punch these bastards have. Send a message to their flagship with instructions to form up with—"

The sentence hung on his lips. On the screen, he saw something unthinkable. His hopes shattered.

Several Russian ships in the advance guard opened fire on the *Nottingham*, a heavy cruiser in Granger's task force. Captain Barnes's ship. More advancing Russian ships joined in. Within ten seconds, the *Nottingham* broke in half, spewing wreckage into space as the newcomers blazed past and bore down on the rest of his task force.

CHAPTER SEVENTY-SEVEN

Volari Three, Volari System
High Orbit

VOLZ WATCHED IN DISMAY as the singularity disappeared, reappearing seconds later, he supposed, at the center of the heavy cruiser nearby, the *Palisades*. It contracted for a moment before exploding in a dazzling blast. He veered away at the last second: even so, the debris from the blast showered his fighter, causing alarms to go off as several small holes ripped open in his hull.

"Sorry, Ballsy. I ... I couldn't shake these fighters...."

Pew Pew's voice was solemn. He'd tried to launch his osmium brick, but a throng of enemy craft had enveloped him—far too many for Ballsy and Spacechamp to knock loose. His voice sounded as if he was blaming himself for the deaths of the thousand souls on the *Palisades*.

"Not your fault, buddy. Come on, we've got one more singularity to plug."

His three squadmates collected into a tight diamond formation as they soared toward the remaining minia-ture black hole, shimmering as the surrounding rarified molecules, dust, and debris swirled in a tight vortex, cast-

331

ing off intense x-rays, ultraviolet rays, and of course, blinding white light. He blinked, and shadows from the light's memory seemed etched into his retinas. He wanted to believe Captain Granger, that this was it. This could very well be the final time he'd have to face down one of these monstrosities.

The singularities were almost an affront against nature. A place where reality broke down, space compressed to something smaller than a point, time seemed hopelessly at its mercy, and on the other end....

Something. There was something on the other side to come back from, and it wasn't just death.

"Ballsy, too fast, man!" Fodder's voice blared in his ear, and he realized he'd pushed on the accelerator full-bore, blazing straight toward the singularity.

Fly faster, Ballsy.

He shook his head and eased back on the controls. "Sorry, got carried away. Fodder, Spacechamp, and I will handle those fighters coming toward us. Pew Pew, deliver the package when you see an opening. Looks like Roadrunner squad is attempting the same thing—let's see if we can't catch the bastards in a crossfire. Move!"

In a well-rehearsed maneuver, Volz—who'd been flying point—Fodder, and Spacechamp peeled off hard in three different directions as Pew Pew maintained his course. They wheeled around, blasting at the stray bogeys, picking off the ones that tried to take aim at Pew Pew and his osmium brick.

He was closing. Less than a kilometer. Time seemed to compress as Volz watched his friend streak toward it, weaving in and out of intercepting fighters, avoiding the explosions of others as Spacechamp and Fodder caught them in their sights.

And the brick was away.

"Woohoo! Yeah, man, I—" Pew Pew started celebrating into his headset.

But he was premature. With a sickening lurch, the osmium brick banked out of the path of the singularity as a Swarm fighter slammed into it. A second fighter collided with Pew Pew's craft, and he spun out of control, out of sight. On Volz's scope, he lost contact with his squadmate's fighter, the other pilot's electronics fried and dead.

Fodder screamed into the comm. Spacechamp swore.

In the commotion, Volz thought he heard Commander Pierce's voice. Something about omega runs. Ram the singularity. He heard the CAG order Fodder in.

Fly faster, Ballsy.

"Well boys," Fodder began, clearing his throat. "If death's good enough for my brother, it's good enough for me. Take care, friends, and remember—" he punched his maneuvering thrusters and veered away as he finished, "—don't fly like—"

And in another sickening collision, his fighter lurched as a Swarm craft rammed him, sending him tumbling away end over end, soon disappearing out of sight in the dim blue glare of the terminator line of the atmosphere below.

Both brothers gone, within moments of each other.

And the singularity grew larger.

CHAPTER SEVENTY-EIGHT

The Waypoint, Near Sirius
Brig, ISS Lincoln

"LAST QUESTION, EAMON," she began with a heavy sigh. The gun was still aimed straight at his forehead, just a foot away. He slowly raised his hands, though he couldn't fathom why—it was obvious he had no way to fight back, no way to stop the inevitable. He saw the look in her eyes. She hated him. Loathed him. That much was clear.

"You won't kill me."

"I will. There's nothing that can stop that now. I either kill you now, or...." She cocked the gun. "Or, I let you live for a few more years and make you my bitch." She chuckled softly. "You chose the wrong president to cross, Eamon. I've littered the political landscape with bastards like you. People who put their own interests, their own profit, their own hormones ahead of the good of our society."

He clucked his tongue. "Oh, please. You do the same. We all do it, Barb, don't—"

She pulled the trigger. The cell exploded with a loud percussive shock wave from the blast and his hands instinctively went up to cover his face. When he opened his eyes moments later, he saw her still standing there, gun still pointed at his head. He turned and saw a hole gouged out of the wall behind him where the bullet had ricocheted.

"Don't call me Barb, Mr. Vice President. Now listen closely. You have a choice to make. Either I own you for the next three years—you do exactly what I tell you, when I tell you, how I tell you, for how long I tell you and with the attitude I tell you, serving at my whim, beck, and call at every minute and second of the day, every day—or this bullet goes into your brain and I can notch a small win for humanity by relieving it of your continued miserable existence."

His jaw moved but no words came out. He could barely hear her—the ringing from the gun still overpowered his ears.

"Say it again, Eamon."

"I ... I will."

"Good." She lowered the gun. "And understand this. I'm putting this gun back into my handbag. But it is still aimed at your face. One wrong step, one wrong *anything*, and I fire. I've got a confession out of you that will make the entire human race scream out for the reinstatement of not only the death penalty, but immolation, water boarding, castration, the rack, disembowelment, and every other ghoulish practice our society has outlawed over the years. It'll all come back, just for a brief moment— just for you—if you step out of line."

The door opened behind her. Men and women in white lab coats stepped forward.

"Put your arms through the bars, Mr. Vice President," she said.

Numbly, without a word, he obeyed. One of the men clamped a sort of restraining device over both arms and attached them to the bars so that they stayed motionless no matter how hard he struggled.

"Don't fight it, you'll only make it hurt more."

His eyes grew wide as one of the attendants stepped forward with what looked like an ultra-high-tech gun of sorts. She held the tip up to a spot on his forearm and pulled the trigger.

He screamed. White hot pain shot up his arm like molten metal. "What the hell are you doing!"

She paced the outside of the cell. "Insurance, Mr. Vice President. I'm tracking your every move, I'm listening to your every word, and I'm reading your every emotion. You sneeze, and I know it. You lie, and I know it. You get laid, I know it. And if you do any of those things without me telling you to, the device in your arm will release a toxin at a word from me and you die instantly." She paused, glancing sidelong at a technician. "Or was it terrible, mind blowing pain? I can't remember, can you?"

The tech chuckled, and then pressed the gun up to half a dozen more spots on his arms—each causing him to shriek in pain—before reaching the device through the bars and onto his torso. The gun fired at least twenty more times—he lost count at ten—each one stinging like the world's largest and most violent hornet had burrowed into his skin and started eating him from the inside.

Finally, the tech stepped away. "There," said Avery, pleased. "That's ... what, thirty? They all do the same thing, but I thought thirty would be a nice failsafe if you suddenly tried to take one out. They're made out of silver, you know, Eamon? Thirty pieces of silver shoved up your ass as a testament to your treason. The human race nearly died because of you. And now, through you, I'm going to save it."

She motioned to the guard who had escorted the techs in. With the press of a button, Isaacson's cell door clicked open, and the restraints attaching his arms to the bars fell away to the floor with a clatter.

"Follow me, Eamon. We've got work to do."

CHAPTER SEVENTY-NINE

Volari Three, Volari System
Bridge, ISS Warrior

"ALL SHIPS, FALL BACK! Form a perimeter. Task Force Granger Three, cover the Granger One ships—they're getting slaughtered." He glanced at the tactical readout and watched in horror as the new arrivals tore through the task force led by Admiral Zingano. One ship blew, then another. Three light cruisers got caught in between the advancing Russian ships and a handful of Swarm carriers and were cut to pieces within fifteen seconds.

The *Warrior* shuddered as more anti-matter beams struck the hull and red lights started flashing all over the ship schematic at his console, indicating numerous breaches. He heard the XO shout orders over the din on the bridge, sending emergency response crews to the damaged areas of the ship.

His console beeped with an incoming call from Zingano and he mashed the comm link button with a clenched fist.

"Looking pretty grim here, Tim," said the admiral.

"We'll hold. We had the advantage before the traitor bastards showed up. We'll still prevail, Bill, and now we'll take the Russians down a few notches too."

"Tim," began Zingano. Granger could hear the hesitation in his voice. "We're outnumbered. This is suicide."

Suicide. How appropriate, after all the suicide runs he'd ordered against the Swarm, he was leading up the last, final fleet on a final suicide mission himself. But it felt right. Somewhere, deep inside, it felt like the right thing to do. Something whispered in his ear that this place, this world, was *still* the place to be.

"Yes, Bill. It may be suicide. But it's necessary. Think about it—when will we ever get this chance again? It's clear from the Swarm's response that *this is* their home-world. Why else would they force their allies out into the open like this? It was far more beneficial to them to keep their relationship with the Russians secret and ambiguous. It was throwing us off balance. But now we've forced their hand. We took the initiative and surprised them, and now *they're* off balance. They've called in their allies to defend their planet. The only explanation is that if they lose this, they lose everything. There's something about this place, Bill. Something about this place that has made them willing to put all their chips down. We need to win this fight, then raze the surface. It's our only option."

His logic was convincing, he knew. But asking the admiral to potentially sacrifice all their lives on a last ditch effort at wiping out the Swarm might be too much.

But to his credit, the other man swore, and laughed. "Tim, you old bastard. Fine. Let's turn this around. All hands, all ships," Zingano raised his voice, keying the commlink into the entire fleet, "people, this might look like a setback, but they're only fighting harder now because their backs are against the wall. We've got Granger with us. We've got *The Hero of Earth*. We've got half the entire fleet of United Earth and all its member worlds. And our cause is just. We will prevail. Zingano out."

"Sir," began Lieutenant Diaz, "these Russian ships are cutting through the smart-steel armor at an alarming rate. Nothing like the Swarm three months ago, I mean, they clearly haven't cracked our quantum field modulation frequencies or anything, but—"

Granger approached the tactical station. "But what?"

One of the other tactical crew members jumped in. "But the Russians are using some type of ... well, it looks like a positron-based particle beam."

"Anti-matter?" Granger shook his head. Looks like Avery wasn't the only one engaging in anti-matter research over the last few years.

"Positrons technically *are* anti-matter, sir, but there are no anti-protons or anti-neutrons present. Not like the Swarm's anti-boron beam. Just a whole bunch of free positrons in a bath of high energy photons." The tech looked up. "Basically a really big laser, but with anti-electrons along for the ride, and they're having a field day with the quantum modulations of the smart-steel armor."

Granger grunted. "Anything our ships can do to counteract it?"

The tech shook his head. "No, sir. No amount of re-modulation could fix this. It seems that free positrons fundamentally disrupt the quantum field of the smart-steel, no matter what its modulation."

Damn. The Russians had been playing them for years, supposedly contributing to smart-steel research, all while developing a back-door weapon to defeat it in case they ever found themselves on the opposite side of a conflict.

"Fine. The *Constitution* to the rescue. Again." Several bridge crew members glanced up at him, confused. "I mean, the *Warrior.*"

Damn. He missed the Old Bird. "You know, we've never given our temporary home a nickname."

Lieutenant Diaz looked up. "Old Wolfram."

Granger paused. "After the governor of New Dublin?" he said, confused.

"No, sir. The original *Constitution* was nicknamed *Old Ironsides* because the iron cannonballs just bounced right off the hull. Our hull is ten meters of tungsten. The old name for tungsten is Wolfram. So therefore—"

"Got it. That'll do." He turned to Ensign Prince. "Turn Old Wolfram about, Ensign. Looks like we get to be the battering ram again." Cocking his head toward the comm he continued, "Strike Force Granger One and Granger Two, stick with the Swarm. Strike Force Granger Three, back up the *Warrior.* We're going to go hand the Russian's asses to them. Follow us in—we'll take out as many of their positron beams as we can, then you clean up."

Finally. After two months of ordering other ships and men and women to their deaths, he was about to do the same to himself. Turn the *Warrior* into another brick. He watched on the screen as the dozens of Russian cruisers grew larger on the screen as the *Warrior* approached, and soon, they were upon them. Granger punched the internal comm. "Hang on, everybody. It's about to get choppy."

CHAPTER EIGHTY

Volari Three, Volari System
High Orbit

"SPACECHAMP, YOU'RE UP!" The CAG's voice sounded grim, and reluctant. As if he were doing a detestable duty. He was, Volz knew. How anyone could order someone to sacrifice their life was beyond him. He knew he'd never be a CAG, or a captain, or an XO, or anyone who could have that burden thrust upon them. Ever.

He heard a confident voice pipe back, "Aye, aye, sir! One Spacechamp brick coming right up!"

She sounded so full of life. So lively. Like death was nothing to her. Like she'd already accepted her fate long ago, not resigned to death, but treating it like flying to see an old friend, or announcing she was going on a hot date.

Fly faster, Ballsy.

He couldn't let her. Not another one. Not on his watch. He'd lost Hotbox, Dogtown, Fodder, Pew Pew, and of course, *her.* Fishtail. He wasn't going to lose another one.

"Stand down, Fishtail, I'm going in," he said. He pushed hard on the accelerator.

"Sir...?" He could hear the confusion in Spacechamp's voice, and he immediately realized what he'd said.

"I said, stand down, Spacechamp. This one's mine." He pushed the accelerator to maximum. *Fly faster, Ballsy.* "You get to stick around and clean up the mess. So long, Spacechamp."

He streaked toward it, weaving through a squad of Swarm fighters that seemed intent on ramming anything that came within a kilometer of the singularity.

But he was too fast for them. Liberated of his desire for life, he felt alive. Nothing could touch him. Nothing. He veered toward the light, toward oblivion, toward his fate. And on the other side?

Death.

Fly faster, Ballsy.

He plunged in, and all went white.

CHAPTER EIGHTY–ONE

Volari Three, Volari System
Bridge, ISS Warrior

DOZENS OF RUSSIAN positron beams ravaged the *Warrior*'s hull, but she held. "Target all positron beam installations. All fighters, this is *Warrior* Actual. Target all positron beam positions. Ignore the fighters."

They plunged into the Russian position, and the *Warrior* shook with the impact of nearly a hundred beams. Fortunately, the ten meters of tungsten held up to the energy of the positrons. Though the petawatts of laser energy was another thing entirely. Soon, the hull was pockmarked with deep holes carved out by the Russian beams.

But the *Warrior* held her course. "Redirect starboard fire toward Russian ship at five mark one," said Granger, seeing the previous cruiser's defenses had been neutralized. He grinned as he saw the *Eddington* and the *Philadelphia* swoop in and pummel the prone Russian ship with mag rail fire, and within ten seconds the vessel was spouting debris and fire as the internal atmosphere ignited and streamed out into space, carrying the smoldering bodies of dozens of crewmen. Poor kids—suffering for the poor choices of their leaders.

Minutes passed. Gut-wrenching, heart-pounding minutes, but minutes that saw them carve up a dozen ships and pass them off to the task force. Granger surveyed the rest of the battle. Task forces One and Two were holding up against the Swarm. Barely. It was going to be a tight battle.

But they were going to make it. Maybe—if their luck held.

"Russian fleet down to sixty percent of their force, sir," said Diaz.

"Good. Swing around to twenty mark five and target those ships over—"

More flickering on the screen, announcing something that was starting to get on Granger's nerves. More ships.

"Sir! Nearly a hundred more sensor contacts!"

He put his head in his hands. "Please tell me it's the rest of IDF."

"Sorry, sir." The sensor officer turned to him with a pained look. "It's the Dolmasi."

CHAPTER EIGHTY_TWO

Volari Three, Volari System
Bridge, ISS Warrior

GRANGER HAD WONDERED when those bastards were going to show up. In fact, by his reckoning, they were late. He scanned the tactical readout and was surprised—whereas before they'd only come to the Swarm's rescue with a dozen ships or so, this time they'd arrived in force. Over a hundred ships. Each nearly as deadly as a Swarm carrier.

It was over.

The comm crackled to life. He heard Zingano yelling out of it, explosions and shouting in the background. It was chaos aboard the *Victory*. "Granger! We're out of here! All ships, full retreat. Emergency q-jumps. Get back to the staging area at Britannia."

Granger watched the tactical display. The Dolmasi ships swooped in and flanked the Swarm carriers, providing a formidable backdrop to an already formidable enemy.

They weren't firing yet.

"Standby, Admiral," he said, waving over to the comm.

"Standby? Tim, this thing is over. Dead. Tits up."

"Understood, Bill. Just give me one minute." He turned to the comm station. "Put me on with the Dolmasi flagship."

They still weren't firing. They were just hovering there, behind the Swarm carriers.

"You're on, sir. Dolmasi flagship on visual."

Granger turned to the screen, even as the ship lurched to starboard under the assault of a few Swarm carriers that had come to assist the Russian fleet from the *Warrior*'s assault. A familiar sight greeted him.

"Vishgane Kharsa. Hello again. I advise you to keep your distance, or you will suffer the same fate as the Swarm and Russian—"

Loud, choking laughter greeted him. "Captain Granger! You've been a good friend. A powerful ally. You will be rewarded."

Granger's heart sunk. His stomach turned to ice. Was it true? Had he unwittingly been led by the Swarm into this situation? He'd been a tool the entire time. The Swarm's method of summoning nearly the entire IDF fleet here, to their homeworld, to the seat of their power.

Where the combined might of the Swarm, and the Concordat of Seven could more easily destroy them. With their five other alien "friends." *Where were the others anyway?*

Zingano's voice hollered in the background. "Granger, what the hell is he talking about?"

It was time to tell the admiral how foolish he'd been. How he'd known for over a week now that he'd once been under Swarm control, and—most likely—still was.

But first, one last ditch attempt to scare off the Dolmasi.

"I'm warning you, Kharsa. Get the hell out or I'll—"

"No need, my good friend. You've done enough already. Stand back and witness the fruit of your many labors."

The screen blanked out, replaced by a view of the battle, which had once again begun to turn south—the appearance of the new threat had sapped the hope from the entire IDF fleet. Here and there, a cruiser winked out as it q-jumped to safety.

The Dolmasi started firing.

Granger blinked. He couldn't understand what he was seeing.

"Diaz, am I seeing this right?"

Diaz nodded slowly. "Confirmed, sir. Sensors show the Dolmasi are, indeed, firing on the Swarm carriers." He looked up at the screen as one of the massive carriers exploded. "With remarkable effect."

It was a dream. It couldn't be possible. But the viewscreen didn't lie and the sensors confirmed it: the Dolmasi, flanking the Swarm carriers from behind, were cutting their way through the enemy fleet, ripping the Swarm to shreds. Carrier after carrier broke into pieces, exploded, and careened through the atmosphere.

The battle was turning. Decisively.

Over the comm he heard Zingano yelling orders to the rest of the fleet to reengage, and Granger shouted his own orders to his strike force. "Hammer and anvil, people. Tag team with our new friends. *Eddington*, *Philadelphia*, and *Arizona*, take your light cruisers and assist at thirty mark ten. *Oregon*, *Wales*, and *Paris* focus on that Russian wing where the Dolmasi are already hitting them!"

On the screen, the field of battle was still a fireworks display, but this time, instead of IDF ships falling back and shattering under the withering fire from the enemy, it was the Swarm and Russian ships receiving the brutal lashing. The Dolmasi, apparently, were a force to be reckoned with, especially when they showed up in such vast numbers. The Russian fleet wilted before them. The Swarm carriers lurched and veered out of the way, caught in the crossfire between the new arrivals and IDF, which had redoubled its fire.

And soon, the battle was won. The Russians—what was left of them anyway—began q-jumping away. The Swarm carriers had dwindled down to no more than a dozen, and they soon found themselves surrounded by both IDF and Dolmasi cruisers. Within another five minutes they were vaporized.

It was over.

Against all odds, in spite of bad turn after bad turn, from hopeless and final defeat came the unseen victory.

But how? Why? Granger wasn't one to look the gift horse in the mouth, but they needed to know if they weren't next. That the Dolmasi, having turned on their masters, wouldn't now turn on their new *friends*. "Hail Vishgane Kharsa's ship."

Prucha nodded. "Onscreen, sir."

The alien's triumphant face flashed onto the wall. "Captain Timothy Granger. Congratulations on your victory. It was well earned."

Granger bowed his head slightly. "And congratulations to you, Vishgane. You've apparently thrown off your overlords. Well done."

Kharsa choked out another laugh. "So we have. And more than you know."

On the other half of the screen, the rest of the battle was being mopped up as the fleet targeted the now homeless and flailing Swarm fighters. The planet still turned serenely below. Their true target. It was time to finish up what they came here for.

"Now, if you'll excuse me, Vishgane, we need to raze the surface. If we destroy this world, the Swarm will surely fall. Without their home they will be crushed."

Kharsa shook his head. "You will do no such thing, Captain."

"Excuse me?" He knew there was a catch. "Vishgane, this is the Swarm's homeworld. If we destroy this, we break their backs. We don't understand everything about Swarm physiology or culture or technology, but I'm sure that if we destroy their home base that—"

"You will do no such thing, Captain Granger, because this is not the homeworld of the Valarisi."

Granger's stomach clenched. "It's not? How do you know?"

Vishgane Kharsa smiled. "It is not. Because it is ours. It is the Dolmasi homeworld. And with your gracious help, we have now liberated it."

CHAPTER EIGHTY-THREE

Volari Three, Volari System
Conference Room One, ISS Warrior

THE SILENCE IN THE conference room was awkward, to say the least. Admiral Zingano, Vishgane Kharsa, and Granger sat alone in the small room off of the *Warrior's* bridge.

"What do you mean, Vishgane, when you say you *encouraged* Captain Granger here to liberate your world?" Zingano turned to Granger, his eyes flashing with anger. "Tim?"

Granger shook his head.

"It is simple, Admiral," began the Vishgane. "The captain was once under the influence of the Valarisi, just like us. But, just like us, he managed to find a way to throw off their influence. Somehow, he regained his freedom. We do not know how. But once an individual has been under the Valarisi's control, their influence never completely goes away. Traces of the Valarisi still course through the captain's blood. Just as it does with us. It is how we deceive them, letting them think they still control us."

Zingano swore. Granger put his head in his hands and repeated the profanity.

"Tim, how long have you known?"

Granger looked up at Zingano. "I've had the dreams, of course. You knew that. But, the Vishgane suggested as much to me the last time we met." Granger glared at the alien. "And the last time we met, you destroyed several of my ships. Thousands of men and women. What do you say about that?"

The Vishgane bowed his head, and held it there. The pose was one of humility. Or was it shame? Granger was still trying to decipher the alien's mannerisms and speech, as they were, well, alien.

"We are truly regretful, gentlemen. It was necessary. At the time the Swarm was watching everything I did. If I didn't ... put on a good show, as you would say, then the charade would be over. They were holding our world hostage, and would surely destroy it if they detected any deception on our part. Billions of my people would have died. The sacrifice of your people will long be sung about among mine."

Zingano pounded the table. "Bullshit. We are not your pawns." He glared at Granger. "And how did you do it, Vishgane? How did you make my friend here do your dirty work?"

"Easy. We have a common bond. We are still part of the same great family, even if our parents no longer control us. You went somewhere, Captain, when your ship fell into that singularity. But it was not here. You did not come to our world. You went somewhere else."

"Where?" Granger felt like a fool, having been played, but he at least could figure out the mystery. What had truly happened to him.

"That much is clear. You went to the Russian's singularity production facility."

Zingano swore again. "The *Russians*?! The singularities are a Swarm weapon!"

"They are. The Russian ships have never been able to generate the amount of energy required to weaponize the singularities. But it is Russian technology, to be sure. They produce them, and the Valarisi deploy them." Kharsa folded his short, scaled fingers on the table in front of him. "And it was to their production facility that you went, of course, when you emerged from the other side. All singularities are made in pairs. And each in a pair acts as a gateway to the other. Like what you would call a wormhole. Under the right circumstances, what enters one will emerge from the other. And you emerged from the other, near death. The Russians found you. They brought you aboard their station. And, at the behest of our former masters, they injected you with Valarium...." Kharsa hesitated. "I believe you would call it ... Swarm matter."

Zingano glared at Granger as the alien continued.

"The Valarium cured you, Captain. It revivifies living tissue. It hunts down viruses and foreign contaminants, for it itself is a virus. The most advanced virus we have ever encountered. And it changes you. Allows you to organically tap into graviton fields—the core of meta-space communication. That is how they communicate, Captain. How they control. And when we touched, when I shook your hand," Kharsa looked down again. "You'll forgive me, Captain, that is when I placed within you the false memory. I saw your memories aboard the Russian station at their production facility, I saw the world you orbited, and I replaced it with an image of *my* world. When you then looked at it, you felt *my* desires. *My* longing for my home."

Granger nodded, understanding. "I felt like it was here. That *this* was the place to be. Where we had to come with the fleet."

"Everything that I felt for my homeworld, you felt for this planet. And so, when you saw it for the first time, you knew you had found it. You took your own memories of your time as a friend of the Valarisi, you tapped into my feelings and determination to take back my own world, you remembered the false memory I placed within you of this world, and the result was something we'd hoped for. We knew this was a great gamble. A risk. But it paid off. You came. In force. And the result is our freedom."

More silence, as the disturbing news started to sink in.

"Wyatt. Hanrahan. The pilots—Martin and Palmer and Dogtown." Granger began. "They were all swarm infected, weren't they?"

Kharsa nodded. "Yes. The doctor two months ago. Hanrahan and the pilots recently. When I shook the colonel's hand right before yours, I looked into his mind and saw the five of them were under the Valarisi's control. So I directed him to kill the pilots. In the scant moments I was holding the colonel's hand and communing with him, I decided the fewer security holes you had to deal with, the better."

"So, the Swarm is defeated then?" asked Granger.

Kharsa looked at, and shook his head. "Regrettably, no. This was less than half their strength. And remember, we were but one of a great family of seven people. Six formidable friends of the Valarisi. Now that we have betrayed them, the full might of the other six allies will be summoned. The Valarisi do not abide treachery."

More silence. "Fortunately, the identity of the seventh ally is now revealed. We had worked out the locations and identities of four of the other allies—the Valarisi prefer to keep us separate so that we do not communicate. But today's battle confirmed it."

It couldn't be. But it made sense, of course. All the signs pointed to it. Granger only nodded as Kharsa finished his thought.

"The seventh ally is humanity."

Zingano snorted. "You mean the Russians. Bastards."

Kharsa nodded. "The Valarisi do not see you as separate factions or people. To them, you are one society. One race. Your political divisions are unimportant to them."

"Then why are they trying to destroy us?" said Granger. "Why the invasion? Why the bloodshed, if they already consider humanity to be their friends, through the Russians?"

"Because, Captain Granger, the Valarisi can not abide division and confusion. In their eyes, they see you as a malignant tumor that must be rooted out. Seventy-five years ago they encountered you, and like every other race they found before, they tried to conquer and convert you. But they started late in their cycle. You put up such a stiff defense that they realized it would take them far more time to convert you than they had planned, so they left, and let you be for a time. They needed to begin the next cycle."

Granger nodded. "Proctor was telling me about this. So they just stopped because their evolutionary cycle was over? Just like that?"

"Just like that," said Kharsa. "It's built into their genetic code, Captain. They're hard wired to return home and commence the next cycle when the current one elapses. But this time, they were interrupted. Your people—the Russians, as you call them—found the Valarisi. Communicated with them. Traded technology with them. Gave the Valarisi a weapon that was so devastating it changed the entire calculus of their cycle. They decided to accelerate—to commence the expansion phase of their cycle far earlier than usual."

Granger shook his head. "And that's when they invaded Earth again. Right where they left off." He paused. "But where do I come into all this? How do you know me so well? The first time I encountered your ships you seemed to know me and my ship as well as I do. And your command of our language and your knowledge of—"

Kharsa held up a hand. "That is because we have met before, Captain. For you it was nearly three months ago. For me ... it was five."

The realization began to dawn on him. "What are you saying?"

"Five months ago, I was at the Russian singularity production facility. It was our task to integrate the new technology into the Valarisi's ships. That is also part of their evolution—they have no hands, no feet, no way to physically manipulate the environment around them. There is no need when you have other races to do that for you. So it fell to us to upgrade their ships. We were about halfway done when, to our surprise, the *Constitution* appeared out of nowhere. Streams of air and smoke and debris coming from deep holes in its hull. The Adanasi—or, Russians, humanity—they were instructed to take you. To convert you. To alter your ship and send you back to your world as—" He seemed to struggle with words.

"As a Trojan horse?" Zingano filled in for Kharsa.

The Vishgane smiled. "Precisely. You, aboard the *Constitution*, were to fly back to Earth at that time—two months prior to the planned invasion—and with several dozen singularities of your own, were to destroy your centers of leadership. Your military positions. Then, the

Valarisi would come in behind you, land a thousand carriers, unleash a swarm of Valarium distribution vehicles into your cities and towns, and convert the rest of you. As they've done for tens of thousands of years."

Unbelievable. He was going to be the vehicle of Earth's destruction. In the past. Somehow, one of the singularities transported him to the *past*.

But it didn't work. He'd found a way to defeat them. Even if he couldn't remember how.

"But I didn't do that. I didn't travel to Earth. At least, not in the way they had planned. Earth was saved."

Kharsa nodded. "True. Earth was saved from that first invasion, from the *Constitution* returning with singularities targeting its surface. It was saved. But not by you."

CHAPTER EIGHTY-FOUR

Volari Three, Volari System
Conference Room One, ISS Warrior

IT TOOK GRANGER a moment to understand the Vishgane's meaning. Earth had been saved from a Swarm-controlled Trojan horse: Granger. In the past. By someone else. Before he could ask who it was, the comm beeped.

"Sir, you'll want to see this," said Ensign Prucha from the bridge.

Granger started, grabbing his armrests, before jumping up and dashing toward the door. He motioned to Kharsa to follow, and within moments he, Zingano, and the alien were striding onto the bridge.

"Sir, it just came out."

"What came out? And from what?"

Diaz pointed to the viewscreen. A fighter. From the looks of it, it had recently come through an intense battle. He scanned the markings—it was clearly one of the *Warrior*'s.

"Commander Pierce, all fighters have been aboard for over an hour, right?"

The comm computer relayed his question to the CAG, whose voice soon came over the speaker. "Aye, sir. All surviving fighters are accounted for."

"Then who the hell is *this*?"

Another voice came over the comm.

"Lieutenant Tyler Volz, sir. I ... I flew into a singularity. Just like you. And I'm back. And I brought an old friend. She needs the doc, sir. She's in a bad way."

Granger's knees began to weaken as he stumbled into his chair, overcome. He didn't even need to ask who it was.

Volz continued. "Fishtail is alive, sir. But barely. Her pulse is faint."

Someone he sent to die for him. Someone else he'd used up, used as weapon, as a stone in a sling, as a brick through a window—they were *alive*.

Granger's voice cracked: "Keep her alive son. Medics will meet you in the fighter bay."

CHAPTER EIGHTY-FIVE

Washington D.C., Earth
Vice President's Residence

THE PRESIDENT REARRANGED his secret service security detail, so it was with her own personal agents that Isaacson made his way from the executive spaceport to his residence. The new officers escorted him to the door, shut it behind him, and when he was finally alone he collapsed onto a sofa nearby, rubbing his arms.

That bitch.

They ached. The devices Avery had injected into him didn't go in gently, even though they were most likely tiny—no bigger than a pill. No bigger than his remaining dignity, he supposed with a wince as he felt a sharp twinge near his elbow. He held the arm up and examined the wounds left behind. They pockmarked his skin, an accusing trail that went all the way up to his biceps. Several angry welts screamed out from his chest too.

He'd kill her. He really would this time. No hesitation. No remorse.

Instantly, his head exploded in pain and he cried out.

Moments later, as the pain subsided, he realized his comm card had been beeping. How long? He pulled it out of his pocket and tried to open his eyes—the room was only dimly lit, but the light seared his sight after the unexpected blast of pain in his head.

It was a voice memo. He tapped it to play.

Avery's voice rang out from the card. "You won't kill me, Eamon. You won't because you can't. You're an impotent little slug. Yes—that's right, I know what you think. I know what you feel. I told you—I own you completely now. Every thought. Every feeling. You'd better learn to guard yourself or I'll just have to keep this pain button clicked to maximum. Your life is over, Eamon. I killed you back on the *Lincoln*. You're dead. The only way for you to live again is to do exactly what I tell you, perfectly and willingly, until this war is over and our civilization safe. Then, if you've proved yourself, you'll be reborn. I'll grant you a new life, Eamon. All your own. Without the old battle-ax hovering over, telling you what to do.

"Now, go to bed. Do nothing else. Get some sleep. You're going to need it. In the morning report to the executive mansion for your first assignment."

He sighed. She was right—he was dead. His thoughts were not his own. His feelings were not his own. He was a prisoner in his own body. Worse—he was a slave in his own body. In appearance, one of the most powerful men in the galaxy, but in actuality only an automaton.

He'd kill her.

Dammit! Another short burst of pain reminded him of her constantly monitoring presence.

A sound made him jump off the sofa with a start. Someone was moving in another room.

He crept around the corner, peering into the empty kitchen. He heard it again—it was coming from his bedroom down the hall.

Padding softly across the carpet down the hall, he pushed the door open to his bedroom, only to relax when he saw the source of the sound.

Conner, you brilliant bastard.

He flushed and swelled at the sight. Just like he described her. Beautiful. Young. Exotic. Laying invitingly on his bed, with eyes that said *now*.

His belt came off. He struggled with the clasp on his pants. She raised an inviting finger, motioning him forward. *Oh god, she's amazing.* Like wildfire, a heat rose up from his groin, electrifying his chest to the point he felt almost lightheaded. It had been way too long. Nearly a week.

His head exploded in pain again.

"No!" he said. "No, no, no...."

Maybe it was a fluke. He let his pants drop to the floor.

The pain intensified. Pulsed with a regular, unnatural rhythm.

With a sigh, he sat down on the corner of the bed and pointed to the door.

"Out," he mumbled.

The woman hesitated.

"Leave."

She swore, slid off the bed, and pulled her clothes back on before slipping out the door.

His comm card beeped again, and with a reluctant sigh he reached down to his pocket near the floor and tapped it.

The president's voice grated on his ears. "Don't worry, Eamon. You'll get some action. But only when I tell you. And only if you've been a very, very good boy."

CHAPTER EIGHTY-SIX

Volari Three, Volari System
Sickbay, ISS Warrior

THE MEDICS HAD CARRIED Fishtail to sickbay, and with good reason: her face was smashed, her lungs collapsed, and her blood pressure was so low that the nurse said her heart would stop at any moment.

Granger ran to sickbay with Zingano and Kharsa and a handful of marines in tow. At the door to sickbay a young man stopped him. A pilot from the looks of him, who eyed Granger warily.

"Stand aside, son."

"You were there, Captain. You were there. With the Swarm. With the Russians. Just moments ago. And ... and, now you're here." He struggled for words. "I ... I—"

"I understand your confusion, Lieutenant, I don't understand it myself. But I'm here now. And so are you. And Miller."

Volz's face contorted in grief. "Not anymore. Her heart just stopped."

With a curse, Granger shoved the young man aside and walked into sickbay. A nurse and his team worked frantically on the body of the pilot he'd sent to die, but from the looks of their faces, it was over.

He was numb. The woman's blood stained the table where she lay, spilling onto the floor and staining the gloved hands of the medical staff. He'd never had to face the consequences of his painful decisions with such ... such viscerally gruesome immediacy. He'd always ordered from afar. The ships would receive his orders, and they'd fly against their targets, and it was over. He'd never seen the aftermath up close and personal. Not like this.

Proctor stood in the background, apparently recovered enough that she could be out of bed. Her hand covered her mouth. Bandages wrapped her shoulder where Doc Wyatt's bullet had struck, but she looked like she'd be just fine with rest and—

Holy hell, he thought. Proctor. Doc Wyatt. He'd been infected with Swarm. But then Proctor had cured him.

Granger had been infected by Swarm matter, which had cured his cancer. Kharsa said the matter acted like a virus that killed every other competing virus and foreign contaminant. That the Russians had injected him with it, saving him, and condemning him to Swarm control at the same time.

But he'd been cured of Swarm control, too.

And if he could be freed from the Swarm....

"Proctor, you still have active Swarm virus?"

She nodded, and produced a small vial from one of her pockets.

"Then what the hell are you waiting for?"

She shook her head. "I ... I can't, Captain."

He stepped forward and grabbed her arm. "What do you mean you can't? I'm cured. Doc Wyatt was cured. We can still save her."

She shook her head again.

He squeezed harder. "Do it. Inject her. While we still have time."

She looked at him. "Captain, Doc Wyatt is dead. The antidote didn't work. It killed him."

Impossible. He looked at the body. The medical team had stopped their efforts, and the nurse swore before sighing. "Time of death, twenty-two hundred hours, five minutes."

No. He wasn't going to have her here, alive, brought back from the brink of death, a fate that resulted directly from *his* decision, his actions, only to lose her again. He spun back around to the Vishgane. "You. You found a way to subvert Swarm control over your people. If we inject her with Swarm matter, you can keep her safe!"

He shook his head. "I'm sorry, Captain Granger. Our physiology is quite different from yours. Our method would most assuredly result in her death, too."

He looked back at her. The broken body lying on the table, still dripping with blood. The bruises still blue and purple and the bones still broken.

"Do it."

Proctor stared at him. "Captain?"

"I said, do it. Inject her."

"But the antidote will only—"

"I know what the goddamned antidote will do! Inject her with Swarm matter anyway. We'll figure out the cure later."

Shaking her head, Proctor fumbled in a drawer for a meta-syringe, and, loading the vial in, she pressed it against Miller's bloody neck.

He motioned to the nurse. "Continue life saving efforts. Get oxygen into her lungs. Keep it flowing."

The nurse looked confused, eyeing the captain warily.

"DO IT!"

The medical team sprang back into action, one of them shoving the oxygen tube back into her throat, the others pumping on her chest to induce blood flow to the brain, working just enough oxygen up there to keep it from dying before the Swarm matter had the chance to repair the damage.

It didn't take its time. To everyone's shock, she suddenly breathed, gasping for air. Her eyes opened. Her chest rose and fell. She reached out and grabbed the arms of the two medical techs nearby.

Proctor sidled up to him. "And what if we can't find a way to counteract the Swarm virus, Captain? We can't risk having her spread it. We still have no idea how virulent it is once inside a human host. If we hadn't stopped Doc Wyatt and Colonel Hanrahan they might have been able to infect the entire crew. What if she tries to do the same?"

He watched as the medical staff worked on Miller, sealing up the wounds, setting the bones, injecting her with what he assumed was pain medication and something to induce tissue repair. "Then I kill her again, Shelby. But at least this time I get to look her in the eyes when I do it."

The head nurse, who'd taken charge in place of Doc Wyatt, cleared sickbay. Vishgane Kharsa left, escorted by the marines, back to the shuttle bay where he returned to his ship. Zingano left, with instructions to Granger that they meet to talk within the hour. Soon only Granger, Proctor, and the young pilot who'd come back holding Miller's dying body remained.

"You did good, son."

Volz nodded, but said nothing.

"Look, son, I may have been under Swarm influence when and where you last saw me. But that's over. And we've just won the biggest battle with them yet. And they're stripped of one of their most powerful allies. We've got them on the run." He turned to look at the pilot—the young man didn't look a day over twenty-five. Granger recalled distant memories of looking so thin and athletic. "We're going to win this war, son."

The young man met his eyes. "Are we, sir? Only heroes win wars. All we've got are millions of dead. We get our heroes, but only as martyrs: they die in the very act of becoming a hero."

"Bullshit. People like us win wars. Not heroes, not legends. Us. Me and you."

They looked each other over, a momentary silence passing between them. Medical scanners beeped in the background.

"She's not dead, Lieutenant," Granger said, pointing to the young woman on the table. "She's a hero, and she's alive." He fingered Volz. "And you're not dead either."

The pilot nodded. "No, sir. I'm not dead. And neither are you. The entire Earth watched *you* not die."

The Hero of Earth.

Granger was about to respond with contempt at the idea that he was a hero, but he stopped, wondering if maybe the kid had a point. Sure, regular people won wars. That meant regular people were the heroes. He *was* ordinary. He could be a hero. Could he be comfortable with that? Even knowing how many bricks he'd tossed, how many ships he'd ordered to their fiery deaths?

He nearly retorted something back, but stopped: Miller's eyes were open. And staring straight at Granger. He stepped forward and nodded at her, glancing to see that the restraints the medical staff had put on her arms and legs were secure to the bed. "How are you feeling, Lieutenant?"

She smiled. He never met Miller before, but this smile seemed ... off. Haughty. Amused.

"Our good friend. We are overjoyed to see you again."

Granger frowned. He glanced at the restraints one more time before stepping right up to her bed.

"What do you want?"

"We've told you this before, Captain Granger. To be friends, that is all. We are safer that way. You are safer. We all are safer, and prosperous, and secure."

He scoffed. "Safer? One could say that slaves are the least safe of all. Neither they nor their masters. Didn't work out so well with the Dolmasi, did it?"

She mimicked his scoff. "A minor setback. They've been replaced in the Concordat of Seven by the Adanasi, our truest, most faithful, profitable allies. Of which you are part. Peace has already been made, Captain, on behalf of your entire race. Submit now, and join with the rest of the Adanasi. Take your place at our side. The friendship of the entire galaxy awaits. We will ally with worlds without number. And they will rejoice."

He puffed a mocking breath of air. "No deal."

Miller sighed. "It was worth a try." She fixed her eyes on him. "Captain Granger, just as with you, we now know everything this person ever did. Every fact, every bit of knowledge, and every turn of phrase. Every colloquialism. I'm sure you'll recognize this one."

"And what's that?"

Miller's gaze turned cold.

"You ain't seen nothing yet."

Thank you for reading Warrior.

Sign up to find out when Victory, *book 3 of The Legacy Fleet Trilogy, is released: smarturl.it/nickwebblist*

Contact information:
www.nickwebbwrites.com
facebook.com/authornickwebb
authornickwebb@gmail.com